Cokcraco

"Paul Williams has written a novel that provides
every conceivable narrative pleasure. *Cokcraco* is a
brilliant satire of letters set against the backdrop
of post-colonial Africa. I cannot praise this novel
highly enough."

– Elizabeth McKenzie, author of *Stop That Girl!*

Cokcraco

. . . .

a novel in ten cockroaches

by

paul williams

[Lacuna]
2013

Published in 2013 by Lacuna
   http://www.lacunapublishing.com

Lacuna is an imprint of Golden Orb Creative
PO Box 185, Westgate NSW 2048, Australia
http://www.goldenorbcreative.com

Cover design: Golden Orb Creative
Text layout: Golden Orb Creative
Typeset in Trinigan FG (titles), Adobe Caslon Pro 12/14.4 pt (main text), Cochin 12/14.4 pt (Bantu text), and Minion Pro 11/13 pt (feature text).

National Library of Australia Cataloguing-in-Publication entry

   Williams, Paul, author.

   Cokcraco / Paul Williams.

   ISBN 9781922198082 (paperback)
   ISBN 9781922198099 (ebook)

   Subjects: Satire.
               Creative writing--Fiction.
               Criticism--Fiction.
               Universities and colleges--Faculty--South Africa--Fiction.
               Australian fiction.
               Homelands (South Africa)--Fiction.

A823.4

Contents

From da kokroach point of view, humans are irrelvant. Kokroaches no like em. Doan want em. Do not even tink bout em. Doan care for deh conversations. Books we like to eat, not read. We wish humans dead so we can eat em too.

— Sizwe Bantu, *The Cockroach Whisperer*, 2010

Storytelling ...
more venerable than history,
as ancient as
the cockroach.

— J.M. Coetzee

1

Blaberus craniifer
· · · · · · · · · · · · · · ·
Death-head cockroach

> The death-head cockroach or *Blaberus craniifer* is marked with a dark spot on its thorax, which, with a stretch of the imagination, looks like a skull. It will eat anything, even faeces, to satisfy its hunger. It has wings, but is incapable of flight, and chooses rather to confront its enemies by emitting a repulsive odour. It is most commonly found in so-called Third World countries, and because of its markings is often the victim of negative projections.

You're driving down a red dirt road in the middle of South Africa, having turned off at the intersection of nowhere and nowhere. You're lost. You're late for a meeting. The air-con in the rental car doesn't work, and you're wearing a European suit. You should stop and ask for directions, but you're male, genetically programmed never to ask for directions.

Three men stand in the road. One brandishes a panga—a machete. One points the barrel of an AK-47 at your face. The middle one holds up the open palm of his hand and bangs on the bonnet. You stop the car.

'Where you going, *umlungu*?'[1]

'Open up here, sharp sharp, man.'

Your blood runs cold.

No, no, no. Your blood does not bloody run cold. Only the blood of ectothermic creatures, like frogs, fish, geckos, crocodiles, chameleons, snakes, spiders, centipedes and cockroaches, runs cold. Your blood

---

1   *Umlungu*: Zulu (n). Derogatory. White man. Origin: white foam on the beach, i.e. white scum.

pumps hot and fast through your body, and your brain sends frantic messages to your fight or flight centres: your heart, your limbs, your brain. Epinephrine increases your heart rate, constricts your blood vessels, dilates air passages, and you're ready for a fight … or more likely in this case, flight.

Think. *Think!* You should drive right straight at them, through them; knock them over like bowling pins. But your leg locks into a cramp on the pedal. Two faces press against the passenger window. The leader—the one with the AK-47—stands his ground in front of the car. No false moves, the fearsome eyes say. Try not to stare at the barrel of the ubiquitous AK-47.

Mikhail Kalashnikov, your invention is alive and well.

The one with the panga raps on the glass. Tak. Tak. Tak. 'Where you going, *umlungu*?'

Your voice, no matter how hard you try to sound calm, is hoarse and shaky. Don't show any fear. Pretend all is cool. 'To … to … to the university.'

'Heh, heh, heh.' The young man performs a mini-dance of triumph in front of the car.

Is it too late to pray to the god whose existence you have denied all your life?

This country is the crime capital of the world; South Africa is in *Guinness World Records* for the highest carjacking figures. A motor vehicle is hijacked every forty to fifty minutes. More than twenty-five motor vehicle drivers become victims of hijackings daily. South Africa also gets the gold medal for murder and rape: a murder every thirty seconds, a rape every fifteen; one in four women have been raped; one in ten tourists has had something bad happen to them. And here you are. Fifteen seconds tick away and the country is waiting for its next victim.

You're dead.

And they're waiting.

It's a rental, you want to say. It's not mine. Take it. I have no cash. No cash. No gold. But your tongue is thick and dry. Your skin—your white *umlungu* skin—is clammy.

'Can we have a lift?'

You must look even whiter now. 'What?'

'A ride. We need a ride to the university. Can you give us a ride?'

They're playing with you. Even now you can drive off, before they get in. A choice: drive and get shot in the back, or give them a lift, so they can slit you from mouth to genitals, discard your lifeless body in the green and red Zululand backdrop. You know. You've read the stories.

> South Africa has a very high level of crime, including rape and murder. Thieves operate at international airports and bus and railway stations. Keep your belongings with you at all times. Due to theft of checked baggage at airports, you should vacuum-wrap all items where local regulations permit. You should keep all valuables in carry-on hand luggage. There have been incidents involving foreigners being followed from King Shaka International Airport to their destinations by car and then robbed, often at gunpoint. You should exercise particular caution in and around the airport and extra vigilance when driving away. Some taxis and car rental companies are fraudsters ...
>
> *Crowded-Planet* (2013): p. 120

Go on: rev the car, knock them down like skittles, swerve. The reckless hero escapes, tyres squealing as gunshots crack the back windscreen.

But no.

'No worries.'

They pile in. Two in the back, one in the front. AK man clatters the gun against the door as he wrestles with it. Panga man slides comfortably into the back. The third man has a scar that slices his face into two lopsided halves.

'Drive, drive.' AK man indicates the side road to the left where the green sign points into the furrowing valley. *University of eSikamanga, 3 kilometres.*

A nightmare. A bloody nightmare. What kind of a welcome is this to South Africa? You're sick to the gut. You want to throw up. But then, what did you expect? That you could drive through South Africa and *not* be hijacked?

The leader places his feet on the dashboard and props his AK-47 against the door.

You're careful not to turn your head, but out of the corner of your eye, you take note of the curved banana magazine, the wooden butt drenched in sweat, the notches—*notches!*—on the matt black stock. The weapon looks plasticky, homemade, as if he's assembled it from parts of other weapons.

'Where do I go?'

'Through here.'

'*Bundu* bashing,' adds the man from the back seat.

So they do mean to arrow you into the cane fields, back you up against a low anthill and murder you. All for this tinny Golf GTI rental. You can hear the shots already, muffled by the six-foot-high sugar cane.

'Drive—left … left … now straight, straight.'

You drive as straight as you can on the snaking roads.

'You a professor or something?'

'Don't distract the driver, Caliban.'

Caliban? You steal a glance at the man in the rear-view mirror. Remember to identify the carjackers for the police. Caliban. Scarface. Panga man. AK man. Three, four notches.

'That's Kaliban with a K. KU- KU-KU-Kaliban, Professor.'

'Drive, drive.'

You drive.

You count two kilometres of bumpy roads which have been gouged out of the red mountains, and you have to zigzag around goats and stones and ochre earth spills. A mini-bus plastered with 'I love eSika-manga' stickers shoots past, missing the car by inches. You should flash your lights to signal for help. Pull up on the brights. Three times. Morse code. Do they even know Morse code here? A weak stream of water wees onto the windscreen and the wiper blade judders across, smearing red dust—now red mud—across your line of vision. Now you can't see at all. Slowly the wiper does its job.

'Straight!'

Yeah, right. An AK bullet straight to the head.

'By the way we're the New Strugglers. This is Joel, Caesar …'

'Kaliban!'

'Sorry … Kaliban. And I'm Eric Phala.'

Their gang, their group, their little carjacking syndicate: The New Strugglers. What a name for a gang! And what caricatures. They are cartoon characters, confirmation of the worst stereotypes from South Africa: the black thug with panga, the AK-wielding carjacker, the silent brooding youth with a scar splitting his face in two.

'The New Strugglers for a new South Africa.' The man gives a guttural laugh. '*Viva* the new struggle!'

They smell of heavy deodorant and hair oil as if they are going to a party.

Some party.

A cow saunters across the road. You brake, looking for an opportunity to do something rash. But you can think of nothing. Red rivulets of paths criss-cross the countryside. Another cow prodded from behind by a boy with a stick crosses the road ahead.

'Just drive—he'll get out of the way.'

There must be people who live near here, people who can help you. But all you can see is six-foot-high sugarcane.

'Okay. Okay. Stop here.'

This is it.

You slow the car, and the red dust catches up, clouds the windows and front windscreen. The three men bang open the doors and climb out, the AK-47 again clattering against the door handle, the panga against the window. You're spitting dust, but have to ask. 'Where are we?'

The AK is pointed at your head. The sun is screaming (or are those cicadas?). The man with the scar grins. 'This is it, *umlungu.*'

It is at this point that your life is supposed to flash before your eyes. You know you're going to die, so you quickly review your life, and realise— too late—how precious every moment up to this point has been. If only you hadn't stopped at this intersection; if only you hadn't come to South Africa at all, if only she hadn't left you … if only you could rewind your life, just a little, just a few minutes. Why the hell did you drive down this back road?

This is the point when you feel an AK bullet in your brain, your soul rises up from your body, and stares forlornly from the branches of a tree at your dead white male protestant heterosexual corpse.

This is the point where you should wake up, sweating, heart racing, thinking—whew—it was only a dream. And what a nightmare.

The man swings the AK to point through the green jungle to a red flash of roof, a metal aerial glinting in the sun. 'Through there.'

Caliban—Kaliban—grins into the front window and bangs on the roof. 'Thanks. Thanks, man, for the ride. Nice wheels. Nice wheels.'

You steel yourself for the climax, the confrontation, but when you open your eyes, they are plunging into the green foliage, following a thin red path. Then they are gone.

The world stops for a second; even the cicadas stop screaming.

As soon as you can stop your leg from shaking, you drive on, wary of a trick, a trap, ready for the clatter of bullets in your skull.

But no.

Ahead, as you round the corner, you see red and white boom gates, a guard house, three men in green uniforms lolling in the shade. But it is no mirage. You take three deep breaths, pry your sticky hands off the steering wheel, slow your heart. Look down the path that has swallowed them up, and up again at the banner.

'The University of eSikamanga', announces a sign arching over the road in English and Afrikaans, the language of the former oppressor. Universiteit van eSikamanga.

> From the point of view of da cockroach, all languages are da languages of the Oppressor.
>
> — Sizwe Bantu, *Seven Invisible Selves,* 2008

You drive under the arch, and your car putters to the booms. Your heart is still pounding way too loud and fast but your mind is numb, as if you have indeed been murdered and are on the other side, your ghostly self still insisting you have a body, and you are driving an imaginary car to a spirit university entrance.

A security guard leaps out into the road. He looks real enough. 'Whoa, whoa!' Another walks in front of the booms, holding a clipboard, his peaked cap low in the glaring sun. He bangs the bonnet with an all-too-real fist. 'Stop! Stop, *wena.*'

You stop.

You eye the man's pistol tucked away in his pocket.

You speak. The words, surprisingly, come out as words that you can, and he can, hear. 'Th … th … those men … ?'

The guard pokes his cap into the front window. 'They think I don't see … ? I saw them! I saw them!'

Guard number two holds out his clipboard. 'We try not to encourage giving them lifts, Professor. Especially those ones. *Skabengas*.[2] *Tsotsis*.[3]'

'You … know them?'

Guard number one shakes his head, meaning yes. Guard number two clicks his tongue. 'Troublemakers.'

'One had an AK …'

You are not sure they understand you. A BLOODY AK, you want to shout. But perhaps that is normal around here. Perhaps everyone carries weapons in South Africa. The guards certainly do.

He hands you the clipboard. 'Welcome to the University of eSika-manga.'

'Cokcraco' by Sizwe Bantu

(The Present Tense, Vol. XXV, Feb. 2002, pp. 36-40)[4]

In the city of Durban, KwaZulu-Natal (in the imaginary country of Azania, Afrika) a man rented an apartment near the beach, in a derelict but expensive neighbourhood behind Point Road. In Apart-

---

2   *Skabenga*: South African (n). Slang. Rascal, scallywag.

3   *Tsotsi*: South African (n). Slang. Thug, dodgy character (from Nguni *tsotsa*: flashy dresser).

4   There has been much critical speculation regarding the title of this story. Jones (2008) maintains that the anagrammic dyslexia says much about the displacement of the 'other', and 'the cockroach motif has been a favorite symbol for displaced people everywhere'. Others have made much of the missing letter 'h', pointing to Bantu's commentary on how dialects of English omit the 'h' in speech, as in " 'e 'as an 'airy back". But the most plausible, if intellectually and aesthetically unsatisfying, explanation is documented by Wesson (2010) who points out that the original manuscfuptis of Bantu shows that he is a notoriously bad typist and contstantl;y miseplles words, as if he is typing in grtea haste. See for eample his commonly misspelled 'form'; for ;'from'. Wesson suggests tthat Bantu was simply tryig nt otype the word 'cockroach' and his fingers slipped on the keys, indicating that when inspiration strikes and the words pour out ,yo udo not have the dexterity to keep up. Elsewhere in his manuscripts, we see cockroach spelled ckroahc, cokroahd, and even codchroarh.

heid days, the area had been a whites-only area—and was still largely whites-only due to the exorbitant rents set by unscrupulous and invisible landlords. (I'm only talking of the insides of the apartments, of course: the streets were the habitat of prostitutes and street children.) The man—let me call him a Modern Afrikanist for now—who rented the flat lived alone.

The flat afforded a sea view, or so the landlord had told him. The apartment block was crowded in with other dilapidated buildings, but if he craned his neck out of the kitchen window on a clear day, he could see a blue patch of sea between the Nedbank towers and The Wheel. Taxi-drivers, prostitutes and street brawlers below made the street a noisy place at night, but once he had bolted and double-locked his front door and slammed the street-facing windows, the Modern Afrikanist would be left in silence to pursue his artistic endeavours.

Unfortunately, the main feature of this flat was not its privacy, nor its silence, but the scuttling of serrated legs and rasping of carapaces against the linoleum. In Durban, cockroaches grew three to four inches long.[5] He would find them everywhere: when he turned on the tap, they shot out; when he made tea, he found them dead and soggy in the kettle; when he poured cereal, he found them sleeping disguised as Honey Smacks … He didn't like squashing them—they made such a mess. Instead, he spread toxic white powder for them in the kitchen cupboards; he plugged up the taps; he sealed his food. But they kept coming. He resorted to spraying the crevices, cracks and running boards every morning before he went out. He would return at night to find piles of cockroach corpses in the bath, on the kitchen table, in the bed, and lining the skirting board to every room.

His initial repugnance soon grew into a hesitant fascination for these armies of determined creatures, who by their suicidal insistence claimed residence here. Over supper (Bunny Chow bought from The Star of India downstairs), he found himself staring at a particularly large dead cockroach on his dining room table. Its jagged legs, its oval shape, the light reflecting purple and orange off its back spoke to him.

---

5   Although Bantu here refers to the African or Oriental cockroach (*Blatta orientalis*), scholars have agreed that the cockroaches in his paintings and sculptures are more likely to be the death-head cockroach (*Blaberus craniifer*) because of the striking markings on the thorax.

I am black, but comely, it said. Behold, I also am formed out of the clay. He was particularly intrigued by the black marking on its head, a third eye watching him from another dimension.

He was suddenly ashamed. The Modern Afrikanist was an artist: he prided himself on an aesthetic appreciation of the world: so why should he exclude cockroaches from his artistic apprehension of the universe? They had value. They had form. They had beauty.

So instead of brushing away the dead cockroach in disgust, he set up easel and paints on the table and painted its portrait, with garish Fauvist colours, and generous gobs of paint, smeared on with the gusto and urgency of Van Gogh.

Pleased with his evening's work, he hung the picture on the living room wall. The next day, after breakfast, he shaped in black modelling clay a giant Rodin representation of the dead creature. And as he was loath to throw away the cockroach corpse, he varnished it with lacquer, and set it on the mantelpiece under his painting.

From here on, he no longer swept away dead cockroaches, but collected and sorted them according to size, texture, colour, and death-posture. He pasted the tiny ones onto a canvas and painted them —bright blue, orange and green—into a landscape, and hung the work of art on the wall in his kitchen. Monet would be impressed: up close, the painting was a knobbly packed death trench of cockroaches; from a distance, it was the North KwaZulu coast line, with sweeping, wavy cane fields, complete with workers dotted in the stalks, and smoke rising in the distance where old cane fields were being burned.

He glued the large cockroaches along the rim of his bookcase to make a pleasing pattern of ridges and bumps, taking care with the feelers so they would form a pattern of aerial lightness.

As more and more cockroaches died, he created more works of art. In a few short weeks, his furniture was covered with varnished cockroach designs, seven magnificent paintings hung on his walls, and a trinity of three large statues sat on his tables in raw clay, an essential gesture of cockroach emerging out of the formlessness of his previous prejudices. Soon there were no more walls to use: he covered his lampshade with cockroach designs; he made a sofa cover from the smooth corpses of cockroaches; he covered his desk with the oval pattern; he pasted them all over the bookcase. He now loved cockroaches—their form, their slender shape, their nestling together. A dozen new projects spun from his mind onto paper in the middle of the night—a cock-roach-paste sculpture, a cockroach doorway, a cockroach carpet, a cockroach Azanian flag.

Ironically, as the months passed, he ran out of cockroaches. Either there were no more in the dark spaces behind the walls of his flat, or they had got wind of his intentions, and had migrated to better home-lands, where there was more to eat, and where macabre, varnished corpses of their brothers and sisters did not stare at them from walls and bookshelves and headboards.

But the Modern Afrikanist was still bubbling with inspiration; and so he went out in search of raw material. He scoured the rubbish containers at the end of the street and collected roaches in plastic bags lined with white powder. He frequented the back end of The Star of India restaurant, the stench of a make-shift toilet behind the shish-kebab stall on the corner, and the stair wells of his apartment building. He arrived home every evening with his bag full, sorted them out by shape and breed (Asian, Smoky-Brown, Parktown-Prawn black), glued broken feelers on the big ones, repaired broken wings, legs, and carapaces, then set to work.

The paintings were beautiful: here is one of the Indian Ocean he couldn't quite see from the kitchen window, clear skies, zero humidity, the brown smog that skulked over Durban vanquished; here's another of the street below, devoid of prostitutes and taxis and street gangs, replaced by a post-Apartheid rainbow community of people; and here is a self-portrait of a clear-faced, hopeful Modern Afrikanist, looking out onto the horizon of the Afrikan Renaissance. Each painting breathed hope into the world.

The heat is hellish.

The car is protesting as you drive onto campus. Its needle strains way into the red, its fan whines, its engine stutters.

And you're late.

You follow Alice-in-Wonderland signs that coax you around round-abouts to Building D: HUMANITIES. The English Department is on the second floor.

You park in an empty lot, adjust your tie, gather your belongings and walk smartly towards Building D. You hunt first for a toilet. You need to rearrange yourself, compose yourself, straighten the crumpled suit, splash the fear off your face.

Here's one on the first floor. GENTLEMEN: STAFF ONLY. But the sign has been mutilated with a knife, and a palimpsest has been scrawled over it in black pen: THE DOORS OF ABLUTION BLOCKS SHALL BE OPEN TO ALL.

You hunt in vain for a mirror but find instead four screw holes on the wall and a dark patch where a mirror has been removed. The water from the cold tap comes out scalding hot, and the hot water tap produces cold water.

The sweat has dried on you to a lacquer finish, a thin varnish of fear glazed onto your soul.

Your body always betrays you. Every time. But stick it in a suit and tie, itchy grey socks and black leather shoes, crisp shirt and collar, and you can disguise its animal nature well enough.

The long English Department corridor smells of smoke and burnt rubber. Half way down the passage, you pass a gutted office—and stop to peer in through a dark black hole where the door has been beaten in with an axe. The gold plaque on the door, blackened but still legible, reads DR THAMI MPOFU, ENGLISH.

You take out the printed copy of the email you have folded tightly in your pocket and squint at it in the bad light.

Hi Timothy

Shall we say, ten am on the 15th? Let's meet in my office.

Building D, second floor, left along D corridor.

You can't miss it.

Thami Mpofu.

Yellow tape criss-crosses the yawning cavity, and inside, the entire office is burnt out. What were once plastic blinds on the windows are now curled molten blobs of black dripping down the wall onto what was once a desk. Empty bookshelves stand charred against the wall. Just your luck. Come all this way and the guy's been burnt to death in his own office. You walk past many shut doors, heavy oak stout doors with sombre signs labelling them as Professor, Doctor, Lecturer, Adjunct Temporary Tutor and so on. At the far end of the corridor, you spot the door you have been looking for: Professor J. Zimmerlie, Acting Chair.

In any other universe, you would wonder what the hell an 'Acting Chair' is.

You get the impression that they are watching you on CCTV, though you have seen no cameras, for even before you knock, the door opens.

'Professor Zimmerlie. Dr Turner is it? Glad you made it.' The man offers a limp yellow hand for you to shake.

The *umlungu* is dressed in a tight dark suit, white shirt, tie, cufflinks, shiny leather shoes. He is the whitest man you have ever seen. And you mean that literally. He is so white, he looks geckoish. And good god, you stare—try not to stare—at the stitches on his head, scars now, faded pink Frankenstein stitches about two centimetres long, neatly caterpillared across his left temple.

Behind him, another man thrusts out his hand. 'Hi, I'm Mpofu. Thami Mpofu.'

He is the opposite of Zimmerlie, if people can be opposites. He exudes a healthy dark glow, and grins with a self-confidence that you see can never be shaken.

'Ah, Professor Mpofu. I … your … office … ?'

'My office is temporarily indisposed,' says Mpofu.

'There was an accident,' says Zimmerlie. 'A fire.'

You detect a flicker of embarrassment between them. No, more than embarrassment: a lie.

'We Zulus have a saying,' says Mpofu. '*Khotha eyikhothayo* … The cow licks the one that licks her. John has kindly let me use his office and facilities.'

Zimmerlie presses his fingers together. 'Thami has an *apropos* proverb for every calamity.'

They speak like one creature, a two-headed monster. Opposites, but twinned, symbiotic opposites.

'Come in, come in.'

The walls of the office ceiling are plumped with books, framed certif-icates, photos. *The Journal of Southern African Literature.* Leavis's *The Great Tradition*, Harold Bloom, Kristeva, Derrida, Barthes, Foucault, Saussure, *Structuralist Poetics.* The books speak for themselves. You are now entering the world of Literary Criticism, another world, another language. And there are shelves of literature, too, with a capital L: *The Collected Works of Chaucer, Shakespeare, John Donne, The Romantic Poets, Thomas Hardy, DH Lawrence.* Be warned: this is the world of Literary Criticism, and these are Literary Critics.

A LITERARY KRITIK

KritiK: a person who rubs his or her legs together to make a noise. Not to be confused with a KriKit, the singular of the game played with a bat and a ball by humans dressed in white. Not to be confused with a KoKroach, another hardy insect that has outlived the dinosaur, and doesn't Kriticise anybody.

KritiK: Arch enemy of writer.

A strange thing, a literary KritiK. Always seKondary. Though KritiX themselves do not think like this. KritiX always trail behind writers, mopping their words, examining their faeces for meaning, signifiKance, signifers and signifiers. Would it not be better to be the writer yourself? Maybe that's what KritiX are, failed writers, wanna-be writers, and this whole industry of literary aKademia is a green pool of envy and failure. The right brain telling the wrong brain what to do.

But we shouldn't disparage them: they're a dying race, and no longer have anything to feed off. XtinKt. Once they bred in the sewers of univer-sities all over the world, and now all we have are their empty KarKasses. No one reads anymore.

— Sizwe Bantu, *Seven Invisible Selves*, 2008

The window looks out on an idealised African image: rolling green hills, dotted with grass huts under a deep blue sky.

They haven't let you speak yet. You put it off as long as possible, rehearsing the words, slowing your breathing down. The sweat has dried sticky and cold on your skin in the arctic air-conditioning in the room.

'Sit, sit. You must be tired. How was the trip?'

You sit. Consider. Should you tell them about the sixteen-hour flight, the Durban hotel you stayed in the night before adjacent to a *shebeen* that played loud music to the early hours of the morning, the air-conditioning in your overpriced rental car that didn't work, the last few minutes of terror when you were sure you'd be dead?

'It was fine. No worries.'

'No worries? I like that.'

'He's Australian. Australians don't have worries.'

'Australians have a sense of humour.'

'You'll need a sense of humour to work here, Dr Turner.'

'Tim. Call me Tim. Or Timothy.'

A suit does wonders. Paste a self onto your shimmering non-being, and people believe you to be solid.

'You're replacing a man who has been suspended from office,' says Mpofu.

'It's been a terrible business.'

'As we Zulus say, *Umlomo, ishoba lokuziphungela.*' He offers no translation this time, but you nod anyway. You do a lot of nodding. The puppeteer up there in your brain jerks the head string way too often. But that is what humouring is.

> The differAnce between pretending to be what people wAnt you to be and humouring them by Acting in a certain way is quite indistinguishable. Always mAsk; AlwAys pretend; AlwAys protect yourself. But don't inhabit the mAsk. Don't feel inferior: only Act as if you Are inferior. Be deferentiAl, but don't yield.
>
> – Sizwe Bantu, *AfriKan Metaphysics*, 2007

Zimmerlie sighs. 'He's fighting the case, of course. Suing the department, the university, has even made a personal case against each of us.'

'The case could go on for months, years …'

'A delicate issue,' says Zimmerlie. 'We shouldn't talk much about it.'

'The less said the better.'

'There's a trial, an inquiry, an investigation.'

You have to ask. 'Who … ? Who are you talking about?'

'Makaya.'

'A horrible man.' Zimmerlie holds up an enormous weight of air with his hands to measure, you guess, the enormity of the horror. 'It may be a semester, or perhaps longer—we just don't know—because now he's refused to accept dismissal and there's a board of enquiry—and he's taking us all to court …'

'Dr Turner, if he is fired, there'll be a permanent post here and there's a good chance you'll get it—we didn't want to bring you all the way from Australia for nothing.'

'What's this?' Mpofu takes the blue-bound thesis from your hands. 'The novels of Sizwe Bantu?'

'My doctoral thesis, in case you're interested, is on the novels of Sizwe Bantu.'

They don't seem to be, so you offer more: 'You know, the author who made himself famous venerating the cockroach.'

Blank, unreadable faces. Zimmerlie's furrowed eyebrows. Mpofu licking his lips. Go on, prod their memories. 'African International Book Prize. Nova Award?'

Zimmerlie takes the thesis from Mpofu and riffles through the two hundred pages as if it is an animation flick book. 'Interesting.' He hands it back without reading a word.

Mpofu speaks in a tone that can only be interpreted as patronising. 'He's a rather contentious writer around here.'

Don't react. Don't. Don't gawp in amazed disbelief. Grit your teeth. Smile. 'Oh, really? Contentious?' Don't say: Sizwe Bantu is the Greatest African Writer of All Time.

'Not very well thought of around here,' adds Zimmerlie.

Don't say: he lives around here. Surely you know him, honour him revere him, even just as a local writer?

Surely Bantu?

For this is Bantu territory. The hills you can see through the window are the hills pictured on the cover of Bantu's third novel, *Seven Invisible Selves*.

But of course—and you should know this—people are blind to talent in their own backyard, and a prophet is never recognised in his own country.

An embarrassing unpleasantness hovers over you, like the smell of a gutted office and burnt rubber. Silence. The swallowing of thick Adam's apples.

Zimmerlie claps his hands together to banish whatever bad spirits have entered the room. 'Well, Timothy, Thami and I have some business to attend to with Admin regarding your appointment. Why don't you stroll around campus and get a feel for it, and return in, say, half an hour?'

*

The idea of a quick campus tour is quashed the second you step out of the air-conditioned English Department. The air blasts your face like a furnace, and the sour humidity curdles your stomach. Have you forgotten so quickly where you are? The sun dazzles every reflective surface; you swear that the tar under your feet is melting. And there is not a soul out of doors. The air-conditioning units on every corner of every building roar; what must be cicadas compete from low grey bushes. It is not a place to be outside at midday.

And—an aside—why the colonisers named this the Dark Continent must have been some kind of joke. It is full of light everywhere, refracting off all surfaces. It is drenched in sunlight. And the land is green. Fertile. Fecund. Fruitful. The jacarandas here are really purple, not like the insipid pastels back in Victoria. And the poincianas are magnificent trees with blood-red dripping leaves.[6]

6   Footnotes are tiresome things, interrupting the reader's '*jouissance* of the text' (if any) and plunging his or her eyes down to the bottom of the page to read some unnecessary and distracting, often self-consciously arrogant 'extra' but vital information added by the author. Look at me, they (the words) shout, or worse, look at ME (the author). Even more annoying is when they spill onto the next page. Ironically those who argue for the use of footnotes are those who maintain that they (the footnotes, not the people) are there to avoid disruption of the flow of the main narrative. They are most common in academic

You pace the sparkling cinder-paths, determined to get a perspective on the place. Each building—science faculty, arts block, Admin, each lecture hall—has been magnificently designed. The Admin block even has turrets, towers and flying buttresses. The science block is a cool, modern green—enormous slabs of concrete and sweeping open stairs lead up to large sliding glass doors. But each window, each glass-fronted door, is obscured by an intricate brick breeze-block pattern, as if to stop people looking in or out.

You savour the idea: this is a university, a place of the mind, and more, it is an African university, twelve thousand kilometres away from everything you were not, and twelve thousand kilometres closer to someone you will become.

You reach a green park, neatly squared off and labelled 'Freedom Square', its benches slouching against shady trees around a perimeter of buildings, and decide that this is the centre, the focus of the campus, a good place to stop and get perspective on the place.

Beyond, you can see Bantu's bumpy and hazy hills, huts and dust. Freedom Square—a place where no doubt some bloody history—demonstrations, water cannons, tear gas, police baton charges—occurred, where students, vanguards of the revolution, wrestled their freedom from the Apartheid regime. *The Doors of Learning Shall be Open!* You saw the grainy news clips on TV as a child—but today, the square is sterile, empty, barren. The struggle, it appears, is over.

A scraggly, fur-matted, mewing kitten presses against the metal leg of the bench. You bend down to pet it, but it scratches your beckoning hand and runs off into the grey-green bushes behind. You observe with cold horror that its eyes have been gouged out.

In the centre of the square, signs point in higgledy-piggledy directions to Bekezulu Hall, to the Sports Field, to LAAC (whatever LAAC is), to the Staff Tearoom, Student Services. But you are seduced by the one pointing to the library. The humming machines promise sweet cool air, and you are dripping with sweat. You push through the glass

works, where terms need to be explained, or outrageous claims need to be justified, or irate or confused readers need help. The idea is that they can be ignored. Ha! Just try to read past one of those little numbers, and you are distracted, the flow of your narrative *jouissance* is stopped in its tracks, and you have to see what it is that the author has deemed so important that you have to halt your reading and find the corresponding number at the bottom of the page. Thank god, you say, these are not end notes, or hyperlinks.

doors. Inside, a vast open-plan dome, like a church, opens out. Very air-conditioned.

The library is empty. No students anywhere. But staff librarians quietly shuffle behind glass-walled offices. One woman at the checkout counter looks up as you pass her desk. You meander through the corridors of books, and then sit at a catalogue computer. You type in 'Sizwe Bantu'.

Search results show that this university has all Bantu's major works, in hard copy and electronic form. *The Great South African Novel* (2006), *AfriKan Metaphysics* (2007), *Seven Invisible Selves* (2008), *The Five AfriKan Senses* (2009), *The Cockroach Whisperer* (2010), and *Cokcraco and Other Stories* (2011).

Whew.

But when you search for availability, all of them show up empty. Withdrawn. Unavailable. Missing.

---

i Yam the cockroach who everyone ignores.

i Yam the loud fart in the elevator everyone pretends did not happen.

i Yam the spot on the teenager's nose just before her first date.

i Yam the disembodied obscenity scratched on the wall of the church.

– Sizwe Bantu, *AfriKan Metaphysics* (2007)[7]

---

7   The reader will recognise several plagiarised/sampled/intertextual references, this time to Zimbabwe writer Dambudzo Marechera's poem 'Identify the Identity Parade' in *Cemetery of Mind*, ed. Flora Veit-Wild, (Harare: Baobab Books, 1992): 'I am the loud fart all silently agree never happened'. The phrase 'Disembodied obscenity' is taken from Njabulo Ndebele's story 'Fools' in *Fools and Other Stories* (Readers International, 1986). Words, Bantu is saying, are all borrowed, recycled, used up, and all we can do is rearrange them.

*

'Ah, Mr Turner.'

Mpofu hands you a document, stamped and signed. 'As we arranged over the Skype interview, Admin are very agreeable to a twelve-month contract for starters. And as soon as our little problem is cleared up, we can advertise a permanent position. And if we play our cards right, you could get it.'

'Thanks.'

A moment's hesitation.

'A word of warning ... we'd be amiss if we didn't say ...' A lightning glance at Zimmerlie; a slight nod in return. 'You know you're walking into the lion's den?'

It is not difficult to guess what they are going to say next. 'You mean Makaya ... ?'

Zimmerlie nods. 'Makaya is a dangerous, vindictive man. When he hears that you are taking his position ...'

'The political minefields in this campus are complex, Timothy, very complex. We have to watch our backs.'

'We want to protect you from the kind of spiteful attacks that occur on this campus in the name of academia.'

Are you surprised? Where have you been anywhere in the world where spiteful attacks in the name of academia do not occur? But you widen your eyes appropriately.

'We need someone to take over a very restless class of one hundred first-year students who have been left in the lurch and messed around by ... by ...'

'That recalcitrant man.'

'And the Honours class is ... how can we put this? Rather ... belligerent.'

'Aggressive.'

'Makaya tossed all textbooks out of the window. He had got them doing silly creative writing exercises instead of studying real literature.'

'That's the urgency. You could start on Monday?'

'Yes, of course.'

'Of course,' says Mpofu. 'He has all sorts of questions. Salary, accommodation, syllabus.'

'The details we can arrange later. The important thing is—you can start Monday, get those students off our backs ...'

'Where will you be staying?'

'Not sure. I was thinking of eSikamanga?'

Zimmerlie frowns. 'Thami lives in Assegai, thirty k's north, as do many of our faculty. A large city with all the modern conveniences.'

'Professor Zimmerlie,' says Mpofu, 'lives in eSikamanga. He loves it there. By the sea. A small town right on the Indian Ocean, about thirty k's south. Those are your choices. I can put you in touch with an estate agent ... ?'

'That would be good. How are the waves?'

Zimmerlie nudges Mpofu. 'I told you he was an Australian. Now ... I know this is very short notice, Timothy, but there is a requirement of any new faculty member to ... to ... er ... present a lecture to the staff and faculty of the university, to introduce yourself, as it were.'

'Sure. I can do that. When?'

'Is next Friday too soon?' Zimmerlie wrinkles his brow.

'No worries.'

'Marvellous! And do you have a topic?'

'I will. Probably something like ... "Playing with Words while Afrika is Ablaze"?'

'Intriguing. And you can have this ready for next week?'

'Yep. Too easy.'

Zimmerlie clears his throat. 'Is that a yes?'

*

You march down the dark corridor to the EXIT sign armed with *The Complete Works of Shakespeare*, Chaucer's *The Canterbury Tales*, *Modern African Stories*, a solid phalanx of literature to teach. The gist of it is, Makaya neglected—even dropped—literature from the syllabus, and taught instead Creative Writing. And you are here, so you gather, to put that all right.

It is no matter. You don't care what you are teaching. You have already decided to humour these men, to glide along over these matters. Makaya, for all you know, might be quite a decent bloke. You are determined from the outset to remain above it all, as neutral as Switzerland, as wry, ironic, as Bantu himself, unsullied by politics of the academy.

But your sense of wellbeing is short-lived. A door to the left swings open, and a short, stout man bursts out and sends you sprawling. The books Mpofu has given you thud on the red polished floor. The man reaches out a hand to help you up. 'Sorry, didn't see you there, *china*.'

Double take, then smile, as if this is normal. The man has orange hair. You cannot stop staring. 'Turner,' you say. 'The new replacement lecturer.'

The man pulls his hand away as if he is afraid of catching some contagious disease. '*Wena?*'

You scoop the books off the floor to make a quick exit. But it is too late. The man has seen. 'Shakespeare? Chaucer?'

'I'm teaching Shakespeare, yes. And Chaucer.'

'Dead white males? To African students who are trying their hardest to throw off the shackles of colonialism?'

How do you respond to a loaded question? Point the gun away from yourself. You indicate the closed door at the end of the corridor. 'Professor Zimmerlie ...'

'Zimmerlie!' The man uses the word as an expletive.

'Yes, Zimmerlie. And Mpofu.'

'Mpofu! I should have guessed.'

'And you are ... ?'

The man ignores your outstretched hand and shoulders his way down the corridor. His footsteps echo past the series of dark office doors, and at the end of the hallway, framed by a halo of light, he turns and squints back into the darkness, sunlight setting his red hair on fire. 'Bastards.'

It looks, on your first day, as if you have inadvertently made an enemy.

COCKROACH INTERVIEWER: Why do you not like humans?

COCKROACH: Humans are *nasty* pests, known for their insatiable greed. These parasites will feed on other *animals* as well as their own kind. Once they colonise a territory, it can be a real challenge to eliminate them. Humans carry many toxic diseases and leave a trail of destruction wherever they go. Their love of turning pristine wildernesses into sterile concrete nests and burrows is well documented.

– Sizwe Bantu, *The Cockroach Whisperer*, 2010

2

Supella longipalpa

· ·

Brown-banded cockroach

Often found in bedrooms and living rooms, brown-banded cockroaches (*Supella longipalpa*) are hardy creatures that shun the light, lay their eggs under furniture, and scavenge off humans. These creatures are the most common cockroaches found around the world. A popular misconception is that cockroaches are dirty creatures that carry disease: nothing could be further from the truth. Cockroaches are the garbage collectors of society and if allowed to go about their business, will keep a house clean and free of food waste. Toxic when eaten raw, they nevertheless are a popular culinary delicacy in certain parts of the world.

The road to eSikamanga[1] is lined kilometre after kilometre with good intentions—Zulu goods for sale: beads, carvings, grass mats, hats, bangles. Vendors crowd every dusty intersection. You would stop, but of course you don't. It's also lined with carjackers.

As the car crests the hill, your heart lifts to see the sparkling Indian Ocean, the sweep of enormous sand dunes, the gold beaches.

You have dreamed of this moment.

Careful not to slow down at intersections or give anyone rides, doors locked, windows down, you cruise along vacant streets and parks until

---

1 eSikamanga is off the beaten track, a beautiful town with kilometres of unspoiled beaches, and has the air of not having being 'discovered' yet, as well as a laid-back lifestyle enjoyed by residents distrustful of change in any form. But, surprisingly, Zululand's most idyllic coastal hideaway is off the grid. Residents voted to exclude it from tourist listings, block all advertising on the internet and to discourage large-scale tourist activities. There are no hotels or bed and breakfasts, and residents do not encourage visitors.

you reach the eSikamanga Mall, a stretch of low buildings with large verandas, boasting a SPAR Supermarket, Chemist, Zulu Souvenirs and Curio Shop, Estate Agent, and Mrs K's Take-Aways. You are also pleased to see a police station in the prominent centre of the square, a hunched building bristling with aerials, completely enmeshed in barbed wire fencing. Amazing how theoretical one's anarchism can be.

You pull back a strongly sprung front door and plunge into the ice-cold air of the dimly lit estate agency. A woman with red bifocals pushes back tired grey-blonde hair from her eyes.

'And what can I do for you?' Her eyes are narrow, her lips pursed.

'Timothy Turner, from the University of eSikamanga.'

'Oh! Professor Zimmerlie called me with the good news. Said to expect you. Thank god. They've found someone to replace that dreadful man. I hope for your sake you never have to meet him.'

'I'll do my best.'

'Mrs Steyn.' She thrusts out a hand. 'So, Dr Turner—it's Dr is it, or Professor?—I have exactly what you're looking for.' She taps a long red fingernail on the glass counter top. Under the glass is a map of eSika-manga, a grid of streets sandwiched between two snaking rivers and a large blue estuary. 'We have a nice town house for you here—going for four thousand a month: three bedroom, two bathroom, one ensuite ... very clean, modern. ... Electronic security. ... Neighbourhood Watch.'

'I ... I was looking for something more ... modest. I ... don't know how long I'll be staying, you see.'

'Oh, don't worry about that.' She crouches over the counter in a confidential invasion of personal space.

Some people occupy more space than others, see their bodies as missiles or blockades, and colonise your space, extend themselves in an aura that radiates far beyond their body space. They squash you into a little corner and thrust their physicality at you to make you acquiesce. Mrs Steyn, intentionally or not, thrusts out her breasts at you in some territorial display of aggression. You could be wrong—this would be a ghastly error of cultural judgement—but you feel she is challenging you to a battle with the world, one she has to win at all costs.

'Those are only rumours about his reinstatement. You'll be here a long time ... a year's lease to start? Professor Zimmerlie told me you have a twelve-month contract.'

It is all to do with bodies. We pretend we are rational beings, consciousnesses, and drag these bodies apologetically (as a white man, you speak for yourself here) but there is another language we speak all the time, the language of the body. And women, you are told, have sex organs just about everywhere. Mrs Steyn's relation to you is ... in a broad sense ... physical, sexual, through the body, not through the mind.

You loosen your tie, that ghastly British invention designed to choke and pinch your neck. In fact, you now realise, the suit is a way of denying the body altogether, bracketing it off from everyday discourse. 'I just need a one-bedroom. I don't mind an older place. Nearer the sea, perhaps? And a shorter lease to start.'

'Do you have family here?'

'No ...'

'And you're from Australia?'

'This is a smaller town than I thought.'

'Everyone knows everyone's business here, Dr Turner. And that's a good thing: we look after each other. Australia, hey? Why come here?'

'Call me Tim.'

'My sister moved to Perth a few years back. Refuses to come back here to visit. Lovely place. You know Perth?'

'I'm from the other side, actually. Never been to Western Australia.'

'Hmm.'

You browse the photos of houses for sale on the adjacent wall. 'Haven't you got anything cheaper ... smaller?'

'Most single professors live in the block of flats called Strandloper. They pay from six to ten thousand Rand a month. They're large apartments, safe, secure ...'

'This for instance.' Your finger hovers over a picture of a thatched cottage standing on its own in the midst of a wild garden. In the background, a misty blue ocean fogs the sky.

'Oh, you wouldn't like that. It's ...'

Acid rises in your throat.

' ... too small and run down. Hasn't been let for years. Running water a little temperamental; gas heating; you have to buy the canisters from the general store. Garden uncared for. And for security reasons, most of us live in gated communities.'

'So, just how bad is the crime here?'

'Oh, nowhere's safe these days, but I did mention our Neighbourhood Watch at Strandloper?'

You tap the glass. 'How much?'

'The cottage? I could let you have it for … six thousand at a squeeze. But you'd be sorry. You'll regret not paying the little extra to have comfort and security.'

'Could I have a look?'

She looks at you over her bifocals as if she has only just noticed you are in the room. 'Fine.' She bangs open a drawer, scrapes her chair, snatches a key chain off the hook on the wall behind her, and then motions you to follow her outside to a white Mercedes, where she fusses with jangling keys, unlocks the car, disarms some complicated alarm system and lets you slide into the white leather front seat. Then you are swishing down the roads towards the residential area on the west side of town.

The Post-Apocalyptic Guide to Parochial
South African Towns Buried in the Past

eSikamanga is a squat, hunchback town which, because of some curious disposition of the land, turns its back on the sea. The high sand dunes and the swampy area between the Manga and the Mswaswe rivers squeeze the town into an unhealthy, uncongenial spot in the mangrove swamps. The town is a vestige from the Apartheid era, very white, a neighbourhood-watch-starts-here type of town.

Crowded-Planet (2013): pp. 122-123

She drives past glass-fronted houses with pools and fountains on large multi-acre grounds, private jetties jutting out into the lagoon through the dense green scrub. In her last valiant attempt, she cruises (by chance, she claims) past Strandloper, an offensive walled-off row of town houses, with a blinding white reflection from the sun on the high walls. Three strands of electric fence top the wall and a sign warns intruders (in three languages) of the danger of electrocution if they even dare to think of breaking in. She nods at the walls; you shake your head; she drives her Mercedes impetuously down a narrow gully of a street towards the sea. She turns down into a dirt road to the left, named Seaview Street, the sign almost completely screened by palm trees. The lane is strewn with dry palm fronds and rotting leaves; a deep ditch of dried red mud runs down the middle of what must have once been a driveway. She takes delight in roaring her car over the bumps and roots, as if to say: see—this is not what you would want to rent.

The property is surrounded—as all others are, nothing unusual here, apparently—by a high electric barbed-wire fence. She stops at the gates, looks around and then unlocks it.

'Most attacks occur at the entrances of the security gates,' she says.

'Most people seem to live pretty much like prisoners in their own houses,' you reply.

Parrot-blue eyelids, laden with heavy black mascara, blink at you. 'In Australia you don't have high security walls around your houses?'

It is of course not a question: it is an answer to a question. She sighs. 'Like in the old days. I bet you don't even have a key to your house.'

But your fears of being in a high security prison are soon allayed. Once inside the grounds, the perimeter fence is swallowed up by greenery. The drive opens out into a wide expanse of green lawn which fronts a bad copy of the photo in the estate agency. The cottage, it seems, is sinking in the mud of a recent flood. The walls are red up to the windows, and the roof is strewn with fallen branches and leaves from the overhanging trees. A line of brown and green mould circles the house at shin level. She parks in front of the veranda door. Two large birds fly off in alarm from a paw-paw tree's yellow fruit. She drums her fingernails on the steering wheel. Surely her client will now acquiesce, shudder and return to Strandloper with all due haste? Instead, you step out of the car and onto the red polished veranda.

'Wait!'

You turn to see a blur of grey fur dash past your feet, followed by a long tail. Then more blurs, more tails. They leap from the veranda wall onto the trees and swing through the branches. One bounces on and off the bonnet of the car, bounds into a tree and disappears. You watch the passage of a troop—ten, twelve—through the treetops.

One last one leaps on the roof of the car and clutches the aerial. You stare at its human face.

'Cute.'

'Vervet monkeys are not cute. Damn pests. Shoo! Shoo!' She claps her hands and waves her arms at the monkey, but instead of bolting, it bares its yellow teeth and red gums. Then it swings up into the trees, and the branches shimmer as it catches up with its troop.

'You can't leave anything outside. They'll steal whatever they can lay their thieving little paws on. And never leave windows open.'

You turn to the cottage.

Sure, it is mean, its windows covered with gauze netting. Cracks spider down the walls; the front door is overgrown with a fierce creeper that is reluctant to yield as Mrs Steyn pushes through into the dark entrance hall.

'Electricity needs to be turned on. But Dr Turner … ?'

'Timothy.'

'There's no phone line or TV connection. No internet connection. You'll have to ask the telephone company to …'

'I don't need a phone. Or TV. Or the internet. I came here to get away from all that.'

'Oh, really?' She yanks up a blind at the far end of the room, and grey light streams through a high window.

'I can't believe the mess.' She bends to overturn a box and a large cockroach scurries into a crack in the skirting board.

She knows you won't like it. But you do like it. Not because you are perverse, and want to break her will—well, perhaps there is a slight element of that too—but it has something. It feels good. Exactly the kind of place you had in mind when you imagined this trip. And—most importantly—you can hear the crash of the sea. You force open a door onto a back veranda and breathe in the briny air.

Amazing, you think, how different a self you can be with different people. The stutter, the grey invisibility has gone, and you are a solid presence before Mrs Steyn. Something about her you like, but there is also something about her that nauseates you. Most of all, you are solid and real. You like yourself in this role.

With a flick of her wrist, Mrs Steyn indicates the back wall of a three-storey house that obscures any view of the ocean. 'I wasn't planning to rent this out, and as you can see I haven't rented it out for a while.' She catches you running your hands down a yellow surfboard propped up in the corner. It is dented, chewed off at the end, and granuled brown from all the wax. 'Oh, I'll have that removed ...'

'No.' You hold it up to get its feel. 'I might like to try it out, if that's okay.'

Mrs Steyn presses her lips tightly together. 'The sea around here is dangerous, Dr Turner. No one swims here. There are sharks ... there have been shark attacks.'

'Leave it here anyway. I like it. Ambience ...'

She marches into the kitchen and peels a 'Surf Wax' sticker off the window with angry nails while you tour the rest of the cottage, stumbling over boxes, pulling up blinds.

'I'll take it for four thousand.'

'I said six thousand.'

'Look at the condition of it!' You tap a broken window pane and the remaining triangle of glass shatters on the veranda outside. Oops. 'Four thousand.'

'Call it five and it's yours.'

'Month to month lease.'

'Are all Aussies as hard-nosed as you?'

You smile. 'Yes, or no, I can't win that one.'

'You won't need a deposit, as your job will stand as surety. Our office doubles as the building society. The university will transfer your salary through us, so you need to open an account on your way back. And give us your mobile phone number too, won't you?'

'I don't have a mobile.'

The silence on the way back to the mall is horrible, as if she is waiting for you to confess that you do have a mobile phone after all, or that you will relent and plead to be taken to Strandloper *post-haste*. But you hold your ground.

*

Dear M,

They say the depth of the pain is measured by how many kilometres away you have to travel to stop feeling it. I am now 9,837 kilometres away from you. They also say that you only will stop feeling pain when you stop writing to the person who causes it. I must stop talking to you in my head. I must stop seeing everything through your eyes. Stop doing everything for your approval.

They say too (who is this they?) that when she stops playing herself as the feature film in your life, you will be cured.

But for now, a flick of your blonde hair, wide eyes, a hand reaching forward, an old song playing in my head.

Yours
T

*

You stand in the frame of the front door, savouring the moment. It is a moment of triumph, really, your stand of independence, your rebellion against the past, your dream. For haven't you imagined this moment, free of sticky pain, the joy returning, yourself emerging as a separate being?

The cottage stinks of mould and rotten seaweed. You creak across the wooden floors to the bedroom, where you find a bed covered with a pink blanket and pink pillows, a dresser sagging in the corner, a pink rug, blotched with cockroach droppings. Back in the living room, a pile of depressed suitcases draped with a cloth serves as a table; there is also a dusty sofa, a stiff office chair, and a rickety bookshelf eaten away by termites at the back. In the kitchen stands a silent Frigidaire (which you regret opening). A dripping tap has stained the sink. The small stove works on gas—you flick the canister with a fingernail and hear a hollow ring.

The windows are mostly glass free. Rusty gauze, linted with years of human skin particles, cage each window to protect the house from the monkeys, presumably. Never mind the panga men and AK-wielding thieves. But the security system comes fully equipped with a panic button, and no one, Mrs Steyn reassures you, can get past FREEMAN security.

And there are boxes everywhere, as if the previous tenant was evicted before he had time to move out his stuff. The boxes are sealed, heavily taped, and labelled BOOKS, CLOTHES AND SHIT, SNORKELLING GEAR.

You haul your suitcase from the boot of the car into the house, and change into shorts and t-shirt. You store the suit on the wire hanger in the bedroom cupboard, shove the boxes off to the storeroom, and sweep the sand and cockroach droppings out with a straw broom you find in the kitchen closet.

On the makeshift table, you set up the Sizwe Bantu collection. You arrange the novels, prop up a grainy photograph of the author's famous quote (*Worship yourself: be your own guru*) against the books, and place a large varnished rubber cockroach in the centre of the display.

*

Blurb from the back cover of *The Great South African Novel* (first edition, 2006, reprinted 12 times; this edition, 2013):

Sizwe Bantu is considered by many to be the greatest living novelist in the English language.[2] Spanning five decades, his ambitious narrative project has been consistent in its focus to explore the "nerve centre of being" and "unveil the masks of our … civilization."[3] He has dissected the sexist, racist and speciesist "myths of our time"[4] with intellectual courage and honesty, and has pushed the boundaries of the genres his fictions inhabit. He has won so many awards for his writing that it would be tedious to list them all. He is most renowned for his cockroach stories and his use of experimental second-person narratives and wry irony. He has succeeded in being both a popular and a literary writer, ploughing through that distinction with ease, and taking delight in leaving piles of overturned critics writhing on their backs in his wake. Simultaneously, he has attracted a cult following of believers, fervent admirers who live and breathe Bantu, and carry rubber cockroaches in his honour.

A formidable recluse, Sizwe Bantu has never appeared in public, has never shown up to claim any of his multiple awards, and does not give interviews. No one knows where he lives, and though his novels are invariably set in the urban and rural thickets of KwaZulu-Natal, they have an allegorical, ahistorical air about them, as if he has never lived there.

*

2   Pantheon (2013), 'Bantu, a Disembodied No Man' in *New York Times Review*.

3   Tom Watt's comment on the back cover of the 2008 Penguin edition of *Seven Invisible Selves*: 'Bantu's vision goes to the nerve-centre of humanness. His incisive narrative seeks not merely to reflect back to us the horror of our human condition, but to peel off our black and white skins and unveil the masks of our so-called civilisation.'

4   Sizwe Bantu, 'Sivilization' in *The African Presence*, Vol. 2, March/April 2005, pp. 31-34. Bantu, quoting another great South African writer, speaks of two types of literature, one that seeks to reinforce the myths of 'sivilisation', and one that dissects these myths.

You find a box of matches and a pack of six white candles in a kitchen drawer. You strike the match and light a candle, melt its rear end and mash it onto the windowsill. You place the placard on which you have hand-written the author's poem 'Imbrase kontradikshun' on the wall.[5]

IMBRASE KONTRADIKSHUN

I

I am

I am against

I am against kontradikshun

I am against those who are against kontradikshun

I am against those who are against those who are against kontradikshun

I am against

I am

I

The sun burns orange through the smeared windowless frame. Sweat pours off your face. The words wash over, through, in you. You begin— finally—to relax. To be yourself, whatever that is.

5   In this anarchist poem, Sizwe Bantu calls attention to the anarchist poem it parodies, Zimbabwean author Dambudzo Marechera's 'The Bar-Stool Edible Worm,' in *Cemetery of Mind*, ed. Flora Veit-Wild, (Harare: Baobab Books, 1992) and *Scrapiron Blues*, ed. Flora Veit-Wild (Harare: Baobab Books, 1994) and available online at <http://www.poetryinternationalweb.net/pi/site/poem/item/5862>.

All the stores are closed, sealed off like the rest of this town in a heat haze, but Mrs K's Take-Aways is open, and the smell of stale cooking oil greets you as you enter the doorway—beaded with old rusty bottle tops from glass bottles—yes, they still sell fizzy drinks in chipped bottles here. You order two 'K Burgers' and two portions of chips from a young woman dressed in an orange apron who stares at you as if you have just teleported from another planet. Perhaps you have. When she speaks, she throws furtive glances back at the curtain that separates the customers from the kitchen. The stilted conversation consists of the most formal of conventions. You try out your pidgin-Zulu. '*Sour Boner.*'

'*Sawubona.*' She is too polite to correct you or break out into paroxysms of mocking laughter, as she should.

'Can you wrap one up for a takeaway … I'll eat one here.'

She nods.

'Any chance of a milk shake?'

'We have run out of milk, but I can get some from the store.'

'No, no, don't bother, a Coke …'

You wait half an hour in a humming under-air-conditioned room. The checked red and white curtains are drawn, and the waitress bustles in the kitchen. Smoke chokes the room, and oil spits. When the order arrives she curtsies, delivers the meal on the tips of her fingers, and retreats.

You feel silly: you have watched American tourists in Australia exclusively frequent McDonalds and KFC, and putter around the Gold Coast as if it were Florida. And here, you suspect, you are moving around in a well-constructed, but poorly imitated Western orbit. So far, not much is different.

How was Africa? Zululand?

Oh, you can hear yourself saying, *much the same as here.*

The fat oozes from the chips, and you have to wipe your hands on your shorts, as there is no napkin. The burger, a poorly constructed skyscraper of undercooked meat, pickles and onions on a disintegrating white bun, slips and slops over the plate.

'Wait, I'll have those. Those are local, aren't they?'

'Local?'

You point to a golden doughy plait on the counter under lace and hovering flies.

'What are they?'

Koeksisters is what they are, but you hear 'Cook Sister'.

Your stomach regrets eating them as soon as you take the first gooey mouthful. Surely this syrupy, oil-laden heavy dough is not a South African traditional pastry? But as the waitress is watching from behind the bead curtain, you smile and eat the whole thing, nodding. 'It's good. Good.'

In Australia, no one leaves a tip at a takeaway. You consider that leaving a tip is a condescending insult that re-installs class hierarchy and power relations. But here, you have been told that it constitutes most, if not all, of the waitress's wages. You leave the money on the table, but the waitress hides until you are well outside before she clears the table, and then stands by the checkered curtain watching.

> Avoid isolated beaches and picnic spots across South Africa. Walking alone anywhere, especially in remote areas, is not advised and hikers should stick to popular trails.
>
> *Crowded-Planet* (2013): p. 160

Some hours later (there is no need to describe the diarrhoea), you are driving down Msaswe Beach Road, gliding on fine brown sand roads into the high sand dunes, following the signs TO DA BEACH. (No, it doesn't really say that, but it feels to you as if it should.) The image of the surfboard in the corner of the cottage (and now its manifestation in the boot of the car) has already determined your next move. The dirt road winds through the dunes for a kilometre before opening into an empty car park. You park the car on the sand area under a tree, climb over a dune and spy a deserted beach prostrating itself before the Indian Ocean. A gleaming river on your left is sign-posted *Mswaswe River*, its brown stream disappearing into the golden sand, and on your right, a mile or so away, another river, or large expanse of water, pools into a gap between the high dunes. You are barefoot; the sand burns into your soles; you have to dance all the way to the sea line.

Mrs Steyn's wagging finger is not going to deter you. You're Australian for god's sake, as everyone keeps reminding you. Run straight into the waves. It's slimy warm, bitterly salty, rough, and much warmer than the waters off Victoria. Gargle and spit, draw off the energy of the ocean, let the waves toss and pull you into its currents. Surf into the grainy brown sand, again and again, washing the sticky bad faith of the day's encounters with people.

Celebrate the body.

Celebrate nature.

Celebrate the energy of this symbiotic relationship between the body and the world.

The waves are all dumpers. They pull you into a backwash and hurl you gritty-mouthed onto the ocean floor. You swim as far as you dare beyond the breakers, and then let them roll you back in. The water is murky, and only when you are floating in the calm behind the breakers do you ponder the fact that muddy estuaries make an ideal breeding ground for sharks.

Instantly, the brown water populates itself with dark shapes. The skin of the sea breaks out in dorsal fins knifing towards you; your leg brushes against the hard grey flanks of what can only be a school of Zambezi sharks—Bull sharks as they are known in Australia. In high panic, you strike out for shore but make no headway. And what about riptides, those currents that suck you out to sea instead of towards the shore? You ply your hardest, but underwater currents drag you back further than the waves can propel you forward. Your arms ache, your head throbs and your chest is ablaze. Don't panic. Swim sideways. Don't try to confront the current directly. Go around.

You tack sideways out of the sucking current. The dark shapes follow, encircle you. After blind minutes, you catch the surf and, propelled by a large wave which bursts into millions of particles of sand, crash onto the beach. You look back through a star-spinning haze at the sea.

Nothing like a good shark attack to throw you back to your senses.

I must stop seeing myself in the second person.
I must stop seeing myself through your eyes, M
I must stop seeing my 'self'
'I' must stop
I must
I

The dorsal fins pursuing you cut back behind the breakers, not able to come closer. You drag your heavy body onto the shore. The roaring ocean clutches at your feet and draws back with the breath of a million shells and stones and grains of sand, angry that you have got away.

You have been washed up the coast a hundred metres, at the mouth of the estuary of the ever-changing Mswaswe River. You wade across, against the current of a warm, tea-coloured tide, to a lagoon nestling in sand dunes. The sand shimmers, mirages of water stream down them, rubber green Triffids grow out of them. Wind scurries down them and dust devils whirl at their bases. You climb up one of the dunes, and roll down the other side, sticky and granulated with sand, into the lagoon. Lie in the shallow yellow water, and then swim across, slicing the skin of the red-brown depths of the lake with your hands. When you reach the far shore, a green sign with uneven white lettering glints at you. You cannot read it at this distance, so you wade closer.

IT IS DANGEROUS

TO SWIM IN THE LAGOON

BECAUSE OF

SHARKS AND CROCODILES[6]

---

6   Saussure states that the relationship between a sign and the real-world thing it denotes is an arbitrary one. There is not a natural relationship between a word and the object it refers to, nor is there a causal relationship between the inherent properties of the object and the nature of the sign used to denote it. The sign relation is dyadic, consisting only of a form of the sign (the signifier) and its meaning (the signified). Saussure saw this relation as being essentially arbitrary, motivated only by social convention.

You pull yourself out of the water, give a quick scout for nobbly crocodile backs, and wonder how far these creatures can track someone on land. You have beached yourself in a mangrove swamp. You trudge through a muddy clearing, and lopsided fiddler crabs scatter to your left and right. Mangrove trees thrust up spiky roots to trip you. Reeds crowd in around you. The smell of the earth is primeval. You have to stamp the ground to clear it of crabs who flee sideways, scuttling away into tennis ball-size holes.

You climb up and leap off a dune and onto another until you are out of the slime, gleaming with sweat and covered with coarse golden granules. Your skin tingles with the drying salt, and you feel better, much better. This is complete freedom. No one about.

It's an odd thing: you can only be yourself when you are absolutely alone. The minute someone appears, you leap into some other self and begin acting. Why? Is it possible ever to be yourself, like you are when you are alone? Or are you still in some ghostly mask while you are alone too, unable to rip off this acting self? What is the real you, the real self that is not constructed, or habit-formed by genetics, nurture, and ecopoliticosocioshit? You don't know. It feels good being this self, this Rousseauian free man. But perhaps the good feeling has more to do with the fact that you have succeeded in one of your selves, that you have just procured a job, wormed your way into a pleasantly secluded cottage 9,837 kilometres away and bought yourself a space in which you can be yourself, whoever you are.

*

The word 'I', like the word 'self', is a word that has fallen into ill-repute. There is no such thing. You initially named your doctoral dissertation 'Constructing the African Self' but then had to erase all the selves in it, on advice from your Lacanian supervisor. *The 'self' is a false construct,* she'd said. *You have to use the word 'subject'. And for god's sake, stop using the personal pronoun in your academic work. Who is this 'I'? Haven't you realised that the author is dead, and that even if he isn't, he does not know what he is talking about?*

*

Your meditation, conscious as it is, is made even more conscious by the sight of a lone figure walking miles away on the dunes, watching you, as if to test you, to see what chameleon colour you turn. You are suddenly too aware of yourself, how you appear to this man. Or woman. At this distance and in the haze of the sun, you only see a stick figure. The person is walking, meandering in aimless circles, but always returning and staring out at the sea. Or at you. Reassured that you must also be an unrecognisable stick figure, you continue what you are doing, which is tracing your feet in the sand, feeling the texture of the granules, and staring at the brown haze over the sea. Then the person waves. So he is watching. Annoyed, you wave back, conscious now that you are doing what the self you are now would not do. Get lost! you want to say to this watcher, but instead you wave heartily back, to keep the peace, to show you are a friendly, fellow human being.

That evening, alone in a dark house (no electricity yet), you eat the second K Burger and chips glued together with white grease. Faint echoes of Dire Straits waft across from the house behind, but they are no match for the frog chorus at the end of the property, or the screeching cicadas on all four sides of the cottage. Animals scuffle in the bush. You strain to listen to the haunting guitar of Mark Knopfler's 'Private Investigations', played with thumb and fingers.

You discard the pink sheets and lie on the open mattress, tossing and turning, listening to mosquitoes buzzing and geckos tapping on the ceiling until you drift into a haze of dead sleep. But at midnight you wake, sweat-drenched and harassed. The previous occupants of this house are still around. Whoever lived here before has imprinted his sweaty, restless nature in the air, and the room is full of ghosts.

You crawl out of bed and light the candle. The room immediately fills with shadows of hugely distorted Timothy Turners leaping around. You reach for the volume at your bedside, *Bantu's Complete Works*, flip through to a page chosen at random and begin to read.

∧

∧ ∧

"The Hermit Cockroach"

I am a spirit hovering over the water,
A soul brooding over the formless void,
Waiting to incarnate.

What is the shape of my soul?
Am I black, white? Male, female?
My soul does not wear a label,
Does not hunch its shoulders,
Does not carry centuries of programmed
Guilt or shame or degradation or complexes.
I live in the words and conventions but am NOT.
I am other.
I pretend, yes, but I am always aware that I am lying,
Humouring;
I am not my body or my roots
I am not my skin.

I am a soul, a spirit, an ageless, sexless, raceless being,
Yet I am the fullness of my sex, my race, my age at the same time.
I am uncomfortably lodged in the kontradikshun,
In a particular space and time,
Dependent on the shells I inhabit for survival;
I need to eat, sleep,
Commune,
so I husk myself until
I get too uncomfortable
And then—

I move on.

v

You blow out the candle, slap the incessant mosquitoes. No air-conditioning, no fans, no cool breeze here, just the pounding waves on the rough shore rocking you to sleep.

3

Periplaneta americana
· · · · · · · · · · · · · ·
American cockroach

> American cockroaches (*Periplaneta americana*) are the largest cockroaches found near human habitation and can fly, although they do not get their wings until adulthood. Prolific breeders, they can hatch up to 150 offspring a year. Interestingly, the American cockroach which has spread all over the world is thought to have originated in Africa and was possibly brought across in slave ships in the 1600s.

You wake at five thirty a.m. to a rustling of leaves, cawing and scratching. Outside your window, a squadron of birds with oversize beaks and scruffy black and white feathers are feasting on the paw-paws. Are you seeing right? They look dinosauric, rhinosauric, prehistoric. *Shoo. Shoo.* You bang the window sill. *Bugger off.* Only then do they dip and dive in a curious arc of flight above the house. Makaya! Makaya! Makaya! they call.

The sun prises open the horizon and blood oozes through the cracks.

You stumble through the garden—barefoot—to salvage a paw-paw and twist it off its stalk. *This was supposed to be my breakfast, you thieving bastards.* You slice it open with a pen knife, scoop the black pips out and grind them into the red earth. Then you sit on the back step to eat and watch the sun ripen through the trees. The sea pounds at the coastline.

In the bathroom, a scorpion claims your green toilet bag, and its tail arches as you try to reach for your toothbrush. It is small—three centimetres—but these buggers are deadly. You clamp a shoe box over it and carry it to the edge of the lawn where you shake it off into the rubbish heap.

You are used to creatures that kill with one bite, sting, suck, or zap. Your five-year-old niece nearly died of a paralysis tick bite in North Queensland. The Australian bush is dripping with brown snakes, black snakes, tiger snakes and taipans (to name a few of the more deadly species). But here in Africa you don't know the bad guys from the good guys yet.

And then there is the gecko that clings to the ceiling of the bedroom all night catching mosquitoes and making kissing noises every time you try to drift off to sleep. In the morning it occupies the bathroom while you shower. It follows your every movement, watches you take a crap, and cocks its head at the clanking of the toilet roll against the wall.

> Lizards drop their tails as decoys to allow them to get away from predators. All lizards have detachable tails. Which is why humans need tales too, to trail along behind them, to give them balance. And what are tales for? The analogy swishes its way through the jungle. Detachable tails are for self-preservation, to distract predators and entertain unwelcome visitors. Leave them wagging like tongues so that the teller of the tale can escape. But beware the tales that do not detach. Scorpion tails have a sting at the end. Cockroaches, on the other feeler, have no tales to tell, so to speak.
>
> Sizwe Bantu, 'The Tale of the African Lizard'
> from *Ubuntu!* Vol. IX, pp. 23-24.

There are the insects: long-legged spiky *hexapoda*, shiny black monster centipedes, a freeway of ants, each the size of your thumb, beetles sporting rhino horns. Spiders—again you are used to huntsmen and funnelwebs—but here monsters lurk in every corner, black widows under the kitchen counter and the chairs, and aliens with swollen abdomens, their backs crawling with a million baby spiders—the stuff nightmares are made of.[1]

---

1   Superstitions have given rise to many myths about cockroaches; for example, the myth of the dreaded African kissing bugs. One bite will make you itch forever, and not an ordinary itch, but a sexual itch that drives you mad with desire, and leaves you unable to ever satisfy your lust.

You pour your cereal into a bowl of preserved milk and out scramble five live cockroaches. They swim valiantly in the milk to reach the sides.

'Bloody hell.' You scoop them out, contemplate eating the cereal, but decide against it and pour the mixture into the flowerbed outside. The packet is crawling with cockroaches, so you dump that too.

Cockroaches have made themselves at home in all your packets, even chewing the cardboard that holds the cereal. Three large Oriental/African cockroaches scurry away as you open the pantry door. You find the nearest weapon—a tea towel this time—and whack them to death. One escapes, crippled, a serrated leg left behind in the sugar bowl, but you smash it with your shoe as it tries to squeeze into a crack in the floorboards.

Your love of the cockroach is only theoretical, symbolic, literary. You wonder about Bantu's obsession with these pests: is his fascination with the *Periplaneta*, *Blaberus* and *Blatella* species also only theoretical, or does he keep them as pets, revere them as tiny gods of the oppressed? Does he study their behaviour to get inspiration for his material?

It is time for work. In spite of the cold shower, you are already sweating. You have to dunk your head under the tap before donning the suit.

Surely this is madness? How soon will you be able to shed this skin? But the suit, you have to remind yourself, is the uniform of the supercilious sneerers. And you are now one of them. Funny that. You go to university, ranting and radicalising, not realising you are one of the elite, and then you finally capitulate and take your place as oppressor of yourself.

But if you look smart, the rental car looks a right mess. It is wet with dew. Mud has splashed up the doors and bumpers and caked dry; road dirt has sprayed up onto the windscreen and roof; and the tyres look a little depressed, if not entirely miserable. The exhaust makes a farting noise if you rev it too high.

You arrive on campus at seven thirty. No armed gangs of thugs or ambushes intercept you this time, but just past the Mazisi Kunene turnpike, an *impi* of Zulu warriors wheels onto the verge of the freeway ahead of you and marches in squadrons of four abreast along the verge. They are singing some war song, their bare chests glistening in the sun, spears whacking their shields in time to the beat. Cowhide shields, knobkerries, spears, the lot. Is there a war on you don't know about? Or a remake of the movie *Shaka Zulu* you have stumbled into? But other cars whiz by unperturbed, so you do the same.

Even this early in the morning, the university is rivuleted with students in jeans, joggers and sandals, t-shirts with corporate logos, and backpacks. You squeeze past giggling triplets of women, heavy phalanxes of men; you listen to loud conversations held on mobile phones by students staring through you at electronic friends. Students slouch in the shade, or drape themselves onto benches, or brush past you, engaged in fervent dialogues about important matters. You understand nothing of the clicking, musical language. What good was that iZulu language course you took on the plane on the way over here?

Sawubona! Wena unjani? Ngi khona.

The Honours classroom is an octagonal over-air-conditioned room with no windows. Ten pairs of eyes follow you across the room and watch you dump *Modern South African Literature* on the podium. Seven women, three men: the student elite of the university.

None of these students has textbooks. You have been warned.

The women sit in the first three rows, cushioned in groups of solidarity. The men, as men do, sit in the dark of the back row, arms folded. One places his runners on the desk in front of him. Another wears his cap backwards on his head. Another in gang-baggy pants holds a phone to his ear.

Your attention is focused on the female student in the front row. Her thick blonde dreadlocks hang halfway down her back, tangled with beads and shells. She wears a black bowler hat at an angle, and her pale green eyes are bright in contrast to her dark skin. She's like a creature from the deep who's been washed and tumbled into existence by a briny sea. The way she stares at you, and the way others look at her, tell you that she is used to being the centre of male admiration and attention. Here is another person who speaks to the world with her body and not her words.

Do you need to casually mention the AK-47 propped up against the cupboard in the corner? And ... is this a panga you see before you, lying on the front desk, stained with dried blood?

As your eyes adjust, you see them—the three hijackers in the back row. Kaliban. The AK man slouched in the front row, his feet up on the desk; next to him, the man with the scar.

Should you call security?

Should you make a leap for the AK?

Or should you simply clutch the podium tightly and swallow hard, staring in turn at the panga then the AK then the students, grinning like an idiot?

'You remember us?'

'Joel.'

'Kaliban—with a K.'

'His real name however is Caesar Langa.'

The nightmare resurrected. Panga man, Scarface and AK man. You swallow.

'The New Strugglers.'

You open the folder and run your finger down the student list. Sure enough, here they are: Eric Phala (pronounced 'pala'); Caesar Langa;

'And you must be ...'

'Joel Matinde.'

'You ... you're students? Honours students? And is this ... (pointing to the AK-47) ... allowed in a lecture hall?'

They grin like crocodiles.

'Forgive me, I'm not from South Africa—perhaps this is common practice here ...' Like the *impi* of Zulu warriors, burnt-out offices, the Frankenstein stitches on Zimmerlie's head—all perfectly normal.

'It's for the play, sir.'

'The play?'

'*The Tempest.*'

The AK, gunmetal heavy symbol for liberation and oppression, shimmers before your eyes. You stare. The AK is crude and badly made: salvaged from parts of guns to be sure, but non-functioning—the barrel a piece of pipe, the butt (with notches) from a plastic toy gun you could buy in any supermarket. The panga—real enough—is also a prop, blunted, daubed with red paint.

'Is this what you were carrying with you yesterday?'

'We're doing *The Tempest* for our group Honours Project,' explains Eric Phala.

'Kaliban, you see, takes up arms against Prospero, liberates the island ...'

'The Kapitalist Kolonisers—both with a K—are banished ...'

'Driven into the sea.'

'I'm Ariel,' says Scarface. 'He is under house arrest by Prospero and has to do his bidding until he negotiates a settlement.'

'Trinkulo with a K.'

'Wait, wait. You're putting on *The Tempest*. With an ... AK-47?'

'A modern version,' says Eric Phala. 'Where the oppressed have weapons to fight back.'

Joel Matinde: 'We rewrote the entire play ourselves. Workshopped it.'

Kaliban: 'The New Strugglers—that's the name of our play group.'

Eric Phala: 'The New Struggle for a New South Africa.'

Joel Matinde: 'The New Struggle for the Post-Apartheid, Post-New South Africa.'

Kaliban gestures to the ceiling: 'You taught me language, and my profit on it is, I know how to curse. The red plague rid you for learning me your language!'

You cannot keep your eyes off the AK, wondering now how you could possibly have mistaken it for the real thing. It is a crude caricature of an AK-47.

You feel, not for the first time in your life, very foreign. Your perceptions are slow as mud.

The woman in the front row hasn't said a word yet. She folds her arms and watches you with ironic superiority.

'And you are?'

She does not answer. The men at the back speak for her. 'She's Miranda! Miranda!'

'Prospero the Kapitalist's beautiful daughter,' says Kaliban.

'But in our version,' says Eric, 'she marries Kaliban, not the prince!'

'And what's your name, Miranda?'

Finally, she deigns to speak. 'Tracey Khumalo.'

'Is that Khumalo with a K?'

Your eyes meet. She tosses her braided hair over her shoulder and the beads and bells clatter and jingle. An echo of a past ache inserts itself in the present, cuts and pastes itself onto her, squeezes your heart for a moment, and then is gone.

Beauty and good looks, which are merely accidents of biology, should not influence how you treat a student, or any person for that matter. And why should such an accident of beauty (and beauty is always relative, constructed) elevate a person's status in the eyes of others? So you refuse to pay homage. Or try not to anyway. But her green eyes follow your every move, like a cat about to pounce on its prey.

'What have you guys got against the letter C?'

She speaks to you as if you are an idiot. 'It's not African.'[2]

You could say something here. But you don't. 'So, who's playing Prospero in your play?'

'We still don't have anyone to play Prospero. We need a white man, and no white man has volunteered.'

You have sufficiently regained your composure. 'Why am I not surprised?'

The men at the back laugh.

You are aware of the baggage you carry, that they carry: that this superficial friendliness is not real, that underneath this banter is a century of resentment against white men, of which you are one. You have to tread carefully. But your instinct is to say to hell with treading carefully. Culture is not god. Culture is a mould growing and feeding on people, a deceptive green furry substance. You believe that underneath all racial, gendered, cultural, religious and political impositions, there is a fundamental sameness, common ground and this is what you need to tap into here. *Vive la similitude!*

For example, they have an ironic humour you can relate to. Their attitude to the world is wry and sceptical, a familiar stance. The distance with which they measure themselves from others is a trait you might say

2   The letter 'c' in IsiZulu is pronounced with a click, not as 'see' or 'kay' as in most European languages, hence the comment that it is not 'African'. This is nothing unusual. Most English speakers don't like the letter 't'. Cockneys and Londoners say 'w' instead of 'th', and when they can possibly help it, leave out the 't' altogether: 'writing a letter' becomes 'wri'in a le'a'. Americans and Australians, however, prefer a 'd' to a 't': 'wriding a ledder'. But Tracey is probably referring here to the word 'Afrika', the name adopted by black consciousness movements during Apartheid South Africa which strove for a New Azania. The 'a' and 'k' were of course a subconscious draw card. Ironically the word is also spelled 'Afrika' in Afrikaans, the 'language of the oppressor'. The word 'Africa' itself is, of course, not African, as Sizwe Bantu tells us in his 'Notes on Azania' (see p. 165, *Seven Invisible Selves*.) Africa is the Latin name for this continent, kindly bestowed on it by Roman imperialists. And if we want to play the *reductio ad absurdum* game, none of the letters 'a-f-r-i-c-a', or even 'k', are African either.

you had yourself. They exude a dark, restless energy. This is a language you have in common.

You gesture to the six women who sit stony-faced in the middle rows. 'What parts are you ladies playing?'

Joel answers for them. 'They're the chorus. They comment on the play in a unified voice.'

'The main parts of the play are traditionally taken by men,' offers Scarface.

'And what do the women think of that?'

'They agree with us,' says Joel.

Tracey twists her body to face the back row and says something in Zulu which is undoubtedly a swear word.

Scarface rises in his chair, but Kaliban pulls him down again.

You cannot keep your eyes off the scar that runs from the corner of his left eye to the right corner of his mouth, his nose split in two by what could only be an axe stroke. You politely try to ignore it, but it is obvious you are uncomfortable. You cannot help wondering: Zimmerlie's scar, the mutilated kitten, and now this.

They notice, of course. 'Hey, *ushomi*,' calls Kaliban, 'don't worry about him. He was in the struggle, and they chopped him.'

'The struggle?'

'The Old Struggle,' explains Eric. 'Against Apartheid. In detention, they chopped him.'

They are having you on, you are sure. He is far too young to have been involved in any struggle. Apartheid ended in 1994 and this man can be no older than nineteen or twenty. But who are you to argue? He carries his scar like a veteran's medal.

'Tell us about yourself, sir,' says Caesar Langa. 'What are you doing in eSikamanga? How did you end up here?'

You loosen your tie. 'Well, let's say I didn't really "end up" here, since this is hardly the end … I applied for the job on the internet.'

When Tracey speaks, her voice is husky. 'Where you from, Dr Turner?'

A year ago you would have been attracted to her, smitten even. You watch her with dissociated fascination. You've been here before, and you know it's treacherous territory, so you just watch yourself watching her. Thank god for scar tissue.

'From Australia. Melbourne, Victoria. My Ph.D. is in African Literature … well, Postcolonial, Post-Apartheid, Post-Struggle Literature. I studied the great writer Sizwe Bantu … and focused on the African Subject in the novels of Sizwe Bantu.'

'Who's Sizwe Bantu?'

'You're kidding me? Sizwe Bantu, you know, the great South African writer!'

'Sizwe Bantu?' She closes her eyes and taps the pencil on her teeth as if to evoke the vast catalogue of African writers she knows in her mind. 'Never heard of him.'

Now she is pulling your leg. Surely. 'That's funny. He's in the book that is set for you this semester …'

She shrugs her left shoulder and the shells, bells and bric-a-brac in her hair jangle and tinkle. 'We didn't use that book.'

'Which one did you use, then?'

She taps her forehead with her pencil. 'This one.'

You cannot help staring at the green eyes. 'That's not a textbook.'

Her smile is bewitching, seductive. But you shake your head.

Eric Phala indicates the books piled up on the end desk—ten copies of *Modern African Stories*, neatly spider-webbed and covered with what looks like a semester of dust. 'We must create our own African traditions, not passively receive those which have been imposed upon us.' It sounds as if he is quoting somebody.

'You didn't use any books at all in this class?'

Tracey pulls out a pink A5 book from her bag. You read CREATIVE WRITING JOURNAL printed in neat handwriting on the front cover. 'We're not naïve consumers of multinational corporate products. We wrote our own textbook. Wrote our own play.' Her words are spiky, her body language defensive.

Eric Phala concurs: 'Creative Writing gives power back to the people. Creative Writing breaks down the elitist idea of a literary canon.'

'And what's in there?'

'Our own authentic experience of the world. The real text. We wrote about …'

You reach out to take her journal, which she is holding up in the air as if to pass to you. A hiss of disapproval snakes across the back row and she hastily plunges it back into her backpack. 'It's nothing really,' she says, 'just a way to make us write honestly.' A mobile phone prods her back and she arches in annoyance.

'I see.'

You stare at her a little too long. 'What?' she says.

'Nothing.'

You remind me of someone I know, you want to say. Someone ten thousand kilometres away whose name begins with M. Someone I am trying to shut out of my heart. Someone familiar, someone unstable.

You sense that her bravado is a mask for her vulnerability. But you are also aware of how you project your own psychological defects onto others.

Time is ticking by on the large clock on the wall. You only have a few minutes until the end of the lecture. You distribute the ten copies of *Modern African Stories* to the ten students, and take your place at the podium.

They fidget and whisper.

'What?'

'Nothing, nothing,' says Eric.

'All right then. Will you please open your texts at page 343 and read the poem you find there: Bantu's 'The Bloody Horse'. Please read for me, Mr Phala, the poem you find before you.'

Mr Phala opens the book, and then slams it shut again. Smiles.

'What's the matter?'

'I don't have it.'

'What?'

'That page is missing in my book.'

'Okay, Caesar, you read it.'

'That page is missing in my book too.' He holds it up.

You walk across and examine the book, check Eric Phala's too, and find the same careful tearing along the centre spine of the book. 'Did you tear this page out, Mr Phala?'

He frowns, as if trying to remember.

'Does anyone have that page?'

All open their books to the same empty space. No, of course not. 'Okay, what happened?'

The class ripples with grins and nudges.

'Do you mind sharing the joke, folks?'

'Dr Makaya ...'

The hum of the air-conditioner grows louder. You are arguing with someone else, someone whose ghostly presence in this room is so strong, you can see his giant shadow over them.

'What? He tore them out?'

Tracey raises her hand. 'Dr Makaya asked us to tear out all the pages that had Bantu in them.'

'I thought you said you had never heard of Sizwe Bantu.'

She shrugs her shoulder. 'Well, we've never read him. Obviously.'

'The cockroach story too? The poems?'

'Everything.' She holds up the index page of her book. Even the contents have been mutilated with black pens, so that Sizwe Bantu's place in the African canon is erased. Her eyes dance, if you are not mistaken, in teasing mockery.

The question in your mind is, of course, why?

This they cannot tell you.

'Fine. I'll read you some, then.' You place your own text on the image projector and zoom in so Bantu's words are writ large on the screen, and then you read the poem slowly, hoping to instil in them some sense of wonder and awe about the greatest writer in African literature. 'And, if you like the letter K, well, you guys weren't the first to play with words like this. Listen …'

The Afrikan I

The Internet Is the solution to the spIrItual dIscomfort
we feel In a materIal voId. Here I am pure voIce, I can speak
wIth my cartesIan self, my dIsembodIed conscIousness wIthout
havIng to use vocal cords or accent or other blemIshes. No one
judges me by my skIn colour, gesture, habIt, nervous tIcs, sex,
century, but only by my thoughts, my pure mInd, my Idea, my true
"I" of ImagInatIon, Impulse, InstInct, IntuItIon and IndIvIduallty …
The mInd's "I", the true"I" of sIzwe, whIch Is not my name,
because no shell can be ME—the nameless wordless "I". I am a
novelIst because the novel Is pure "I" conscIousness.

Yet who am I wIthout my rainbow skIn, my hIstory, my tradItIon?
Whose I am I? BIll Gates's voIce In AmerIkan chatspeak?[3]

3   An oblique reference to the American cockroach, *Periplaneta americana*, that appears throughout this Bantu novel (*AfriKan Metaphysics*, 2007) in the role of imperialist and linguistic coloniser.

No, to be AfrIkan means to rIp out the Is of Korporate KonsumerIsm
So close your Is: None but ourselves can free our mInd's I.

'So what do you think? Caesar.'
'Call me Kaliban, please. I have to get into my part.'
'Kaliban, what do you think?'
He considers. 'Does he capitalise his Is all the way through the book, or did he have a defective key on his computer keyboard?'
It isn't quite hostility, but it is resistance. Maybe you were wrong about the rapport you were beginning to build. You slam the book shut. 'Okay, folks, for tomorrow, please read Chapter One, and we'll discuss it in class. Your first assignment will be based on … what, Mr Phala?'
'We already have an assignment,' says Eric. 'The play.'
'And we keep a journal of all our activities in our notebooks,' adds Tracey. 'We don't impose other texts on our creative impulse.'
This is Makaya talking. You can hear his voice. 'I see.'
'And we'd like you to help us, Dr Turner. We have to put on that play. Everyone's counting on us. We can't let them down …'
'Our families are all invited. The student hall is booked. We've advertised it everywhere.'
It is an olive branch. That much you recognise. You consider. 'All right. Fine. So the deal is, you read Chapter One, and then I'll be happy to listen to what help you need for your play.'

*

You are familiar with such petty academic squabbles, particularly in this case the very well-worn division here between those in English Departments who study 'literary texts' and read and write literary criticism, and those who write creatively, in effect creating their own texts, and discarding both the idea of the literary text as an object to be studied and the essay form as a method of apprehending meaning. Or to put it another way: English Departments have split into 'readers' and 'writers', critics and artists, left brain and right brain, with both sides pooh-poohing the other. And it seems the divisions of this English Department have fallen neatly along the same silly ideological lines. Zimmerlie and Mpofu are literary critics, and Makaya is the advocate for creative writing. Hence his glib dismissal of the 'text', conventional assignments, and reading texts for meaning. And, you note, he has politicised the issue by maintaining that his creative leaning is more legitimately 'African', and Zimmerlie's insistence on textual analysis is colonial, Eurocentric, imperialist.

And you? You don't care really one way or the other. Literary Theory did nearly sink your academic ship, but at least it was rigorous and precise; Creative Writing does seem to be wishy-washy and blindly naïve in its belief that all you need to do is express yourself to find the truth.

But you have to be careful here. Academic squabbles are rarely about the issues they say they are about.

*

Outside the classroom block, on your way to Admin, you find another blind kitten—or the same one—mewing in the bushes.

Makaya is beginning to take shape, to grow in your mind: a man who tears writers out of textbooks, a man whose words students quote as if he is some kind of prophet, a man who has abolished the text and who encourages free expression rather than rigorous critical analysis. And, it seems, a man who demands worship from his followers.

Your appointment later that morning is with Administration (with a capital A, the way people pronounce it here), to get your photo ID taken.

You sit in a blackened room and smile at a lens while an extremely large man pushes and pulls you into alignment with an extremely phallic lens. The students call this man Idi Amin not because he looks like the Ugandan dictator, but because he looks like a large Forest Whitaker, the actor who caricatures Idi Amin in the Hollywood movie. *Smile*, the man frowns, and then—flash—Timothy Turner is a grinning head-and-shoulders mugshot. Why smile? Keep your face contorted for a second shot. Now there will be a frozen lie, of your face, in space and time in a darkened room somewhere.[4]

---

4   Bantu objects to photographs of people as proof of, or as a measure of, identity. No photos of the author appear on the jackets of Bantu's novels, and characters in his books regard photographs as 'frozen lies in time and space'.

> Am Eye white? Am Eye black?
>
> Eye wear meye face backwards.
>
> No one judges me by meye skin colour;
>
> Sizwe is not meye name, because no shell can be me
>
> Eye cannot be freed unless you
> listen, read, open the door
>
> And let me out.
>
> Eye will not exist unless you imagine me.
>
> Create me.
>
> Mould me into existence with the
> clay of your 'I'magination.
>
> – Sizwe Bantu, 'Me, Myself, Eye' in
> *The Five AfriKan Senses* (2009)

'So you're the English lecturer replacing Makaya?'
'Yes.'
'Congratulations,' beams Idi Amin, 'and commiserations.'
'What can you tell me about him?'
The man shakes his head. 'Don't get on the wrong side of him.'
'Too late, mate, I think I already am.'
He laughs. 'As is everyone on this campus.'

At twelve o'clock, you stand in line in the staff canteen to collect lunch on a wooden tray. The food is another cultural first— *Pap 'n' Wors*, with Mrs Ball's Chutney.

The 'pap' is a stodgy porridge of ground white corn, like polenta, dripped with onion and tomato gravy, and the 'wors' (pronounced 'vorce' as in divorce) is an obscene piece of veined fleshy sausage, coiled like some deadly African snake.

From the back of the room, Zimmerlie and Mpofu beckon you to join them.

'Good afternoon, gentlemen.'

What is most remarkable about these two men is not their physical appearance, but the way their bodies seem somehow irrelevant—dragged around with them as annoying appendages. Mpofu lifts a heavy hand to a heavy brow, scratches his chin, surprised indeed to find it there. Zimmerlie shrugs an uncomfortable, ill-fitting body. The skin is too loose. Zimmerlie and Mpofu are minds, not bodies.

'Timothy, I hope your first day has been okay so far. How did the Honours class go?'

The bangle-clad woman at the nearby table looks up, not at your face, but at the knife and fork you are holding. She is eating the pap with her fingers, dipping it into the chutney. As is everyone else. Another cultural *faux pas*. You wipe your lips with the paper napkin and ditch the utensils.

'Fine, fine.'

'They're back on track with the syllabus?'

'They didn't have their books.'

'They didn't have their books?' says Mpofu. 'What on earth have they been doing, if they didn't have their books? What has he been doing with them?'

Should you tell them about the obliteration of your favourite writer from their textbooks? 'From what I gather, they have been doing a lot of … creative writing, free writing, self-expression. Not that there is anything wrong with creative writing *per se*.'

Mpofu clatters his cup down on his saucer. 'At the expense of real learning, real critical analysis of the text, Timothy, there is. Creative writing they can do at home in their spare time. At an institution of learning, no.' He wiggles his head and air-quotes the words 'creative writing'.

Zimmerlie: 'These days, people are more interested in writing about themselves than reading the Great Writers.' You can hear the capitals.

So you were right—about the superficial division of creative versus critical at least. 'They did seem rather self-absorbed.'

Zimmerlie's scar gleams white. 'Graphomania, it's called. Creative writing? Phhhh! Everyone is a bloody writer these days.[5] A book is published every six seconds. And now with the internet, everyone writes, writes, writes … badly. A world of scribblers—no, they don't scribble anymore, do they, they … type … they "chat" they "text".'

You stare back at the darting eyes, the white hair flopping over his face, the clenched fists.

'Graphomaniacs, the lot of them. Milan Kundera—you know him, Timothy? The Czech writer: he calls it graphomania[6]—and now he wants to infect our campus with that disease.'

'Kundera does?'

'Makaya.' He presses his eyes closed and holds a heavy hand to a sweaty forehead.

Mpofu speaks in an urgent whisper. 'The issue is not simply creative writing, Timothy. He wants to abolish all the tried and tested methods of established academic practice.'

So now you know. The battle lines are drawn between old and new, conservative and radical, traditional and pioneering, and more specifically here, between critical versus creative, left brain versus right brain. All of them false dichotomies. Hasn't Derrida smashed this idea of binary oppositions? And your yin and yang Eastern spiritual phase (when you made your pilgrimage to India, your own, Australian, experience of the Other) was all about reuniting the supposed opposites that are mutually necessary for identity. So you bide your time—the big self that you are. You go with the flow, observe, notice, humour them all, and stand far enough away so you don't get sucked in.

'Sshhh. Shh,' says Mpofu.

---

5   Witness, for example, the proliferation of Creative Writing programs in institutions of higher learning over the past twenty years. It is estimated that there are over a thousand graduate programs across the world that offer Masters and Doctorates in writing, and almost every university offers undergraduate courses in Creative Writing. And this is not to mention the programs and courses outside the academy: writing schools, online courses, writing residences and retreats. These programs churn out thousands and thousands of writers per year. Everyone is a writer, one Creative Writing textbook proclaims, and the world is flooded with millions of writers, or people who call themselves writers.

6   Milan Kundera (the Czech writer, 1929—) in *The Book of Laughter and Forgetting* (1988) criticises the proliferation of Creative Writing, and maintains that instead of connecting people and their experiences, it has the opposite effect: 'everyone surrounds himself with his own writings as with a wall of mirrors cutting off all voices from without.'

You stare at the man with orange hair who walks in, a book in his hand. He joins a table opposite yours, and sits. Zimmerlie raises his eyes at Mpofu, and Mpofu gives an ever-so-slight nod of the head in return.

'Dr James Ngwenya,' mutters Mpofu.

'One of our illustrious colleagues,' explains Zimmerlie.

'We've met.'

The man—James Ngwenya—looks at you from across the way, so you tip an imaginary hat—'G'day'—and his response puts you in no doubt as to his feelings. He turns his back on you and scrapes his chair loudly.

'Ngwenya? Doesn't that mean … ?'[7]

Mpofu nods. 'It's a common Zulu name around here.'

Ngwenya does not stay. He has popped in to the canteen, it seems, simply to give you a dirty look.

You watch him go.

Zimmerlie speaks in a hoarse whisper louder than his normal speaking voice. 'Makaya and Ngwenya are like this.' He binds two yellow fingers together.

'We have to watch our backs.'

After lunch, you are free to go home, or retire to your office to prepare classes. Unfortunately, you do not have an office, although Makaya's had been promised as soon as they can pry the bloody man's name off the door and get him to move his crap (Mpofu's words) out of there. Until then, you have to find somewhere else.

The library is alluring. You hurry into its cool white noise. Although a library boasts silence, you can always hear the humming of arguments, the slithering and writing of words, the *tak tak tak* of binary codes and prescriptive thinking, and the silent screams of tortured souls trapped in books, the dead clamouring for your attention.

---

7   *Ngwenya:* Zulu (n). Large voracious aquatic reptile having a long snout with massive jaws and sharp teeth and a body covered with bony plates; found in sluggish tropical waters and swamps. Animistic associations: wily, crafty, treacherous, untrustworthy and predatory.

You avoid the line of blinking blue screens, which substitute for a reading room. You head for the books—the real books—upstairs. Your resistance to technology is not ideological but visceral. And of course once you have read Bantu's articles on technology, there is no turning back.[8]

But these days, if you want to know who someone is, you look for electronic evidence of their existence. If they are not on the net, they do not exist. If they have made neural connections via blogs, Facebook, online publication, they do. It's a modification of the old adage: publish or perish. You only exist as words on a screen. You find the search bar, type in *The African Presence*.

Volume IX number 6. Here you are—Timothy Turner.

It is not vanity. It is assurance that you exist.

Your first article on Sizwe Bantu is neatly digitalised in long imprisonment since 2009: 'Bantu waives Britannia's Rules'.

You worked hard at this paper, editing and rewriting, and agonising over every word, smoothing out arguments, and implications, and finally sending it to a local university journal only to be rejected by both peer reviewers. 'The argument is weak.' 'These are non-questions.' 'There is a lack of theoretical understanding of the basic premises.' 'This is naïve.' 'He needs to read more widely.' 'This has all been said before.'

You felt as if you had been obliterated. Your words erased. But you could not give up. You rewrote the piece, revised it and sent it off again. Again you received smarmy criticism. He needs to read this; he needs to rewrite that; he needs to drop the introduction; the conclusion peters out and says nothing new. You rewrote it again, according to all the recommendations, and resubmitted. You beat those words into sentences, those sentences into cogent, watertight arguments, and this time they accepted it. But it was by this time a flogged dead horse. You felt no joy at its publication. You had been browbeaten into writing something so far removed from your initial impulse that it no longer felt yours. But now you could at least call yourself an academic.

8   See for example, 'Technology as Colonising Discourse' in *The African Presence*, Vol. 4, pp. 35-45, where Bantu argues that modern technology is a ruthless drive for the control of people's minds, a hard-wiring of their brains to think a certain way that serves a homogenous, corporate empire of consumerism, and that to participate via email, use of the internet, in what he calls 'Microsoft English', is to participate in one's own re-colonisation.

But writing is only the first stage of creating yourself. Now someone has to read you. You do not exist unless someone else sees you. Otherwise you could be living in a solipsistic universe, one where no one hears the tree fall.

Be assured: your paper has been read. Modern journals allow for comments and reviews to be posted after the article. You scroll down and read the commentary.

THIS IS ALL KUK[9] is the first comment. And then: *He eats Bantu's shit and then reshits it.*

You scroll down further. *If Sizwe Bantu were dead, he would turn in his grave to read such drivel.*

You close the screen.

Bastards. Who invented such an appalling system where any Tom, Dick or Harry can comment on your work anonymously, like on Facebook? But let it go; let it go. When you publish something, it is not yours anymore: it becomes something else. It is no longer a part of your soul, if it ever was.

But since this first article, you wrote a steady stream of work about Bantu. You learned the language of literary criticism, of literary theory, a language that was measured, unemotional, calculating, the opposite in fact of your passionate feeling for the literature you were studying. How did it come to be that you could write sentences like *And thus it can be assumed that Bantu's irretrievable experimental narrativisation could be read as a type of immanent critique of postmodern dialectic?*

Now you look up your new employers. The protagonists Zimmerlie and Mpofu, as you have guessed, are both high-powered academics, electronically at least: formidable academics, extensively published.

They exist. They are literary critics, or rather Literary Critics, as you correctly assumed. Both Mpofu and Zimmerlie have published a steady stream of articles, journal entries, papers, conference talks, as academics are supposed to do. And they inhabit the language so well.

But Zimmerlie, you note, is not 'current' or 'active' as they say in the field. His last publication is over five years ago. And in academia, to stay on top, you have to 'publish or perish'. Interesting.

---

9 'Kuk' is the Egyptian god of darkness, which would mean that Turner's article is impenetrable or else imbued with a primordial form of mystical darkness. But, more likely, 'kuk' in this context is the Afrikaans word for 'shit'.

Now for the antagonists. Ngwenya is a common name here, like Smith or Nguyen or Lee, but you locate the man immediately. A rising academic, with a flurry of publications all in the past few years.

Makaya too is a fairly common name: the search engine races around the world and collects three million Makayas floating in cyberspace in a matter of microseconds.

Here he is: Senior Lecturer, University of eSikamanga.

You skim through the list of his achievements, his articles, books, papers, talks, and other publications. This man has written substantially on almost everything African: the writers Achebe, Ngugi, Armah, Head. He has served on committees, literature associations, university boards, and editorial panels for journals. The articles, the papers, the publications all say one thing: this is a formidable academic.

So now you know with whom you are messing. And it does not make you feel any better. A voice with a particularly heavy Aussie accent speaks in your head: who the hell do you think you are? What are you doing here?

The answer, though you can never tell anyone, is simply that you are not here for an academic position, or to take anyone's place. You are here because Bantu is here. This is where he situates his fiction. You are on a pilgrimage.

And the hope is of course that something will happen on this pilgrimage—some insight into the mysterious writer, at least. And at most, you dare to imagine an encounter. If he lives here, surely you may even bump into him somewhere? Why not? Maybe you will be shopping at the SPAR and there ahead of you will be a Presence. You will know immediately who it is. Perhaps he will even turn to you and speak. *Can't believe the price of cockroach bait these days, can you?*

But unlikely. No one has said anything about Bantu. In fact he seems unknown here. If he lives anywhere near here, there would be a flurry of publicity. But you live in hope. You can read it in the air, you can smell the scent, hear the music of the poet's words in the music of the language, in the undulation of the hills, in the crashing of the waves. And the cockroaches. Good god! Who wouldn't write about cockroaches if they lived here?

4

Blatella germanica

· · · · · · · · · · · · · ·

German cockroach

German cockroaches are the most common of all, and the image most people conjure when you say the word 'cockroach' is the *Blattella germanica*. They are opportunistic parasites and feed off anything and everything. These hardy creatures also originate in Africa and are often mistaken for the Asian cockroach, though they are much smaller and more agile, especially at night. Why German? Why Asian? Humans have anthropomorphised these creatures as if cockroaches have nationalities and share national characteristics in the limited way humans do. But cockroaches know no nationality or borders, and do not subscribe to a concept of divisive racial characteristics.

'The Cockroach Artist' by Sizwe Bantu

(The Present Tense, Vol. XXVI, Aug. 2002, pp. 43-50)

The Modern Afrikanist looked out of his flat one afternoon to see a ragged man loping down the street. He wore an interesting array of discarded clothing from the rubbish bins of Western society— faded blue dungarees, camouflage jacket, black takkies—and he was pushing a trolley taken from the nearest Pick n Pay filled with his treasures, white plastic bags weighed down with whatever loot he had collected.

Just as the Modern Afrikanist contemplated moulding a clay statue of this disinherited non-citizen of the new South Africa, he watched the street-man zip across the pavement and lunge at a Business Man's wallet. The Business Man (he had not seen him until now) was taking cash from an ATM, and was dressed in a smart suit, tie, crew cut, shiny black shoes. In a flash, the beggar rolled the trolley at the man to prevent him from following, and dashed at speed across the road, clutching what must have been the wallet. From his high vantage point, the Modern Afrikanist could see all—the beggar zig-zagging around the corner, the Business Man pushing aside the trolley with a clatter so it spilled its contents into the road, the man running like a footballer at the World Cup. The beggar snagged himself in a large crowd of commuters—mostly women—at the bus stop, and buried himself in the confusion. But the Business Man—sleek as a tiger—pulled out a hand gun, displayed it to the buildings around—exhibit number one, your Honour, is a 9mm Tokarev—jerked it at the sky, and seconds later the Modern Afrikanist heard the crack of a pistol shot in his ears. The man cringed on the pavement, covering himself; and without further warning, the Business Man stepped forward, aimed the pistol at the man's head and fired. The beggar jerked back, and then dropped flat on the pavement in a curiously zig-zag shape. The Business Man deftly retrieved his wallet, slipped it into his pocket and turned away neatly back to his car. But the women ballooned around him, gesticulating, opening raw red mouths. The Modern Afrikanist could almost hear their yelling. The Business Man raised his pistol again, fired two shots to clear a path for himself and, still holding the gun high, walked backwards through the crowd, slipped into his Mercedes and was gone.

The Modern Afrikanist watched for half an hour. No one came to help the beggar, whose blood had pooled around his head in a dark halo. The buses arrived and the women trooped in, glad to get on their way home, after a long day. The crowds stepped around, over, across the beggar, until finally an unmarked truck (ambulance? undertaker? municipality?) arrived, two men heaved the corpse into a body bag, tossed a bucket of foamy white liquid over the blood, and drove off through the rush hour traffic.

Only now did the questions accuse him: why had the Modern Afrikanist not intervened? Why had he not called the police? He could have rushed outside, tried to stop the Business Man, or at least written down his licence plate. Instead he had watched; no, not simply watched, but gorged himself on the experience, and thus participated in the atrocity.

It was vital that he make reparation: speak up, even if only in the language of art. He had to immortalise the way the beggar was splayed dead on the sidewalk, the way the crowd had mothered him, protested, and then dissipated; he had to capture the frozen moment in time when the Business Man held the gun high, the hesitation when the scene could have gone another way, but didn't.

And so two days later, a beautiful new painting decorated the walls of the Modern Afrikanist's flat—a golden sky, the romantic colours of an Azanian sunset, the commuters in all their historic despair at the bus stop, the white plastic bags billowing like clouds into the sky, and the man displayed on the street like a Z, blood thickly painted in globs, thick strokes of green wind, and the Business Man a thin tense scream of an Edvard Munch figure with a pistol—black and gleaming—in one hand, his face expressing the uncertainty whether he was going to live or die at the hands of the mob, pocketing his rightful possession with the other hand, a brown wallet, which was worth—in his eyes—the life of a non-citizen of a non-existent country in post-Afrika.

One final touch: from the plastic bags that had laden the trolley, the Modern Afrikanist had painted—Dali style—myriads of cockroaches escaping onto the streets and into gutters, crawling over cars, fleeing commuters, street signs, and, unnoticed, climbing up the leg of the Business Man's suit.

A row of corpses swings from your washing line. Only after you have navigated the car through the security gates, funnelled through the elephant grass, tramped across to the cottage and fumbled in your pocket for the key do you see them.

Jesus!

You drop back behind the car, your body taut. Out of the corner of your eye, you detect movement on the veranda: someone is here, waiting for you. You see a glint of metal—AK? Pistol? Panga?

The bodies swing in the slight breeze.

You back into the undergrowth, looking for some weapon—a spade, a thick stick—but find nothing. And of what use would this be anyway against an automatic weapon?

There has been a spree of wanton destruction and vandalism in Zululand towns recently, with attacks on residents which seem to have no motive other than gratuitous violence. Make sure your alarm systems are functioning properly. Be vigilant: if you encounter armed intruders on your property, do not resist or attempt to disarm them; give them what they want: your life is not worth a few Rand or a HD widescreen TV. Install a panic button in every room so that your security company can be notified when you are in distress.

Crowded-Planet (2013): p. 132.

You grope for a rock and feel its re-assuring hardness. Maybe you can bludgeon whoever is waiting for you in the head before he can shoot you. You measure the distance you have to run to get to the alarm button in the kitchen. You will never make it. Perhaps you can drive away. But before you can even turn the ignition key, you will be slumped dead against the wheel.

You peer out from behind the front fender.

The bodies swing again as the breeze rises, a little too easily, too lightly. In a macabre gesture the murderer has dressed the corpses in your clothes: blue Wrangler jeans, blue Gotcha t-shirt, neon bathing shorts. Red underpants. And the clothes—your clothes—have no bodies in them.

'*Sawubona!*' A young woman in a yellow apron curtsies at the front step.

You kick the wheel of the car, pretend that you have fixed whatever needed fixing, and stand up. Dust your hands. 'Who are you?'

She speaks to the ground, her hands held demurely in front of her. 'I'm Toko.'

Thoko perhaps.

'How did you get in here?'

'Mrs Steyn, she let me in.'

'You're the one at Mrs K's who served me … ?'

'No, that's my sister. I'm Thoko, your maid.'

'My maid? I don't have a … maid.'

'Yes. You have maid. All of you have maid. I am the one who will be your maid.'

'I don't want …' You gesture at the clothing on the line. 'Is this Mrs Steyn's doing?'

She looks bewildered. 'No, no. It is me. We decide who will be. Everyone in eSikamanga has maid. So we can all have job.'

She pronounces 'job' with such satisfaction, as if 'job' is the answer to everything she has ever desired. And you note the way she drops her articles, impatiently, as if the English language has too many words, and needs pruning to a more efficient level of communication: subject, verb, object.

'I don't want a …'

According to Zulu traditional custom, as a sign of respect, the woman does not look the man in the eye, and curtseys every time she speaks to him. Thoko thus speaks to your feet, and bobs her head and body down and up every time she talks to you. But her body language is impatiently dismissive, as if you are a fool to be humoured.

You scan the property. There are no panga-wielding men hiding in the bushes, no AK-trigger-happy thugs ready to commit acts of senseless, random violence. 'And how much am I supposed to pay you?'

She laughs. Why your question is funny you have no idea. 'It is all arrange. I do washing Tuesday, ironing Wednesday, and cleaning the house Thursday.' She speaks slowly as if talking to an idiot, to make sure you understand, counting on her fingers.

'I have to speak to Mrs Steyn about this.'

'Mrs Steyn is not the one to speak. I am the one.'

She promises to return the next day to iron your clothes (you who have never ironed your clothes in your life, you who have never seen the necessity to iron your clothes, you who are quite content to walk around with wrinkled shorts and trousers). She ducks under the fence and into the bushes. And this place is supposed to be secure? Electrified? You follow her path to the fence and see the hole between the two strands of wire, large enough for a person to squeeze through. She holds a strand of wire to steady herself as she climbs through.

'Careful, that's electrifi—'

But it isn't.

So much for the security system.

On the washing line, the clothing ghosts wave. Thoko has pegged them all meticulously, even your underpants and socks.

When you are sure she has gone, you do a quick 360 of the property just to make sure. When you are sure you are alone, you discard the suit and plunge into the outside shower. The drain is clogged with long odd strands of the previous resident's soapy hair, and you have to unblock some of the holes in the showerhead with a pine needle.

*

Dear M,

If only I had words to box these emotions, frame them, keep them at bay. But you are a flame licking at my flesh, a needle in my vein, the roar of a thunderstorm, the smell of spring jasmine in the morning. Mixed metaphors, I know, I know. All those clichés rolled into one. How can I go on?

One image remains and burns in my soul, a splinter of glass that goes septic: how, after you left, I scrubbed my carpet and found your long blonde hairs tangled in my scrubbing brush. All that hair. An average human sheds a hundred hairs a day. And here I am collecting them now, thinking: the pain will only cease when I have rid my carpet of all your hair.

T

*

You lie on the bed and stare at the green gecko on the wall. Although a slow ceiling fan leisurely churns the air above, it makes little difference.

You will have words with Mrs Steyn the next time you see her. A maid! Who does she think you are? You are not going to play master and slave here.

It is time to busy yourself with the 'inaugural speech' as Zimmerlie calls it. You take out your dissertation and leaf through it, looking for the papers and speeches you have already written and pressed between its pages. Yes, this will do nicely. But the qualms of discomfort needle you: how wise is it to promote Sizwe Bantu in a place where lecturers order students to tear him out of textbooks? Where your new employers stiffen their necks and bob their Adam's apples up and down when you show them your dissertation on Sizwe Bantu? Or when beautiful women with blonde dreadlocks and green eyes give you condescending smiles of ironic pity at the mention of his name?

You're hungry, and you have forgotten to fill the fridge with food. The only supermarket in town—the low roofed, large verandaed SPAR—is now closed, so you have to be content with a quick trip down to Mrs K's, which is always open. The same waitress serves you. 'You're Thoko's sister!'

'Thoko?' The woman ducks her head. 'No. No. I am not her.'

'Sure?' You scrutinise what little you can see of the woman's face, which is not much.

You order a takeaway and hurry home to eat a queasy chicken sandwich and greasy chips on the back porch, watching the dying sun burn into the glazed sugarcane-smoke horizon.

But after you turn in, and begin reading Bantu by candlelight (you have to read Bantu by candlelight), something—or someone—rustles in the leaves by the open bedroom window. Then you hear a cough. You place the book down on the table and blow out the candle. You crouch down against the bed so no silhouette can find you out. Like a gecko, you hug the walls, edge beneath the window on your hands and knees, and crawl to the kitchen, keeping below the counter top. You feel for the bread knife, and clasp its cold reassurance in your hand.

A foot crunches on the gravel. An ochre shadow slides across to the window and darkens the room. Someone's eyes and thoughts brood over the Bantu collection. You clutch the bread knife tight. You can almost hear him breathing.

The panic button is located under the kitchen counter. You should have paid attention when Mrs Steyn pointed it out; apparently it turns on some alarm, and floods the house and garden with light. With a swift flick of the hand, you turn it on.

Nothing happens. No alarm, no flooding of light to freeze an intruder in the act. Perhaps it alerts some vigilant on-duty policeman at the station who will screech into the driveway in a matter of minutes, with blue lights flashing, sirens on.

But no. You wait for long minutes, hearing the intruder crunch on the gravel around and around the property, looking no doubt for a way in.

It takes you only these few seconds to discover that you are a shit-scared coward, that you have not an ounce of bravery in your body. That all your principles concerning gun ownership could be tossed out of the window. If you had a bloody bazooka now, you would blast this intruder till Kingdom Come.

The steps cease—and the silence is even more eerie. What is he doing now?

You reach for the outside light switch (you don't even know if it works—you have never tried it before), and, yes, a yellow light drenches the porch and back garden. But you see no one. If the light dazzles the intruder, it blinds you too. If anyone is out there, he has now retreated into the darkness beyond the reach of the light.

You want to slam the door, shut yourself in, lock yourself away. You wait five minutes, listen to the thump of your heart, the wind in the palm trees, and then push open the front door and scour the garden. Trembling because of the cold, bread knife in one hand, you patrol the squelching property, gripping the handle, expecting at any moment to be stabbed, or strong-armed from behind. You dance side to side, pirou-etting to make sure you are not. You see leaping shadows of the trees in the sky, green spiky plants, waving palm-tree fronds. What looks like a moist grey snake slips silently through the grass ahead. You watch out of the corner of your eye (you see better at night if you look sideways), hold your breath, and try to calm your thudding heart.

The cicadas begin singing again, giving the all clear. You slice a vine that lies across the path with the bread knife, and return to the cottage, staring at the gaping window in your bedroom. You listen for long minutes to your thudding heart. You will have to secure that if you are to sleep at all at night.

It is irrational, you know, but you consider Makaya. He may resent your usurpation of his position. You can't imagine anyone else. You have nothing of value to a burglar, nothing anyone would want.

You drag a door frame you find lying in the store room and stand it against the window, pull at the heavy boxes you have stacked in the corner, and haul them to prop up your barrier. Now you are grateful to whoever left these boxes, these rotting remnants of a past life. You pack CLOTHES AND SHIT against the door, SNORKELLING GEAR against the window, and for good measure, shove the bed against the boxes.

You lie awake for long minutes, listen to the waves crashing, the night crickets, your heart still pounding. Africa is full of predators, and you are prey.

*

You wake drenched in sweat at five a.m., the roar of the waves battering the coastline in the distance. The clanking fan judders and squeaks above your head. And the birds (they are Trumpeter Hornbills) outside squabble over your remaining paw-paws. You stagger to the kitchen sink and drink from the tap, splashing water over your face; afterwards, you throw yourself back on the bed and lie awake another hour, feeling the warm wind on your skin as it blows through the gaps in the barricaded window. You are surprised to find yourself alive. Nightmares have battered at your shores all night, and shadows of men lurked in the dark corners of your subconscious.

You have a task to perform if you are to sleep soundly at night. After you dress and eat breakfast (a bowl of new cereal, now tightly sealed, and inspected thoroughly before pouring), you wade through the long grass at the bottom of the garden to a rubbish heap—grass, old cans, muddy scraps of plants and piles of mouldy newspapers, a rubber tyre. A buzz of hot insects rises and falls around it and a pungent smell attacks you. You stir a stick into this pile, examining the history of the previous tenant's garbage. Surfing accessories, a mouldy pair of flippers, jam jars and old pizza boxes. Now here is something useful: fishing wire, tangled rolls of it, hooks, barbs, weights; some old wind chimes—metallic, rusted oblong tubes. An old gate. You drag this to the gaping hole in the fence where Thoko entered the property, and tie it securely across with fishing line. Sorry, Thoko, you'll have to buzz at the gate to get in in future. You untangle the line as best you can, and then, at shin level, unravel it around the cottage, tie it to trees, hook it around small plants to form a trip wire to catch any late night intruders. You attach the jangling chimes so that if an intruder stumbles through the yard, the chimes will serve as an early warning system. And, after a few moments of guilty projection into the victim's future pain, you set barbs at gut level, so that any intruder trying to run away or rush at you will be ensnared in the fishing gear. You loop the fishing line over the porch so that you can enter and exit in the day, but once safely inside, you net the spiral loop tightly around the entire house.

The drive to the university is pleasant. The yellow-lined road winds in and out of the dew-laden Thomas Mofolo Forest; the VW Golf sidles along the coastline between a white-flecked Indian Ocean to your right and hills of green sugarcane on your left. The rising sun projects a long shadowed caricature of the car onto the road and hills around, making the tyres look elliptical, the body of the car a pyramid shape and the occupant by the wheel a tall, imposing figure. You thrust a hand out of the window to play with the shadow and a long thin arm waves back from the road. There is little traffic at this time, and you have the road to yourself.

*

'Professor! Professor!'
    From the yellow shade of some species of Cassia tree at the far end, dark shadows beckon you.

'Here's the professor from down under.'

'Caesar?'

He emerges from behind a bush, brandishing his panga. 'No, no, call me Kaliban, I have to get into character. We all do. It's the Stanislavski Method.'[1]

Tracey is holding a script in her hand, and constantly brushing back her hair out of her eyes. The chorus of women bunch together in melodramatic poses: hands on hips, eyes rolling, as if they are acting being actors and acting putting on a play. Eric aims his AK at you. 'Halt, who goes there?'

You hold your hands up in mock surrender. 'How are you going? Who's Prospero?'

Joel peers out from the Cassia tree. 'You ... we hope.'

'Forget it. I can't act to save my life.'

'Just play yourself.'

'The white oppressor? Thanks a lot.'

'Have a look here.' Eric thrusts a script into your hands. 'Ariel is speaking. Just try it ... from line 43.'

Ariel swings down from the branch and lands unsteadily on his feet. 'I have to fly in at the command of my master. I'm a running dog of the white man, you see.'

'Read, read.'

You read. 'Ariel ...'

He lands at your feet. 'All hail, great master! Grave sir, hail! I come to answer thy best pleasure; be't to fly, to swim, to dive into the fire, to ride on the curled clouds.'

Kaliban pounces from the bush, slicing his panga into the air. 'As wicked dew as e'er my mother brushed with raven's feather from unwholesome fen drop on you both! A south-west blow on ye and blister you all o'er!'

Eric, in the role of director, positions the budding Prospero into position. 'You see, he keeps promising Ariel freedom, but weasels out, no matter how much Ariel tries to please him ...'

'Is there more toil? Since thou dost give me pains, let me remember thee what thou hast promised, which is not yet perform'd me.'

---

1   The Stanislavski Method is when the actor uses his or her emotional memory to feel empathy and past experiences to 'realise' the play.

'Prospero, it's you now … read, read …'

You read, addressing Joel. 'How now? Moody? What is't thou canst demand?'

'My liberty.'

'Before the time be out? No more! *Voetsak!*[2]'

'Pronounce it 'foot-sack' …'

'Wait, wait. *Voetsak*? That's not bloody Shakespeare!'

'Yes, yes … very much Shakespeare … ,' says Eric.

'Ariel? Your line …'

'I prithee, remember I have done thee worthy service, told thee no lies, made thee no mistakings, served without or grudge or grumblings: thou didst promise to bate me a full year. A running dog. I have been a white man, black skin white mask, I have.'

'Definitely not Shakespeare this time.'

'Yes, yes,' says Eric. 'Straight from the Bard's own pen. Go on.'

'Okay, okay. Dost thou forget from what oppression I did free thee?'

'No,' says Ariel.

'Thou dost, and think'st it much to tread the ooze of the salt deep, to run upon the sharp wind of the north, to do me business in the veins o' the earth when it is baked with frost.'

'I do not, sir.'

'Thou liest, malignant thing! Hast thou forgot the foul witches Barbarism, Ignorance and Savagery from which I rescued you? Hast thou forgot them?'

'No, my *groot Baas*.'

An audience has gathered in horseshoe formation around the players. They whistle and applaud.

'Excellent,' says Eric. 'You're a perfect villain.'

'Is my audition over then?'

Eric appeals to the crowd. 'Does he get the part? The colonial oppressor?'

The crowd cheers.

'I'd better go.'

---

2   *Voetsak*: S. African (interj.). Offensive, informal = fuck off, piss off. An expression of dismissal or rejection from C19 Afrikaans. Originally from Dutch *voort se ek* 'forward, I say!'

Kaliban claps you on the back. 'Next rehearsal at my place over the weekend. Can you make it? We invite you.'

Tracey eyes you from behind her script.

'I ...'

'Come on, don't be such a white man!'

'I am a white man.'

'So that's a no?'

'Let me think about it ... I have to get to my First Year lecture on Chaucer.'

*

You babble through the First Year lecture without incident. In fact, the First Year class seems eager to please whoever is in authority over them. But after class, a delegation of students fronts your podium and pays you the ultimate compliment: 'We're so glad you are replacing that man.'

'We didn't know where we were.'

'He banned textbooks from the room.'

'*Aish*, that man!'

'What did he do?'

'He made us question our traditions.'

'He made us uncomfortable.'

'How?'

'He talked of private things, intimate things, in public.'

'He has radical, extreme, challenging views. He chastises us for conforming, for wanting to fit into society. He wants us to challenge every assumption and foundation.'

'He says his job is to make sure we do not fit into society and get a job in the system.'

'He is a dangerous man. A dangerous mind.'

*

After class, it's tea time. You disentangle yourself from the students' compliments and make a bee-line for the cafeteria. But bearing down on you is none other than the Crocodile—Mr Orange Hair. You walk faster, hoping to make it to the tea room before he catches up with you, but he strides like a power walker.

'Dr Turner? Going for tea?'

'I suppose.'

'Let me join you.'

You sip tea, stare at his orange hair. He smiles. 'We got off on the wrong foot the other day.'

'What is the right foot?'

'Ha!' He claps your shoulder. 'I had you pegged for one of them.'

'One of who?'

'Zimmerlie. Mpofu. Redlinghuis. The establishment.'

You fiddle with your tie. 'I am one of them.'

He is not sure about your sense of humour. He wags a finger at you. 'I'm not fooled by your act. The students have been saying some good things about you. You already have a nickname.'

'Oh?'

'Prospero. It's a sign of respect when they give you a nickname.'

'Really. Calling me the colonial oppressor is a sign of respect?'

'I hear you are helping with the play.'

'Mr Ngwenya, I'm just here to do a job. I'm not taking sides with anyone.'

Again he laughs. 'You think so?'

'Absolutely.'

'This is South Africa.'

Although the two of you are alone in the tea room, he lowers his voice. 'And in South Africa, there are a few things you need to know ...'

The low-down. This is why he is making you sit here drinking weak washing-up water disguised as tea. He's going to lecture you about your ignorance. That you're a white man. A foreigner, an Australian. Humour him. Go along with him. Nod a lot.

'You see, Timothy, there are things here you may not know. There are deep divisions not visible to the naked eye. This campus is divided primarily between the ANC and Inkatha. The Communist party. The old white Boer still has his fingers in the pie. The NIC ... COSATU ... NUM ... AZAPO ...'

'Wait a minute. Spare me the acronyms. Or at least explain them to me.'

Like most people here, he speaks slowly to you, as if you are linguistically and aurally impaired. 'Inkatha is primarily a Zulu nationalist movement; the ANC, now in power, is a broad democratic movement, non-tribal, non-racial ...'

'And I gather then, by your favourable definition, that you are ANC?'

He speaks as you do to a child (now who is humouring whom?) 'This campus used to be a homeland university. Zulu students; Boer teachers and administrators. Inkatha dominated. The ANC was banned.'

'But surely now, twenty years after Apartheid ...'

He laughs again. 'Apartheid has merely gone underground. Zimmerlie is still white; Mpofu is still Inkatha ... even twenty years after Apartheid, nothing has changed.'

'And let me guess, Makaya is ANC?'

'Mxolisi Makaya is beyond such petty divisive reductions of the human impulse. He does not identify with any political party. Nor do I. But it seems Mpofu and Zimmerlie, by discriminating against him, do.'

Your repugnance for any cultural imposition is showing. You are an anarchist after all. 'The issues, I believe, are simpler than that. Dr Makaya is suspended not because of some political allegiance, but because he's guilty of some transgression. Some overstepping of the line ...'

He sips his tea. 'It's in your interest to remain ignorant, is that it, for the sake of your job, or rather, your usurpation of Dr Makaya's job?'

'Is it? I don't know.'

'You seem a reasonable person. Dr Makaya has suggested that we meet, all three of us, for supper at the weekend. Friday, maybe after your speech.'

'That doesn't sound like a lot of fun. Might be inappropriate, don't you think?'

'And taking his job *is* appropriate? Ha, he'll love that. He's a good one for a laugh.'

'The situation's not exactly a joke, is it?'

'Listen, Timothy, Dr Makaya bears you no malice, that's what he wanted me to tell you. He wants to meet you to tell you that in person, that he is above petty party politics.'

'Well, I have to get to my class now—Honours class.' You stand, shake his hand.

'Friday night?'

'Really, I must go now.'

'Twenty, Second Avenue. Friday evening?'

'I'll consider it.'

You walk stiffly, feeling his eyes on you the whole way to the exit. Don't turn around.

*

'The cockroach has been a symbol in literature since Kafka's *Metamorphosis*. Dambudzo Marechera, the Zimbabwean writer, talks in a "cockroach voice".'

The Honours class is in a jubilant mood, calling you Prospero, making Shakespearean jibes. They are prepared to go along with what they consider your cockroach obsession. 'Who would like to read the poem?' You wipe a bead of sweat off your nose. 'Eric? You read.'

'Will this moon scrap itself off my poems!' reads Eric. 'This twilight zone stretching between English school and my cockroach voice.'

'What does he mean? Bantu uses the cockroach as a central symbol in his works. His protagonists are obsessed with cockroaches. Any ideas?'

Tracey looks up and holds your gaze, her frown etched deep down her forehead as if she is trying to decide something about you.

'Cockroach voice?' says Joel. 'Like this, maybe?' He makes a rasping sound, an old man with a dry throat.

You stare at her fingers as she writes notes, stare at her spidery handwriting and her delicately painted purple fingernails. She is aware of every movement she makes, and aware that you are aware of her awareness of her every movement.

'Any comments or questions? Eric?'

'Why cockroaches?' asks Joel. 'Why not something relevant to the struggle?

'The New Struggle ...' says Eric.

You pass out the sheets of paper you have carefully cut to fit the pages of the book. Ten copies of each story. And plastic bottles of glue. 'I want you to glue those pages back in your book. I have photocopies here—first the cockroach story ...'

They groan. But they co-operate. They spend the rest of the class getting glue all over fingers, desks and books. Eric manages (and you

suspect this is deliberate) to glue the entire book closed and Tracey …
well, she stares at you throughout the procedure with green cat eyes.

'Done?'

She shows you gluey fingers. 'Very done.'

'Does Dr Makaya approve of this?' asks Eric.

You say nothing, just smile your patronising, humouring, glazed
smile.

After class, the students scramble for the door. But Tracey remains
behind, blocks the door exit, picks the glue skin off her fingers as it dries.
'Are you on Facebook? I tried Googling you but nothing came up.'

'Googling me?'

'I want to add you as a friend on Facebook.'

'I told you I'm not available online.'

'Oh well. See you, Prof.'

She turns, swings her braids and sashays out into the corridor.

*

The last person you want to see after class is a scarred professor at lunch
time. You try to avoid him, but a bony finger beckons you over. He
points a paper cup at you, and you nod. Your throat is sandpapered and
you are grateful for the muddy water that passes for coffee.

'How was the class?'

'Ah, Professor Zimmerlie, I need to ask you something.'

'Shoot.'

'About Sizwe Bantu. Makaya tore all the Bantu stories out of the
Honours textbooks. Did you know that?'

His face reddens, and then he coughs, as if he is about to have an
epileptic fit.

'Are you all right?'

He nods. 'Fine. Fine. Nothing surprises me about that man and his
antics. Nothing.'

'Professor Zimmerlie, what is it with Bantu on this campus? Why
does he enrage Makaya? Why is he … controversial?'

'Bantu is a sore point. An issue on this campus.'

'No kidding.' You haul out a glued textbook. 'But I am restoring him
to the syllabus.'

He takes the book as if you are handing him a turd. The glue sticks to his fingers as he tries to page through it. 'I think we need to talk, Timothy.'

'Go right ahead.'

'Not here.' He gives the walls of the cafeteria a hunted look. 'My place. I'd like to invite you for supper. You live in eSikamanga don't you? This weekend? No, you're busy?'

You stare into the man's yellow eyes. 'I suppose so.'

'Here: my card, my home number, my address. Please … it's important … crucial.'

'Okay.'

Grouped around your car in the heat of a humid afternoon are three students. Another sits in the shade of a flowering yellow tree.

'Prof! We need to ask you something.'

It is Joel the student with the scar. With him are Eric and Caesar. 'Call me Timothy. I'm not a prof.'

'Are you busy this afternoon?'

'Well …'

'Can you give us a ride home?'

'Well …'

Tracey steps out of the shade. 'Just ask him straight, man,' she says to Joel. And to you: 'Actually, we have a rehearsal this afternoon, and we'd like you to be there. Is that okay?'

'Where?'

'We'll give you lunch …'

'So where do you all live? eSikamanga? Assegai?'

Eric shakes his head. 'We can't afford to live in eSikamanga. Or Assegai. White man's towns. We live in the township. eManzakulu. eSitabene.'

A 'township' in Australia is a small rural settlement not quite big enough to be a town, what is known as a 'village' in England, but in South

Africa it has other connotations. Townships were, under Apartheid, labour reserves outside white towns, ghettoes where 'non-whites' lived.

'eSikamanga is a white town.'

'Twenty years after Apartheid?'

'It's economic Apartheid now,' says Caesar.

'My tradition is poverty and violence,' says Joel. So where do you live?'

'eManzakulu.'

'You have wheels. You can take us. Not far. Not far.'

'Okay.'

They pile in the back, Tracey in the middle; Eric with his AK in the front riding shotgun.

The guard at the gate registers his disapproval by lowering the booms, and only opening them after Eric leans out of the window. 'Coming through! Professor Prospero. Please stand back!'

You drive over corrugated dirt roads that rattle your teeth and jangle Tracey's beads and bells. Eric directs you by pointing the AK out of the window. 'Straight! Straight! Left turn ahead. Sharp!'

The three in the back jabber in Zulu, until Tracey catches a glimpse of you in the rear-view mirror. 'Speak English,' she says. 'He might think we're talking about him.'

'We are. But only nice-nice things.'

'Tracey wanted to know if you are married.'

She digs him in the ribs. 'I was not. You were.'

'What a question to ask,' you say. 'But no.'

'Girlfriend?'

'No.'

'He hesitates,' says Joel. 'That means he is not sure.'

'Or has too many.'

'I have too many to count,' says Caesar. 'Far too many.'

'Me too,' says Tracey.

'Maybe,' says Eric, 'you should learn isiZulu.'

'I have actually been trying.'

'What words do you know?'

'*i-khomiyutha. i-imeyyili. i-intanethi. i-webhusayithi.*'[3]

---

3   Computer, email, internet, website. Timothy here is having a go at how other languages appropriate English words.

'He's playing with us,' says Caesar.

Eric is still giving directions. 'Here, turn, quickly right, then the bend ...'

'Teach him the clicks.'

You funnel down a narrow road, and dust billows out behind you. You are surrounded by tall green sugarcane. A sign written in uneven letters indicates that you are three kilometres away from eManzikulu.

Tracey leans forward. 'c ... q ... x ... Repeat after me. c ... q ... x.'

Joel pushes her back on her seat. 'The c click. Do as if you are feeling sorry for someone. Ts ts.'

'As if,' says Caesar, 'you are calling to a sexy girl on the street.'

Tracey thumps him on the arm. 'Excuse my sexist comrades. Let me explain ...'

'Try it.'

'Ts ts.'

'Good good. Now try words like *icinga* ...'

'*Eee-tsk-eeengah.*'

The fall over themselves in laughter.

'Okay, the next click,' says Joel. 'q. As if you are pulling a cork from a nice bottle of wine.'

'Like so. q ... q ... q ...'

'Now say *umqombothi* ...'

'That's not a Zulu word ...' objects Eric.

'*Oomclomboatee.*'

'Not bad. And now the x. Like when you are riding a horse. In the back of your throat.'

'Maybe he has never ridden a horse.'

'*Nqobile Nxumalo.* Say *Nqobile Nxumalo.*'

They laugh.

'Am I saying something rude?'

'He is so cool. Didn't I tell you he was cool?'

'You never stop telling us he's cool.'

You look in the rear-view mirror to see her elbow him in the ribs again.

'Here! Here!' Eric jabs the AK into the air.

eManzikulu. You have read about South African townships. You have seen them in movies: shanty towns made of cardboard boxes and the refuse of Western civilisation; crime, sewage running yellow down streets, gangs blocking roads and wielding unjust power. And recently, township tourism has become the in-thing, with white-faced foreigners poking their cameras at the squalor, taking snapshots of everything they aren't, shuddering with relief as they safely return home. Now you are one of them. You even have your camera with you. You stick out because you're the only white person, and judging by the way those dozens of yelling kids are following the car, it looks like you're the first white person they have ever seen.

'See!' Eric points his weapon at the dust. 'Poverty and violence.'

You don't see any violence or poverty. You see green grass, luminously stark against the blue sky, and neat dirt roads, swept red clean. Rows of tiny brick houses line the roads at a discreet distance. And what is most remarkable, there are no fences, no high walls, no security systems. Not that you are going to make any simplistic observation or binary oppositional statements about townships and white towns, but what strikes you is the openness. People are outside. Children are playing in the street. It beats eSikamanga hollow with its electric fences and drab curtains.

'This is my parents' house. They have invited us for lunch after the rehearsal.'

A thin dog is tied by a short lead to a thin pole and attacks you with short sharp barks.

'I have to apologise for my racist dog,' says Eric. 'He only barks at white people.'

His parents emerge, a shrunken couple, very pleased to see you, shaking hands, curtseying, as if you are a visiting king.

At the back a chicken-wire cage full of rabbits. 'Choose one.'

Tracey singles out a white rabbit eating a grey lettuce leaf. 'That one is cute.'

'Definitely the cutest,' you say.

Then you are off again, driving through a neat maze of zig-zag streets for the sole purpose, it seems, of calling out to Eric's friends, who all seem to be sitting on the front porches of their respective houses or are out on the streets.

You are directed to some sort of town square, a clearing of red dirt and a green building.

'This is where we rehearse.'

'Who are those kids?'

'The centre feeds and clothes orphans, and they tend to hang around here all day.'

As soon as you stop the car, you are surrounded by dozens of cheering kids in clothes way too big for them.

'What are they so excited about? What do they want?'

Children are clawing the car doors, and screeching.

'They're excited to see you. They don't get visitors very often.'

They all pile out, and before you are even out of the car, you are swamped by the children.

Eric pushes through the swarm and calls back to you. 'We're just going to check the props room and get the keys, okay. You wait here.'

'Don't worry,' says Tracey, seeing your concern at being abandoned. 'We just have to find the janitor.' And they disappear around the corner.

You think these kids want money, or lollies, but no, they want to touch you, to pull at your clothes, and a very small girl with a snotty nose wants to hold your hand so tightly that you cannot wrestle free. It is an initiation of sorts. Why else would the New Strugglers leave you alone? You smile, and try to wrestle yourself free of their clawing hands. Then a boy spies your camera.

'Photo! Photo!' he chants and the rest take up the call: 'Photo! Photo!'

'Okay, okay.'

As you take the camera out, dozens more kids come running at you from inside the building and crowd around you for the shot, pulling faces for the shot. You take two, three, four snaps, and the poses get wilder, one girl doing cartwheels.

'Now you. You must be in photo,' calls a boy.

'Can I take?' Another boy reaches for your camera.

'Okay. You press this button here. Let the green light go on first so it can focus, okay?'

'Yes, yes.' He takes the camera and walks backwards until he can fit you all in the viewfinder. 'Back! Back!' he calls, and the crowd clinging to you pull you back against the bonnet of your car.

And you realise what is happening—he has turned and bolted, holding your camera to his chest. He turns the corner of the building.

'Hey! Hey!' But the children hold you tight and you cannot get away to chase after him. The children scream with what you take to be laughter. 'He's stolen my camera, the little bastard. Let me go …'

But as you fight yourself free, Eric turns the corner, holding the boy by the arm, and your camera in the other. 'Give it back to him,' he says and without warning whacks the boy on the head. 'He said I could take,' the boy whines. 'It was joke. Joke.'

'Apologise.' Eric grips the boy's ear and propels him towards you. 'Give him back his camera.'

'Steady on.' You take the camera.

'It's a joke. We play trick.'

'Okay.'

You bury the camera in the glove compartment and lock the car.

The door of the community centre opens from the inside and out come Tracey, Joel and Caesar, their arms heaped with material and clothes.

'Now *hamba*, you kids. We need to do some work here.'

The kids don't *hamba* but follow you around like a school of fish after bait, chattering loudly, reacting with exaggeration at everything you do. At first you are perturbed, but by the end of the rehearsal have learned to ignore them.

'Prospero, your robe.'

It is a musty curtain. You drape it over your shoulder.

Tracey places a plastic crown on her head.

You feel wooden. You cannot act, dance, or express such a wide range of emotions as these students can. They have no inhibition, no shyness, no self-reflective paralysis, and they fall into song and dance spontaneously. *The Tempest* is as much a musical, a dance performance as a play, and the words are not spoken so much as delivered with a zest and enthusiasm for each syllable, for each letter.

'Okay,' says Eric, perusing the script, 'the final scene is where Prospero gets tied up and Miranda is rescued by Kaliban. To it! Miranda, you only speak when you see Kaliban enter …'

'Do I have to have my foot on her shoulder?'

'Yes, Prospero. Your cue, Miranda baby.'

'O, wonder! How many goodly creatures are there here! How beauteous mankind is! O brave new world, That has such people in't!'

Kaliban enters, brandishes his panga. 'How now, evil tyrant, who enslaves beauty?'

Your line: 'Unhand her, thou scurvy patch, thou poisonous slave, thou jesting monkey, thou hag seed, *wena ma-inja*.'

Enter Eric with AK-47 stage left: 'What is this maid? Is she a goddess?'

Kaliban: 'Sir, she is mortal; and he … (points at Prospero) … is damned.'

All (except Prospero): 'Drive him into the sea, from whence he came on his bark!'

Eric presses the AK to your temple. 'Die!'

'Hey.' You pull back. 'You didn't tell me this part. I thought everyone lived happily ever after in this play?'

'It's a rule of drama, Prof,' says Joel. 'You bring on a gun in scene one, it has to go off in scene five.'[4]

You find it difficult to stand still (*proud and defiant*, read the stage directions) while he dances around you, pointing the muzzle of the AK-47 at your head. But there is a twist. Miranda throws herself between you and the AK, and drapes herself onto you.

'No! We can redeem him. Reconciliation! Redemption! Re-education!'

She holds your hand. Beseeches the gods. Stares into your eyes.

And in this moment, you know. That look.

Oh no, you want to say. Not this.

Joel claps his hands. The spell is broken. 'Cut. Cut.'

'Was that in the script?'

'It's the Stanislavski Method,' explains Joel. 'We try out scenes in character and that's how we write the play.'[5]

'You can let him go now, Miranda.'

She lets go your hand. 'It must be time for lunch.'

The children follow you out the building, and run after your car, yelling, keeping up until you belt along the dust road and turn the corner.

---

4   Eric is referring to 'Chekhov's gun'. The nineteenth-century Russian Realist writer advised that if you introduced an item into your dramatic narrative, you had to use it, and fulfil audience expectations.

5   Joel here may also be referring to the workshop method employed by Athol Fugard where actors improvise scenarios in order to develop the script through creative practice.

Lunch is around a round table in a tiny living room in a tiny house, with Eric's mother and Tracey serving the men first.

'A beer?'

'*Umqombothi*,' you say.

'Really?' Mr Phala frowns. 'You've been serving your professor the hard stuff? You want some?'

You shake your head. 'Just practising my Zulu.'

Eric brings a crate of Cokes and opens them one each. You can sense that this generosity is especially for your benefit.

You pass the test by eating the *mieliepap* with your fingers. *Ngiya-bonga*, you say. The meat is stewed and stringy grey, swimming in gravy. 'What is this meat?'

'You chose it,' says Eric. 'Fresh, fresh. You said this is the rabbit you wanted.'

So you have to eat every mouthful, and they have given you the lion's portion.

'What do you think of our ghetto, then?' asks Joel.

'It's not a ghetto!' Eric's father says. 'We are very proud of our community.'

'It's very friendly,' you say.

'What do you think are the main differences?'

'Between ... ?'

'Australia.'

You have to think about this. What sweeping generality can you use? You cannot think of one. But Joel sits at your elbow, Eric pushes against you on the other side, and Tracey is hovering over you, her hair dangling over your shoulder as she pours you a glass of Coke.

'Personal space.'

He nods. 'Australia's a big country.'

'No, I mean the cultural thing: the way Australians—and most Westerners—have to have a bubble around them. You don't touch them; you don't enter that space.'

'How big is this bubble?' Tracey's breath is warm in your ear.

'And another one: or maybe I speak for myself here only. We're kind of wooden. Years of political correctness maybe but we have limited our range of emotions, especially public expression of these emotions.'

'This is a professor's observations,' explains Eric to his father, who is frowning. 'He's very intellectual.'

'You have a range of emotions we have forgotten. The exuberance of those kids, for example.'

You are not sure they know what you're talking about. And it sounds very binary, very simplistic, even racist. You blacks can dance and sing sort of thing. 'But I can't generalise. I shouldn't make any judgement based on only a limited experience ...'

*

Dear M,

Your words of course still hurt. "Don't touch me! Keep your paws off me. I don't feel like it today. Or any day." But what hurts more is the way you shrink from me. You'd rather smoke and talk at a distance, than writhe in common sweat. That's why this place is healing. Here everyone touches you—when they greet you, when they pass by, even in a lunch queue: no one minds rubbing up against you, or notices. It is reassuring that I am not alone, that I am human, a physical animal who needs to touch and be touched in order to exist. Today a woman melted over me like heated cheese. Twelve children pawed me, grown men held my hand as they talked to me, as if friendship is communicated through the fingers, through touch rather than through words and ideas. There is a direct connection of heart to body. No space bubble. No mediation between thought and action. I never knew what T.S. Eliot meant in 'The Hollow Men' until now:

> *Between the idea*
> *And the reality*
> *Between the motion*
> *And the act*
> *Falls the Shadow*

Here there is no shadow.

T

*

'Can you drop me back in eSikamanga?' Tracey is literally dripping herself onto you.

'What?'

She pulls back the curtain of dreads. 'The others are staying. They live here, I live in eSikamanga.'

'Sure.'

They wave goodbye, and she sits up front, and waves a long goodbye in return. Eric bangs on the roof. 'Take it easy, my brother.'

You drive along very long dusty roads until you reach the Mtunzini turnpike, and then you are on a smooth tarred highway.

'They really like you, Professor Turner.'

'Timothy.'

The roads whiz by, and you can recognise where you are. Ten kilometres to eSikamanga. Ten minutes of buoyant conversation needed.

You want to ask, but it's a touchy subject: is she Zulu? She's light skinned, her eyes are green, and she speaks in a different English accent to them. But you don't know how to ask without sounding as if race is an issue, so you leave it. Instead you ask an even more intimate question.

'I was wondering how Joel got such a scar on his face?'

'He told you. In the struggle.'

'He was two years old when Apartheid ended.'

She twiddles her braids. 'The struggle continues.'

'No really.'

'The Panga Man did it to him.'

'Caesar?'

She laughs. 'No, the real Panga Man.'

You drive in silence.

And then, because nothing is forthcoming. 'You live in eSikamanga?'

'Sometimes here, sometimes there. I'm rich enough to have two houses.'

'Meaning?'

But she doesn't elaborate. 'Here, here. You can drop me at the shops.'

You cruise into the car park near the Estate Agent, to let her out. But she does not go. She leans across you.

It's a fumbled hug. Over the gear lever and handbrake in the restrictive space of an idling Golf GTI in the shade of the eSikamanga Estate Agent. You hope no one is watching from behind heavy curtains.

'See you, Prof! Or should I say—Prospero.'

'*Hamba kahle!*'[6]

6 'Go well.' This is incorrect. Since he is the one leaving, Timothy should say *Sala kahle* (stay well).

Some people read horoscopes, others the Bible; you read Sizwe Bantu. As soon as you get home, you shower, and drink two beers straight (for medicinal purposes). You lie on the couch and reach for *The Great South African Novel*, flip through for a BRR, a Bantu Random Reading: close your eyes, stick your finger into a page, and open the book.[7]

Your finger rests on the beginning of a well-known poem. The page is so creased that the universe often selects this page for your daily lesson.

> Beware of prytty ladyes in the sprynge
> Those lyte flytting byrds who dance and chyrp and syng
> Who tempt you with wyles, perfume and smyles
> And in whose tayles you wyll always fynde a styng.
>
> Beware yf yn her you seek exystence
> Yf to be seen you need her assystance
> So please desyst, I do insyst
> Your self needs to grow from resystance.[8]

In your Ph.D. dissertation, you featured this poem 'Beware of Prytty Ladyes' prominently, criticising it for its tinge (tynge) of misogyny. You aren't the only one to spot Bantu's women-hating attitude. Widespread commentary pins Bantu as a male-centred writer who sees Woman as the Other, the Temptress, the Seductress who leads men astray. It is a disturbing fact about Bantu. You wonder if perhaps Bantu himself had a bad experience with someone and it white-washed his work with

---

7   Bantu Random Readings are common practice among Bantu's supporters, started as a joke at a conference where in order to make a decision about which speaker went first, the convener, instead of tossing a coin, closed his eyes and dipped his finger into the *Bantu Complete Works* and said: 'Let's let Bantu decide.' Purportedly the words his finger rested on were: 'Ye of little face: he who is thirst shall be fast.'

8   The only reference to 'prytty ladyes' with this unusual spelling is an obscure one, a road name in Harare, Zimbabwe: Prytty Ladyes Lane. A coincidence probably. More likely Bantu spelled it like this to imitate Ye Olde Englishe.

bitterness; perhaps he wrote this poem simply to expel the venom and dab the pain with cool webs of words.[9]

The lesson of this poem goes deeper, of course, than pure misogyny: if no one sees you, do you exist? And how can you base your existence on someone seeing you who doesn't? How do we exist independently of others? If a self falls down in the forest and there is no one there to hear it, does it make a sound? Is writing a way to create a self independent of others?

*

Dear M,

Forgive me. This poem could have been written about you and the damage you do to my heart.

To all echoes of you.

I am sorry, I have often used it to comfort my torn self.

Bantu the healer of tormented souls. That's what literature is, for me, a salve, a salvation for the wounds in my soul. I use literature the way other people use God or drugs, or alcohol.

But those nights were so dark; the smell of frangipani on the wind so intoxicating, your hands so soft, your words so deep. How can I ever heal from that?

T

*

It's late afternoon. A knock at the door makes you scramble for cover again under the windowsill.

'Who is it?' Two figures are silhouetted in the frosted glass of the front door. You stand, straighten yourself out.

9   Cecily Houghton (2009) attacks Bantu as the stereotypical misogynous male writer who not only demeans women in his novels but also obliterates them. There is not one female character in a Bantu novel who is not in a subservient role: they are maids, wives, or else temptresses, whores, goddesses, Madonnas. Women in positions of power are ridiculed as usurpers. Other feminists have ignored Bantu as insignificant. Still others have defended his misogyny. L.K. Chesterton comments that Bantu is merely reflecting a sexist society where women cannot occupy positions of power and still do not really have a voice. 'Women speak in the silence of the text,' this critic maintains, and speak overtly only in one instance, in his story 'Cockroach Liberation', where they assume all power. Turner also comments on it in this thesis, explaining (and maybe excusing) it as an 'irrational outburst of pain, possibly caused by heartbreak'.

'Thoko? How the hell did you get in here?'

Behind her stands a man in rags, a trilby hat in his hand. 'Who's this?'

'My brother is hungry, very hungry.'

The man addresses the floor. 'Your garden is bad,' he says. 'I weed. I clean up the front … the wires. I mow.'

'Now hang on a minute. It's not that bad. And I like it that way. I … I don't need anyone to …'

'He is good,' says Thoko.

'Did Mrs Steyn send you too? Did she let you in? How did you get in?'

The man looks bewildered.

'He start tomorrow morning,' says Thoko. 'Okay?'

'I don't need a gardener.' You wave at the wilderness surrounding the cottage. 'This is why I moved in—for privacy, for wilderness, to get away from people … so no one would bother me …'

She stands her ground. 'You think he is not good?'

'No, no, he may be good, that isn't the point.'

'Weeding, digging, mowing. Tomorrow,' the man says as if it is all agreed.

'Just a drink and some lunch,' says Thoko. 'He will work all day. All right?'

You shake your head, but the words come out anyway. 'All right, all right.'

You feel constrained by cultural rules, by a suit of behaviour. Perhaps it is just language. If you could speak Zulu you would not have to resort to the parody of monosyllabic grunts. For the maid and gardener (even to use those terms here is derogatory) speak in a flurry of sing-song discourse, like the birds (even that is derogatory, Othering). It seems you cannot interact in any way here without playing out the old racist stereotypes.

There is only one thing for it: in a matter of minutes, your feet are pounding on the coarse brown sand, the frothy sea lapping at them.

The sweat stings your eyes, the sun is a poultice, and soon you are rid of them. All of them.

The sea is the solution to everything. When you feel boxed in, you always head for the ocean and let it wash you clean.

You plunge into the surf and trip into the roaring silt waves. Let the sea punish you for your transgressions. Swallow salty brine. Let the sand abrade your skin, let the Indian Ocean roar.

Your skin tingles with the drying salt as you bask in the complete freedom of being alone at last. You lie on your back on the sand, marvelling at the mountainous dunes set against a stark blue sky.

This is better.

You can only be yourself when you are alone.

You begin to climb a tall shimmering dune. It is difficult work as the sand cascades down around your feet like quicksand, pulling you down, sucking you in. But you are determined to get to the top, to get a good view of the sea and river estuary. For most of the time you crawl on your hands and knees, spitting sand, holding back the dizziness of seeing only moving crystals all around you. Now you know what it feels to be a castaway on a desert island—and it is a good feeling.

At the top, you catch your breath.

On top of the dune, instead—as you imagined—of a vista of the eSika-manga valley and estuary, a brown wooden deck juts out over the dunes. You blink away a dozen green suns, squint out of the corner of your eyes. Above the wooden balcony—stained the colour of red ochre—you see black thatch, a high lightning conductor. The wooden balcony resembles a lookout tower with a view on all sides for encroaching enemies. Two small windows peek out from the thatch. You stare for long minutes, wondering why you are so outraged.

The dunes are National Park land: no houses are permitted here. Perhaps this is an old abandoned lighthouse from colonial times, when the British christened this Zulu territory Port Durnford. You scramble up the top of the dune, latch onto the tree roots growing out of the sand to pull yourself up, and reach level ground. This is not a dune as you thought, but a cliff edge.

Although the cottage—for that is what you now take it to be—is open to the beach, the area behind is fenced off with razor wire, a red skull and crossbones placed at intervals: PRIVATE PROPERTY—KEEP OUT.

Like so much of South Africa, the rich wall off their grains of sand from the poor with electric fences, broken-glass-topped walls, and patrolling security guards. But why would someone want to fence off a piece of land in the middle of nowhere, where no one ventures? You stand on tiptoe to see, above the fence, green fronds of palm trees. But the fence ends at the cottage, and the leeward side is open to the beach.

It commands a beautiful view. From where you stand, you can see the Indian Ocean spread out in ever darkening shades of blue, flecked with wrinkling, crawling waves. You can see miles along each beach, from the Manga River gleaming in the sun, like flowing mercury, to the Mswaswe River to the south, a brown pollutant which silts up the estuary. Whoever positioned this cottage chose the prime spot. It has to be a National Parks cottage, or the cottage of a lighthouse owner. But no lighthouse graces these dunes. You struggle with the sand to reach the deck. The balcony circles the house, and you step onto its shady leeward side. Sand has washed over the empty deck, and the wooden walls are sand blasted too. The windows are dark.

You draw away in sudden fright. A man is slumped against a wall in the sun on the deck. You leap back, biting your lip to stop yelling out. The boards creak as you slither down into the sand. But the man does not see you. Or hear you, apparently. You peer out from between the fronds of a drooping green plant; the man hasn't moved.

You edge closer to the deck, lean on it to get a better view, and the wood cracks loudly. Still the man does not move. You shrink under the deck again, and peer up through the cracks, where you can see the heavy shadow of the sentinel. Under the man, drippings of ochre clay have dried on the ground, on the deck, and on the leaves. You touch the rough texture, and then look up at the shadow above.

The man is made of clay—a gargoyle to scare away intruders, perhaps, or a scarecrow sentry in a sitting position against the wall, legs splayed out, staring vacantly. You tiptoe towards the sculpture. It is roughly moulded, a naked man without genitals. The artist, sculptor, whatever, whoever, has gouged out this man's eyes. It is an act of violence, a statement, or vandalism, you are not sure which.

A primitive fear clutches your heart, your sternum and your genitals. You think of voodoo dolls, of vendettas, of primitive curses.

A gust of wind whistles though the wooden boards, and the house creaks. A door slams somewhere inside.

You scramble off the balcony, stumble through the underbrush and run as fast as the sand will allow down the dune.

5

Arenivaga investigata

. . . .

Sand cockroach

> Sand cockroaches (*Arenivaga investigata*) make their homes by burrowing deep into sand dunes. You can spot them by the small ridges they leave in the sand. Sand cockroaches are nocturnal, black, wingless and oval-shaped. They rarely enter human dwellings, but if they do, do not be alarmed: they are not harmful to humans. If they breed inside your home, it is difficult to get rid of them. Once they settle, they may not ever leave.

When tourists visit Africa, they go primarily to see the animals. Speciesist rather than racist, they are not interested in complex politics, or African cultures or peoples, except perhaps traditional Zulu dancing or rickshaw pulling on Marine Parade. You can't blame them, really: they have been fed a steady diet of *Animal Planet, My Wild Friends*, even *Clarence the Cross-eyed Lion* and *Daktari*. And the news delivers them a steady dose of flies, starvation, coups, despotic African tin-pot republics constantly overturned by vigilante armies in trucks on dusty roads. You don't go to Africa for that.

The bush surrounding you is seething with predatory animals. Lake Vilakazi up north is stocked with hippo, and the Reginald Dhlomo game reserve nearby is inhabited by lion, elephant, giraffe and antelope. But the only wild animals you have seen so far are monkey, cockroach and mosquito.

Unless you include human predators.

Look at you, for god's sake: you've wrapped the house in barbed wire, barricaded yourself with walls and doors and paranoia.

> The Zululand ecosystem is among the most diverse and productive wild lands in the world. It is home to a rich variety of wildlife, including the "Big 5" (lion, buffalo, elephant, rhino, leopard), but also over 400 bird species as well as African wild dog, cheetah, hyena, jackal, hippopotamus, and various antelope species including waterbuck, common and mountain reedbuck, nyala, kudu, bushbuck, steenbok, duiker and impala. The waters, lakes and rivers are populated with hippo and crocodile. Beware too of poisonous mambas, cobras and puff-adders that slither their way through the wild areas.
>
> Crowded-Planet (2013): p. 133

*

Dear M,

You would love it here. Africa! The wild of your heart would find its match. The transgressive nature of the place. Here you could come with me up north, do the animal thing, take a tour of North KwaZulu: Lake Mkusi perhaps, with all its hippos and bull sharks and crocodiles. Or Thomas Mofolo game reserve to see elephants and lions.

But what am I saying? I have wrapped my heart in barbed wire to keep you out, yet you continue to prowl around my house in these dark African nights of the soul.

T

*

Eight a.m. English Department meeting. Present: Professor Zimmerlie, Dr Mpofu, Dr Turner. Absent: Mr Ngwenya, Dr Makaya. Door closed.

Mpofu pores over a brightly coloured A3 sheet of paper on the desk. 'What is it?' Zimmerlie's face is white.

You crane your neck to read too.

For their Final Exam,
Thu Nu STrUgglerZ Prowardly PreZent

THE TIME PEST
A modern rattle of the assegais

Direkted by Dr Mxolisi Makaya

Starring
The English Honours Klass
And their Professor as Prospero

Saturday 9th at 8 pm
Bekezulu Hall
R50 entry
SHARP!
Be there or be nowhere

'He's banned from campus. He's forbidden to interact with the students.'

'And now he's acting the main part in the play!'

'Prospero? What next? The ego of the man!'

'Fancies himself a sorcerer, does he … ?'

'We'll have to speak to Redlinghuis about this.'

'Stopped. That man has to be stopped.'

You glow hot, and the excuses form on your lips. But they are not talking about you.

'Can you imagine Makaya prancing around the stage as Prospero?'

'I … er … have not had the fortune to meet Dr Makaya … yet.'

'In two weeks you will. In two weeks, we will expose this man for the fraudster he is.'

'The trial,' explains Zimmerlie. 'Makaya's trial.'

'It's a closed hearing, really. A university investigation.'

Their voices go furtive and low, and they both stare at the walls. 'That is why there is an urgency about this all. And we were hoping that you …'

'That you could somehow contribute … help …'

'Me? How?'

'Have the Honours class said anything about him?'

'Any information that could help our cause?'

'Well …'

'We would appreciate any information, anything they say … any evidence of Makaya's misdeeds … ?'

'I do have this …' You haul out a copy of *Modern African Stories*, the Glued Edition. Mpofu takes the book and tries to peel back the pages but they are glued fast. He looks in bewilderment at you.

'Makaya did this?'

'No, no. But he … told them to tear out stories from their textbooks …'

'It might help. If you could maybe write up a little statement, anything that can be admitted as evidence …'

'We don't want to drag you into this,' says Zimmerlie. 'It would look bad, but …'

'But not as bad as if he wins the case,' says Mpofu. 'This is a matter of urgency, Timothy. Redlinghuis is tearing his hair out.'

'So anything you can give us, we'd be grateful.'

You're late for class. But the Honours classroom is in darkness. You fumble for the light switch and flood the empty seats with buzzing neon whiteness. The air-conditioning is on high (every classroom, every office, every lecture theatre is over air-conditioned so that you have to wear winter clothing even though it is over 40 degrees outside).

You check your watch, and then the timetable posted on the door. There is definitely supposed to be class. And you are only five minutes late. Surely the buggers have not scarpered so soon? You walk outside again into the blinding sun and scour the square for students. All deserted. You loosen your tie. Check your watch again. If you were a smoker, this is when you would light up a cigarette and suck on it. Smoking is always a good remedy for awkward situations. It gives you something to do with your hands.

'Mr Prospero?'

She is sitting on the low wall in the shade of a jacaranda tree, swinging her legs. You strain to see who is speaking.

'No class, today, Mr Prospero.'

'Ms Khumalo?'

You can barely make out her silhouette in the inky shade. You squint your eyes. 'Where is everybody?'

'Didn't you know about the boycott?'

'Obviously not.'

'They're all at the rally. No lectures today.'

'Why did no one tell me?'

'I'm telling you now.'

'You're here. You're not at the rally … ?'

She clutches her notebook tight in her lap. 'I'm going, but I wanted to catch you before I went. I wanted to ask you something.'

'What?'

'Sit, sit.' She pats the stony wall. You contemplate jumping up and sitting where she indicates, close to her—too close to her—and swinging your legs like she is doing. But you are wearing your suit, holding your briefcase: you are in a straitjacket of adult responsible behaviour. And you know not to get too close: a dangerously attractive student and an emotionally unstable idealist on the rebound and out of his cultural depth is not a good combo. So you continue standing.

'What you showed us the other day—Sizwe Bantu—I'd like to read more.'

You pause before you speak, to leach the scepticism from your reply. 'A bit late for that, don't you think? Didn't you rip all the Bantu stories out of the textbook?'

She opens her mouth to say something then shuts it again. Then, 'In retrospect, though, maybe I'm missing out on something.' A skewed smile.

'Well, I suppose he didn't win the Africa International Prize for nothing.'

A long pause.

'So, say I wanted to seriously read some Bantu, where would you suggest I start?'

You tap the briefcase. 'I'd say start here.'

You slide the case onto the low wall next to her and snap open the locks. 'It's best to start with the cockroach stories and then go from there.'

Now you know what a Jehovah's Witness peddling *Watchtower* feels like. 'Have a look through these and tell me what you think.'

She slides the photocopies into her bag. 'Thanks.'

Pause. Silence. Hot baking sun, shimmering tarmac and concrete. Go on, take a puff of your imaginary cigarette.

'Well, if there's no class, I'd better be off. I have lots of work to do.' You turn in the direction of the library.

She slips off the wall, smiling. 'Why don't you come to the Three Rs rally?'

'Thanks for the offer, but no.'

'But you'll get to see your predecessor!'

'I'm not sure I need that.'

She skips to keep up with your strides. 'It's exciting though, this rally. The Reinstate Makaya Rally.'

'In that case, I certainly have a lot of work to catch up on.'

She quickens her steps alongside you.

'Ms Khumalo ... I need to go to the library ...'

You walk faster, but she keeps up with you.

It is a game. The more you run from her, the more she will chase you. You have played this game often, only the other way around. And you are aware too that your prim little moral barricade is not that strong. You are an anarchist, after all, and one part of you wants adventure, to hell with the consequences.

You never make it to the library. Just as you are crossing Mazisi Kunene Park which fronts the library complex (Tracey seems intent on accompanying you), you hear a roar, the stamp of hundreds of feet, the rhythmic chants of hundreds of voices.

'Resign! Reform! Reinstate!'[1]

Around the corner surge a mass of what at first look like trees. Leaves and branches march towards you. 'What the ... ?'

A forest, indeed the nearby Thomas Mofolo Forest, is rushing towards you, singing and chanting. They are students, hundreds of students, and they hold large leafy branches over their heads. Some carry palm leaves, others gnarled jacaranda branches, and others banana leaves. They wave them in unison, back and forth as they march. At the front of the procession, two students hold up a banner—a white sheet pinned onto

---

1   'Resign' presumably is addressed to Zimmerlie and Mpofu, 'reform' to the administrative staff, and 'reinstate' refers to Makaya.

two high wooden poles, the words *Resign! Reform! Reinstate!* painted in gaudy red and yellow.

'Resign! Reform! Reinstate!'

Before you can scoot out of the way, you are both surrounded.

Leaves and branches brush past you. 'RRRrrrr! The three Rs!'

'Guess you get to see the rally after all.'

'Tracey …'

And then voices of panic. 'Run, run, it's Idi Amin! Idi Amin! Run!'

A student points a gnarled jacaranda branch at you. 'Mtshangu's coming!'

Tracey clutches at your shirt sleeve. 'We'd better go.'

The forest of students marches past you, each dancing from one leg to the other in what you later learn is the *toyi-toyi*, the dance of protest. From the opposite side of the square, a yellow Toyota ute (called a *bakkie*) roars towards you, heading off the marchers. You can read the words CAMPUS SECURITY on the van, and see the security chief, the man who took your ID photo, standing on top of the vehicle. He hunches over a tripod and points his weapon—Nikon camera, telephoto lens—at you. He clicks madly at everything in sight, like an insatiable tourist. He does look like Idi Amin now, wearing a plump padded military uniform. Flash! Flash! Flash! goes his camera, and student protesters hold their branches across their faces.

'Idi Amin! Idi Amin! Idi Amin!' The students *toyi-toyi* on the spot. 'Resign! Reform! Reinstate!'

You are the only one without cover. Now you understand what the branches are for.

A convoy of yellow Land Rovers (contents: barking dogs), which has been trailing Mtshangu's ute, drives out in a classic formation, around the back of the crowd, flanking you on both sides, parking in a curved semi-circle. Security guards step out of the Land Rovers and begin setting up what look like rocket launchers. Others point fat-barrelled guns into the air.

The students, hemmed in now on all sides, jostle and bunch around you. Even more disconcerting, you feel Tracey's hand clutch yours. Your other hand grips the briefcase, and you cannot wipe the sweat from your eyes. The sun beats down; the chanting rhythm of the students' song thrums out; the branches dance in the air above you.

The guards are following a set procedure, one you suspect the students know only too well. The students stamp, march, sing, raise clenched fists, writhe in one mass, a rent-a-crowd in a low budget movie. Mtshangu, on the roof of the ute, holds up a megaphone. 'This is an illegal gathering. Please disperse.'

'*Gat*.' Tracey holds your hand even tighter. 'We'd better get out of here.'

What happens next is predictable too. A quick train of events logically follows: one student runs forward, throws the stone that shatters the windscreen of the Toyota that causes the security chief to give the order to fire tear gas that causes the students to throw more stones that causes the dogs to be set loose, that etc.

'Resign! Reform! Reinstate!'

But it is too late. You and Tracey are surrounded by a whirlwind of dogs and security guards and dancing students. A salivating Alsatian presses you against the brick Admin wall. Waves of lachrymatory smoke billow across the grass and catch you in the throat. Mtshangu's Toyota mounts the hill, churning up the green grass. 'Get those people back over here!' A student ducks and dives, coughs tear gas, runs. You pick up the branch he drops and twirl it around to protect yourself from the gas. Mtshangu glares from his *bakkie*. 'Get back. Get out of here.'

The tear gas swirls around you like KwaZulu mist. The students are running for the hostels, those high square buildings you can see in the distance.

'Come on.' Tracey, still clutching your hand, pulls you into a gap behind a tree and onto a path through two brick buildings. Your eyes are burning, your throat raw, your nose stinging. The Land Rovers roar past. Tentacles of gas reach for you, but Tracey snakes through a narrow alleyway, pulling you with her.

'I know a place.'

She leads you through the corridor and you find yourself on the other side of the Admin building.

'Come!' She dives into the low trimmed bushes under the 'Media Studies' sign. You follow, snagging your jacket on some thorny branch. You crouch in the dank earth behind the bushes, lean heavily against a damp concrete wall. The bushes and tree foliage above seal you off.

'Nice hiding place, eh? I found it last time when Idi Amin was after us.'

You wipe the sweat off your face. It is a mistake. The more you wipe your eyes, the more they sting.

'The last demonstration, we marched on the English Department, and it got a little out of hand ... when we burned down Mpofu's office.'

'You?'

'It wasn't me personally. It was after we first heard that Dr Makaya was dismissed.'

'You burned down Mpofu's office?'

She sits down on the ground and pulls her satchel into her lap. And laughs. 'You're cool, Dr Turner. Cool.'

'What's that got to do with it? I'm over this, you know.'

'You get used to it.'

She smiles hard. 'Hey, listen, can I come over tonight? I'll bring supper.'

Whoa.

She pulls at your sleeve. 'Come on.'

'You don't know where I live.'

'35 Seaview Street.'

'Is anything not known about me in this small town?'

'Say around six?'

'I ... well ... er ...' You make all those delaying sounds to give you time to think of what to say. She stands, slides the journal into her satchel, slings it over her shoulder.

'Catch you later, Prof. Six tonight?'

You watch her walk out into the bright sunshine, her after-image a purple swagger. You wipe the sweat off your brow with a trembling hand.

*

On the far side of Mazisi Kunene Park, you spot the back entrance to the Humanities Building. You duck into the side entrance, scour it for any signs of people you know (it is deserted) and then head for the toilets. Your eyes and throat burn. You wash your face and eyes, and then straighten your tie, stare into empty space on the wall where the mirror should be.

But the guilt is still visible in your gestures, the way you straighten your tie, the way you limber your arms as you walk up the stairs. You always feel guilty, even when you are innocent.

The English Department is a serene balm, its dark hushed corridors forgiving. Zimmerlie waits in the doorway of his office. He ushers you inside and shuts the door. Mpofu looks up from the desk where he is hunched over the computer screen.

'You all right? You gave us quite a scare, Dr Turner. Mr Mtshangu just gave us a call, told us that you were … you were. … caught up in the *fracas*.'

'Scared the shit out of me.'

'Got one,' says Mpofu at the screen and clicks his mouse.

'I should have warned you about the demonstration,' says Zimmerlie. 'You okay?'

'I'll be right. Nothing like the smell of tear gas in the afternoon. It might have helped to have known that classes were cancelled today.'

'They're not. Officially.' Zimmerlie feels his forehead for his scar and scratches it. 'Anyway I'm glad you're safe. Sit. Sit. A glass of water? Here.' He pours two glasses, offers you one and gulps the other down himself, clapping a handful of multi-coloured pills into his mouth.

Mpofu scrolls down the screen. 'Got him!'

'What … ?'

Zimmerlie beckons you around the front of the desk to see the computer screen. 'Mtshangu sends us photographs of the demonstrators. We identify them. He makes a report. See … Langa. Ben Langa if I'm not mistaken. Isn't he in the Honours class?'

'Possibly.'

'And look at this. Dr Turner, this is a surprise!'

At first you do not know what you are looking at. The photograph shows a white blurry figure sneaking away from the trucks across a green mound, holding hands with a blonde-haired student in dreads and a cap.

It looks suspiciously like two lovers running in the park.

'Is that Tracey Khumalo?'

Mpofu folds his arms. '*Wakhahlelwa ihhashi esifubeni.*'[2]

2   Zulu proverb: literally, 'he was kicked in the chest by a horse', meaning: he who cannot keep a secret, cannot disguise his feelings.

This silence they are imposing on you, this sweat pouring down your face, this burning tear gas in your throat—is guilt pure and simple They are making you feel you have transgressed. One strike against you: what are you doing at Makaya's rally? Strike two: what the hell are you doing in the bushes with that student? But this is all your projection. They look genuinely concerned, protective even, over you.

Zimmerlie speaks first. 'Isn't she the one who …?'

Mpofu cuts him off.

'What?' you say.

Zimmerlie sighs. 'She's the one who …'

'It wouldn't be fair to you, Timothy,' says Mpofu, 'if we didn't lay our cards on the table. The man you're replacing has been accused of sexual harassment.'

'What?' Blood drains from your face.

Zimmerlie presses his hand to his forehead and massages his left eye. 'Timothy does not need to know all the gory details …'

Mpofu wrinkles his nose. 'On the contrary, John, he does need to know all the gory details. If he has detected a certain antagonism in his students, a certain trauma, a certain defensiveness, he will want to know why. Am I right, Timothy?'

You hope that this is a rhetorical question.

'Makaya denies it. Absolutely denies it. Says we have no evidence of misconduct or sexual harassment.'

'Of course he denies it. He denies everything.'

'He's right, unfortunately. It's his word against hers. And Redlinghuis says that without evidence, we're screwed.'

You manage to interject here. 'Hers?'

'We are not screwed. We do have evidence. It's pretty obvious to anyone. Even to Timothy, an objective, neutral, outside observer.'

Zimmerlie clutches your arm with a bony claw of a hand. 'What did you see, Timothy, as an objective observer in the classroom?'

You saw a lot. You saw defiance, rebellion, subversion. You saw restless energy, idealism, flirtation. But not sexual harassment. 'Not much.'

'Of course not. They clam up. He's threatened them. They're frightened of the bloody man.'

You try to imagine this Honours class frightened of anyone. Of Tracey clamming up. 'Wait a minute. Are you saying that Tracey Khumalo accused Makaya of sexual harassment? I find that hard to believe.'

'You don't know the man,' says Mpofu. 'He bullies, he ...'

'No, I mean, Tracey. She worships the man.'

Zimmerlie shakes his head. 'Makaya sexually harassed her. A complaint was made. He was suspended pending investigation ...'

Mpofu concurs. 'We had him. Then she refused to co-operate.'

'She withdrew the charge?'

'No, no. The charge was ... er ... made on her behalf. But she refused to co-operate.'

'He intimidated her into silence.'

You try to fit these facts to the picture you have of Tracey Khumalo. The confident swagger, the unflinching gaze, the ironic intelligence.

Mpofu senses your disbelief. 'Her mother found out about his inappropriate sexual relationship with Tracey. Her mother filed the complaint.'

'I see.'

'But now Redlinghuis say the charges will not stick. Unless Tracey co-operates. We all know what the man is doing, but the law apparently cannot help us.'

'Unless ...'

'If only,' says Zimmerlie, looking at you, 'if only we could get some type of concrete evidence. Something substantial that will stand up in a court of law.'

Mpofu clatters his teacup on the table. 'What were they writing, did they say?'

'They ... they wrote journals.'

'Did they show you these journals?'

'No.'

'All Redlinghuis needs is hard evidence.'

'What are you saying?'

'No, Thami,' interjects Zimmerlie. 'We can't expect this young man to ...'

'John, you said so yourself. The students open to him, a fresh face, he has access to information we don't have.'

They turn to you. 'We have a request.'

'Tracey Khumalo. She seems to be open to you.'

'Just tell us anything she says about him. Any information. What they did in class, what he said, any written evidence.'

'A journal. You mentioned journals ... perhaps she wrote something down that would be helpful.'

'You want me to ...'

They nod in unison.

'The poor girl,' says Thami, 'needs help. She has been crushed into silence.'

'But be careful, be careful, Timothy. If he gets wind of it, you're ...' He makes the motion of cutting a throat.

'Afrikan Metamorphosis' by Sizwe Bantu

(*The Present Tense*, Vol. XXVII, Feb. 2003, pp. 66-77)

The Modern Afrikanist woke up one morning to find himself transformed into a large cockroach. As he lay on his back, he could feel his glossy carapace slide on the sheets beneath him, and as he attempted to turn over, saw numerous legs waggling above him.

"What's happened to me," he said in his cockroach voice. It was no dream. Horrified that he had been dabbling with too many cockroaches, he tried to pinch himself as you do when you want to wake from a nightmare. He tried to find that self-conscious thought to distance itself from his reality and so discover that he was outside of it. But no. Not only was he a cockroach, but he was one stuck down in a painting. His back when he wriggled enough to see it was painted blue, and when he tried to speak, it was in a raspy cockroach voice.

The Modern Afrikanist had no friends, no family, so no one would come to rescue or find him. He now regretted his solitary lifestyle. He knew only too well the fate of Kafka's Gregor Samsa in *The Metamorphosis*. He knew too that cockroaches could die on their backs like beetles struggling to turn themselves over—a fault in their design perhaps, or a cruel joke perpetrated on them by a cruel human god.

The glue was sticky but had not quite dried, so he was able to lever himself up a little. But he was still stuck fast.

This is karma, he thought, for all the cockroaches I painted into pictures. I wonder what painting I have been painted into? Myself? Perhaps if I could rock to and fro, and escape ... And then what? He'd still be a cockroach. A free cockroach, but still, a cockroach.

The only way out of his cockroach existence—he could see long days of foraging in shit ahead of him—was to think hard, to create self-consciousness, cockroach-consciousness, and thereby create a loop independent of his brain ... a mind ... a self-awareness. But wait a minute: he was already self-aware. What cruelty to be a mind yoked to a cockroach body, a Cartesian pea in an empty shell of a carapace. He looked in horror at his legs—saws, so thin; his mouth a mean orifice, his back already aching, not used to being hunched, his brain labouring hard to use these few bushy cells. And most of all the absence of flesh: he was a dead creature—a cold, dry insect, despised by all. But the one hope: a cockroach is a survivor. Cockroaches have extraordinary survival skills. They have been around forever. And their primitive life form will outlast everybody, including the cruel artist god who has stuck him into this painting.

After interminable hours of wriggling, he broke free of the paint and began to tread out of its gluey bluey mess. The canvas was still wet. He crawled off the painting and into a crevice, hiding in the dark, his feelers twitching, feeling, hearing, sensing, smelling the air. It was an interesting sensation. He could see through smell, touch, taste and hearing.

Words are excrement, he thought. What's in this black shit anyway? To think some people spend their lives sifting through other people's shit!

Hungry, he began to eat a corner of the canvas, savouring the glue, the paint, but especially the paper. This was not going to be so bad, after all. Being a cockroach was a venerable tradition, he argued to himself. What was wrong with a cockroach anyway? Just as he had transformed his repugnance for the little creatures in his flat, he now had to overcome his physicality, his hard cockroach-ness. Embrace it. Use it. Be it. He had often wondered what it was like being a cockroach. Now he had his answer. To be a cockroach was to forsake self-consciousness, to be at the mercy of his baser instincts, desires, habits, his cockroachness. Could he surrender to pure being?

Best of all of course was the white powder he found spread liberally over the floor. So delicious, so sweet, so cold. In his head he heard music, cockroach music, a symphony of buzzing pleasure, the rasp of wings, the joy of pure being as he ate and ate and ate.[3]

Your cottage is dark and low-ceilinged, smells of fried oil, and there is nowhere to sit except that fluff-erupting green sofa. There are no plates, no glasses, no cutlery to speak of (except a very blunt bread knife which has been commandeered for other purposes). The ground-level windows—some with glass, others boarded up—are mud-splashed from the outside. It is apparent that the tenant who squats here lives in fear and paranoia. And he lives in a bloody mess. His swimming shorts lie twisted in the bathtub, stiff with brine. A mug of mouldy tea sits next to a crushed Coke can which has dribbled sticky liquid onto the sandy floor. And there is a rubber cockroach, for god's sake, in the centre of the room, propped up against a ridiculously childish shrine to an obscure African writer, perched on a make-shift crate. A dark blue suit has been discarded onto a kitchen chair, the shirt and tie still done up, sweat stains under the armpits, the suit trousers dangling as if there is a thin invisible man still inside.

And this is your sacrosanct refuge for your true self?

You really should tidy up. You scud dutifully around the cottage, stuffing clothes into cupboards, miscellaneous items (such as empty Coke cans and pizza boxes) behind mattresses; you hide the suit behind the

---

3   Apart from the obvious borrowing from Kafka's *The Metamorphosis*, this piece is a 'brico-lage' sampled from many sources: Marechera's piece 'What's Wrong with a Cockroach anyway?', the South African poet Mongane Serote's poem 'What's in this Black Shit', and William Carlos Williams' imagist poem 'This is to Say'. Although some critics have dispar-aged this practice of 'bowerbirding', calling it plagiarism, others, including Turner, have pointed out that this is a common 'practice-led research' methodology, as advocated by Haseman, Locke and Gucci.

bathroom door, on an only-now–discovered metal hook, and spray the room with a spray can you find under the kitchen sink (*Killem stops 'em dead!*). You regret this. The musty smell is gone, but now the cockroach poison fills the air and makes your eyes smart and your throat burn. Damn. In the bathroom you find another rusted can—this time labelled 'Heyes' (*Heyes wraps up smells!*)—, shake it to find it is still half full, and spray its contents over every part of the room. Now the room is sickly sweet with the aroma of a Spring Breeze, as promised on the side of the can.

As an afterthought, you pluck two purple and green man-eating crocuses you find growing on a cactus outside, and place them in a mug filled with water on the low, cloth-covered suitcase you use as a footrest. (*Lake Sahara*, the mug is labelled, and caricatured on this desert background is the Cookie Monster from *Sesame Street*, saying 'Good Drink!')

Six o'clock.

Six fifteen.

She isn't coming.

Good. Good. You can't handle this now. You hope she doesn't come. This is a game you shouldn't be playing; a game you don't want to play, but you are aware too that she is also playing a game, and it might not be the same game you are playing.

Yet. And yet.

You want to know everything, and she wants to talk. These are the signs you are reading here.

The Bantu shrine should go too. But to hide it away would be to betray yourself; to leave it there would be expose your secret vulnerability; to even think about either option is to give her too much attention already. You shouldn't care what she, or anyone, thinks.

Six forty-two.

You are not going to sit around waiting for her. You position yourself on the sagging couch and flick through a Bantu novel. At each sound, you leap up. But the sounds—the scrabble of feelers and claws in the boxes in the storeroom—are your own tenants.

Six fifty-three.

Damn her. You put the Bantu away. You shouldn't be so nervous. You shouldn't even be thinking about her at all. You wipe the sticky feelings off your hands.

You take out your journal: a clean white notebook with blue lines, red margins, A5, smooth textured skin. You find the ink pen and scratch the date on the top of a blank page. The first pages of the journal are blank. What should you write? The wind rushing through you at the beach, the jewelled sea drops that splash up against you as the waves pounded your skin. The creeping goose flesh as you contemplate that sculpture on the baked deck of a mysterious cottage in the dunes. Play with words, damn you. But the words won't come. The feeling, yes, but not the words. The words are already used up, someone else's words, and you want your own words to put in this book. If only words were drum beats or splashes of oil paint.

*

Wind chimes tinkle in the breeze outside and tin cans rattle against each other. You slam the journal shut and slip it under the Bantu shrine.

She is wearing a blue Hawaiian-print wrap-around dress, heavy perfume and the smell of pizza. She carries a QUALITY PIZZA box, a smooth green bottle of wine. She steps forward, and tangles herself in the invisible cat-gut fishing line you have draped over the entrance to ensnare intruders.

'*Bliksem! Jou opgefokde doos van 'n hond.*'

She struggles, succeeding in further tangling herself in six metres of fishing line, and tinkling the wind chimes. 'Ow, *Etterkop*! Ow, *yusses, man.*'

South Africa is fortunate to have the best swear words in the world. You don't know what they mean but they sound good.

'Don't move!' You step forward to stop her hurting herself on the barbs. You hold up the barbed line from her face and pull the line from around her neck.

She stands with arms in the air while you untangle the fishing line. Once it is all done, her smile returns. 'So, am I a good catch?'

'That's to stop intruders breaking in. A sort of ... burglar alarm.'

'Can I come in now or is there a booby trap behind the front door?'

'Come in, please, come in.' You take the wine bottle and pizza from her.

'You're not doing anything? Am I disturbing you?'

You wildly try to think of something you are doing, something she is disturbing. 'No, nothing. Nothing, just a bit of reading.'

'Nice! Can I look around?'

You pull the last thread of fishing line from her hair. She unslings the satchel from around her neck and throws it on the couch as if she is arriving home after a hard day at school. But she wanders around as if she is a prospective renter, and you the estate agent. She is not judgemental about the decor, nor does she wrinkle up her nose at the strange smell. She stands by the kitchen counter and watches you fumble in the drawer for a corkscrew. She reaches up into the top cupboard behind you and produces two wine glasses and a silver bottle opener in the shape of a man. She opens the ice compartment of the fridge, and takes out a metal ice tray, plopping two ice cubes in each glass.

You go to work on the cork, twisting, turning, pulling until it splinters into a million fragments so that you have to then dig it out. You hold out two glasses of white wine. She takes one, drinks it down in one super gulp and places the empty glass back in your hand.

You guide her into the living room where she spies the surfboard you propped up in the corner. 'Oh.' Now she is kneeling on the floor and smoothing the surfboard with her hand as if it is a long-lost pet.

'How did you get here? I didn't hear a car.'

'Walked.'

'Walked? It's a long way … from anywhere.'

'Short cut.'

'Sit. Sit.'

She flops down onto the sofa, hugs a cushion tightly to her chest and places her bare feet on the table, wiggling her purple toenails. 'Let's eat. I'm starved. Fresh from Mrs K's—you must try her sometime.'

You indicate the old packets of Mrs K's burger, pizza and chicken sandwiches scrunched up into a plastic bag on the just-visible kitchen counter. You set to work cutting up the pizza.

'Dr Turner …'

'Timothy.'

'Timothy, I read the Bantu. I wanted to come straight over. I have so many questions.'

'What did you read?'

She dives into the satchel and pulls out a sheaf of photocopied sheets of paper. 'Cockroach stories. Loved them. Absolutely loved them. And I loved his quote on the front of the cover—"storytelling ... more venerable than history, as ancient as the cockroach".[4]

You still are not sure of her motives. Treat all intrusions into your personal space as suspicious. Perhaps she is spying on you. Perhaps Makaya has sent her to check out the newbie who has dared take his place. Perhaps she is mirroring your actions.

You have to remind yourself: this is the person who accused Makaya of sexual harassment.

Correction: this is the person on whose behalf a sexual harassment charge was laid.

A world of difference, you know.

You wonder: can you lay a charge of sexual harassment on behalf of someone else? Surely you have to be harassed yourself in order to make a claim? Is harassment an objective quantity that can be recognised by a third party? You know you are being naïve, but you cannot imagine Tracey describing her relationship to Makaya as one of harassment. Whatever the case, that sticky charge has been smeared over him. And whether she complained or not is not the issue: the issue is whether he sexually harassed her or not. And you are in no doubt: intuitively you know he did.

How does she really feel? You have no idea of her involvement with Makaya. Relationships tend to knot themselves in complicated insinuations. Perhaps this is her way of disentangling herself. But you are sure of one thing: her entanglement with him must have crossed boundaries. You know this because even now she is crossing boundaries with you. She spills out into the world, this girl. She is spontaneous, immediate and dangerous. Whereas your gesture is to shrink from the world: you are contained, and your emotions have no tentacles.

'What are you staring at, Mr Prospero?'

'Sorry, I was just thinking ...'

4   J.M. Coetzee, from 'The Novel Today' in *Upstream* Vol. 6(1) 1988: pp. 2-5.

Makaya is in the interstices of this relationship. So you may as well tackle this head on.

'So why do you think Makaya asked you to tear out these pages from your textbook?'

You observe her closely to see what effect the word Makaya has on her. She has a mischievous glint in her eye. 'Dr Makaya says that all Bantu's work is *kuk*, if you'll pardon my French.'

She takes another bite of pizza, though her mouth is still full with her first slice.

'*Kuk?*'

'Shit.'

You know what it means. But you are thinking of the comment on your article in the library. 'Really? And how did he come to such an intelligent critical appraisal of one of the greatest writers alive today?'

'Bantu is derivative, he said. Second hand.'

'He told you that? How naïve! Derivative?'

'Dr Makaya may be a lot of things, but he is not naïve.'

'It's pathetic. He tears Bantu out of books …'

She sits cross-legged on the couch, pumping her knees in rhythm to an inaudible beat, and breaks off another hunk of pizza. 'It's not pathetic. It's pure courage.'

'I don't understand.'

'You wouldn't understand.'

'Try me.'

'He's more than just a teacher. He opened our eyes. He pushed us beyond the normal. He broke all the boundaries, he made us feel alive, he helped us realise our true selves …'

'What boundaries?'

This is the moment you have been waiting for. The confession. But when she speaks, you can see masticated cheese and tomato. She takes another sip of wine (mouth still full of pizza). 'Oh, don't be so … old-fashioned. You sound like my mother. You sound like the Suits … oh, beg your pardon, you are a Suit …'

She stretches out her legs on your lap, curls her toes and wiggles them at you. It is a challenge. It is flirtatious. But you have to remind yourself—again!—that you are in a foreign culture, and that you are extremely good at misreading signs. So whatever signs she is giving you, you have to ignore them.

She pours another glass of wine for you, and for herself, and gulps hers down as if she is afraid you will stop her drinking.

'How old are you anyway?'

'Old enough.'

'You sure you can hold all that alcohol?'

She smiles. 'Maybe you should hold it for me.'

'I mean ...'

'I know what it is.' She points her empty glass at you. 'I know what it is. You're jealous, aren't you? That's what it is. You're jealous of him.'

'Ridiculous.'

'Sounds like jealousy to me.' She pokes you in the ribs with her toes (she has by now slid all the way down to a lying position on the sofa).

'You've read Bantu. You can see how good he is. So why tear him out of textbooks?'

Her answer is swift. 'There is no greater writer than yourself. If you see a great writer on the road, kill him. Quote from Dr Makaya.'

'I see.'

'We are all Sizwe Bantus, he told us, and we all have something to say, no need to elevate one above the rest.'

'That's just nonsense.'

'You're so funny, Dr Turner.' She leaps off the sofa. 'Come.'

'Where are you going?'

'Where are we going? To the beach.'

'Tracey ... ?

'I can't talk with that huge rubber cockroach staring at me. What on earth do you have that for?'

You follow her to the front door where she stands looking at the night outside. A cricket that has been chirping loudly stops and listens. A warm breeze blows through the leaves of the skeletal paw-paw tree. She stands by the Golf, and leans against the passenger door, not minding the condensation on her dress.

'I need some wind in my face.'

'Tracey ...'

'I want to show you something about Makaya. About me. Tell you something. But not here.'

You reach for your car keys and slam the front door behind you. You are reluctant to take someone to another of your secret places, but here you are driving through the dunes, parking the car, slamming the door loudly, listening to her laugh echo through the moist air against the dark dune ahead, abandoning your shoes in a suspiciously close relationship next to hers on the path, treading on the surprisingly cold sand, watching the white frothy waves roll and trip and tumble, and finally trailing your toes in the warm sea.

The moon is the only way you can see where you are, who you are. If not for the glinting teeth and odd reflection by your side, you could be walking by yourself, for she is silent. You walk to the edge of the Mswaswe River and stop at the two-foot precipice that the river has carved. You wait for her to speak. She breathes in and out three times loudly and deeply. You count twenty, thirty seconds.

'So what are you going to tell me?'

She leaps off the cliff, lands in the shallow river with a splash, and lies down backwards in the current.

'This!' The river flows over her; her teeth glint in the moonlight. She emerges from the river a luminous monster that drips globules of her plastic self at every step as she lurches towards you with an outstretched hand. You—the stern university lecturer, the White Australian, the frigid Westerner, all of the above—step back. She shrugs her shoulders, tosses her head from side to side, and then walks through the breakers where she hurls herself into the sea.

'Beware of crocodiles and sharks,' you call.

'What?' A wave tips her over.

You watch her thrash about in the black waves for long minutes, her clothes dripping off her. In the crash of the white tops, you see that she is in trouble. She flails her arms, drops under the waves, gasps, and then ducks under again. A dark shadow circles her, shoots at her, and pulls her down. In a second you strip off your shirt and plunge in. Splash towards her, fight the high surf. When you reach her, she has stopped wrestling with the waves, and is submerged in the foamy brine. You scoop her up by the middle, kick at the dark shapes under the water. 'Tracey?' Her eyes are closed, her body limp, and her breathing strained.

It is difficult to pull her to shore with her legs wrapped around your waist, her arms tight around your neck. Her braids hang heavy. But you wade valiantly out of the sucking sea, thump her on the beach, and stand panting at the sight of this heavy mermaid gleaming in the moonlight. You push aside her tangled hair.

She lies still, eyes closed, her chest heaving up and down.

'Tracey?'

She opens her eyes. Her smile tells you that there are no sharks, no rip current. 'That's what I was going to show you.' She grips your neck and pulls you to her.

You are supposed to kiss her. No mistaking this cultural clue.

But no. You prise her arms off and stand. Brush the sand from your hands and knees. You grope for your shirt, pull it over your head and stare out into the blackness. The waves crash in unison ahead, spraying you with shiny flecks of foam.

'Are you mad at me, Timothy?'

You stare out at the black ocean.

'I don't suppose you have a towel, do you?'

'Why didn't you think of this before you tossed yourself into the sea?'

'I never think too far ahead,' she says, 'and that's what gets me into trouble.' You crunch back on the sand, which glitters like fireflies, and sparks when you scud your toes into it. 'I'll make a nice cup of coffee. Do you have *Koffiehuis* at your place? Or rooibos. Have you ever had rooibos tea?'

In the distance, a light gleams. You locate it on a high dune—the cottage with its eyeless, genderless guardian. The light winks like a star in the humid night air.

'Do you know who lives in that cottage over there?'

'No idea. Why?'

'Do you see that light over there?' The light dances in your eyes as you move.

'Come on, Mr Prospero, please, I'm freezing.'

'Okay.' You lead the way between two dark dune shadows to the car, open the passenger front door for her, and drive roughly up the stony hill back into the night. Tracey twists her hair into a long spiral and tosses it over the back of the seat. 'I can't go home like this. My mother will kill me. Haven't you got any dry clothes I could borrow?'

'You can borrow my track suit …'

*

You settle in the lounge, sinking into the sofa while she takes an extended shower. You hear splashing, singing, the shower being turned off, and then silence. You wait. You jingle-jangle the car keys in your hand, ready to leap up when she appears and drive her home.

For there can be no other conclusion to this saga.

It's a perfect on-the-rebound scenario. She throws herself at you; you catch her. Maybe she is on the rebound too, hurt by Makaya, and she has to repair the damage. Two rebounds make a real disaster. Trust me. But fortunately, you have a glass plate between you and the world. A year ago you would have been attracted to her ... you are attracted to her, but you can't let her in.

And besides, nothing makes sense. There is not a whiff of sexual harassment. She is not on the rebound.

But what is she doing here with you?

Her satchel yawns open. Besides the sheaf of photocopied Bantu stories, you spy the A5 hard-cover book. Her journal. You bend over and nudge it open a little.

You look up to see if she is watching you. You pull it out a fraction and read the heading on one page.

Dr Makaya's Aphorisms

You close the book. Let it slide back into the satchel. Stand up. Check the door. She must still be in the shower.

You wait an eternity, two eternities, three eternities, stare at the yawning satchel, pace the lounge (which is not very long) and finally, resolved, walk down the passage and rap on the open bathroom door. 'Tracey?'

Her Hawaiian dress hangs from the bath taps and drips steadily onto the floor, but the room is empty. You follow the footprint-sized pools of water out of the bathroom to your bedroom, and push open the half-closed door. 'Tracey?'

The lump in your bed does not move. She has her back to you, she is wearing your track suit, and her hair—towel-dried but still damp—is fanned over the pillow. Limbs are tangled in the blanket. The lump rises and falls in time with light snores. You back slowly out of the doorway and pull the door closed.

The couch smells of Mrs K's pizza and cheap wine. You pour yourself the last glass and gulp it down as she did, in one swig. You pace the creaking floorboards of the living room and then take the glasses back to the kitchen. You snap off the light so the cottage is plunged into darkness. You creak open the front door and stumble out into the moist night air. A headache pulses in your right eye, a hangover even before the wine has a chance to take effect. You stare into the darkness at the white mist hanging in the trees.

You can see it now: STUDENT ROMPS IN WAVES WITH NEW UNIVERSITY LECTURER; DISGRACE OF MIDNIGHT ORGY; AUSSIE LECTURER FIRED AFTER SORDID LIAISON WITH STUDENT.

You hate yourself for what you are about to do. You slide the journal out of the satchel and open it. Even now you cannot believe you are going to do what you are doing.

Dr Makaya's Aphorisms

1   Don't listen to the voice of the censor. He is everywhere. He is the colonialist Superego, the watchdog of your creativity. Rip him out of your mind! Rip him out of your textbooks.

2   Sometimes even the President has to stand naked.

3   An African university is by its very nature an antithesis of a Western University.

You could stop now.

Just one more page. Two.

You riffle through the rest of the journal, looking at it through the eyes of your employers, through the legal eyes of Redlinghuis, whoever he may be. You are disappointed. There is nothing here to incriminate Makaya, unless you want to put him on trial for vanity and ego strutting. In a way, that is a relief. You skim through the section on the African University.

An African university should create knowledge of a different kind. An African university is not a corporation or a business and should not feed students into industry and commerce. An African university

Wait.

Here is a section on relationships between students and faculty. You pull the journal closer to the flickering candle. Here Tracey's notes are written hurriedly, scribbled as if he is dictating too fast.

> We reject the expedient relationship of master/servant that most universities operate under. That the lecturer is the repository of knowledge and that the student is here to soak up that knowledge. We reject the notion that knowledge resides in textbooks, and can be transmitted through mechanisms of lecturing, studying, osmosis.

> We reject the notion that achievement can be measured via the essay, the exam, the test.

> Knowledge is not a commodity.

> What is generated then is an Ubuntu, a relationship between people, fellow humans interacting intimately.

You note the fallacy—should you say the hypocrisy—of the man who dictates knowledge for students to write down.

It is the next page that makes your heart pump hard, your hands tremble.

It is a printed page, stuck into the journal, an essay. In the margins are hand-written comments. You are unsure whether these are Makaya's transcribed thoughts or hers.

'Sexuality and the African university' – Tracey Khumalo

> Statistics show that "sex between teachers/lecturers and students is much more common than people are willing to acknowledge," said Charol Shakeshaft, a Hofstra University professor. Shakeshaft reports that up to 5 percent of teachers engage in some form of sexual activity *[she calls it 'abuse']* of students. From a survey of students at a North Carolina High School in 1991, 13 percent of the high school's graduates had partaken in sexual intercourse with a teacher (Goldberg, 1995). *[I think he means more than one teacher.]* In another survey given to North Carolina high school students, 14% reported that they had engaged in sexual intercourse with a teacher (Wishnietsky, 1991). *[They could be lying of course, trying to get the teachers in trouble or else exercising a very teenage practice, wish fulfilment.]*

> And university lecturers are even worse *[or 'better' depending on your point of view.]* … Despite widespread concern about abuse of power and conflicts of interest, sexual relationships between lecturers and students often flourish

within academe. 5% of relationships develop into long-term relationships.

Jane Gallop, once Professor of English and Comparative Literature at the University of Wisconsin-Milwaukee, in '*Feminist Accused of Sexual Harassment*', says: "At its most intense – and, I would argue, its most productive – the pedagogical relation between teacher and student is, in fact, a 'consensual amorous relation', a complicated, erotically charged teacher-student relationship." And that measures barring any relationships between staff and students will not only be unsuccessful but will destroy the pedagogical union between the two. *[Good teaching involves some sort of sexual relationship, in other words.]*

"I worry about the effect of the policy on teaching relationships that are not literally sexual but are warm or personal or flirtatious. I worry that they will make faculty wary of any personal or complicated relationships, and such relationships have been – for the four decades that I've been in the academy – typical of some of the best and most meaningful pedagogical relationships. I worry that they will turn these life-changing relationships into a businesslike client relationship."

"There is an erotic dimension to pedagogy. Really getting to know someone intimately. Passion. It's a terribly sexy experience – two people sitting together talking intimately about their feelings for poetry. How do you desexualise that?"

You creep to the bedroom door and watch the blankets on your bed rise and fall. You observe your own swirl of contradictory emotions with wonder: at least you are alive. The glass plate is not as thick as you thought.

But you cannot stand here any longer. You cannot be with yourself in a stuffy cottage where a student you have just betrayed—are betraying—are about to betray—is waiting for you in your bed. Perhaps that is also part of it: you're flattered, something heals when someone opens up to you, wants you.

You tiptoe out of the house, climb into your car and fiddle with the keys in the ignition. The engine growls to life, and the car drives as fast as it can down the jungle lane away from the cottage. You need to think, you tell yourself. You need to get away from the self you do not like, that self who reads students' journals with a view to betraying them, students who are sleeping in your bed, waiting for you to join them. There are too many desires in the ether here: other people's desires, not yours, wanting you to do, to be, grasping hands clawing you in every direction.

Your sweaty hands grip the steering wheel but they still shake. You drive to escape the clenched knot in your stomach, the dizzy heady spinning, the gleaming spider's web spun around you. Those green eyes. Her laugh. The way she flings herself into the sea. The way you could so easily abandon yourself to the madness of an illicit relationship. The delicious feeling of reckless abandon.

But Makaya is in the way, even of this fantasy.

You drive through the dead town, following the path of least resistance. Night lights gleam onto the houses you pass, or rather onto the high walls with electric fences that screen the houses from view. You are heading for the highest point of the town, a rocky mount shoring itself against the dunes on the west side of town. You have some unformed idea to head for the cottage you have discovered in the dunes. But you have no idea where it would be, coming at it from this side of town. You pick a likely but unimaginatively named street—Second Avenue— and cross into what is part of the nature reserve. The road winds up and around, punctuated with weak street lights and the shadows of crouching, watching trees. But where you expect a clear view, a car park and perhaps a view over the Indian Ocean at the top, the road dead-ends—a high wall and a gate, through which you can glimpse, in blazing night lights, a huge house perched on the top of the very hill you are trying to reach. You count three storeys and a dozen windows, all lit up with blazing yellow lights. You stop the car at the wrought-iron gates and shove the gears into reverse. You flick the headlights onto high beam to see the golden plaque hidden by thick creepers by the gate:

MAKAYA

The night closes black around you and the wind blows cold. You thrust the car into reverse, grind the gears and stall. Pump the accelerator and try to start the car again. Fuel fumes fill the interior through the gap under the handbrake: don't flood the bloody thing. You stare at the blazing mansion. A new, darker emotion is taking root, replacing the blind panic that led you here.

Inexorably. Like a black hole drawing you closer. You cannot escape his tractor beam.

Just as you turn the wheel of the car to reverse out of the narrow driveway entrance, a top window of the house opens and a silhouette of a man looks out. You see head and shoulders, and a hand come up to a mouth. He is staring, you realise, at the brash headlights pointed at the house and gate. You stare too, but the silhouette reveals nothing of the man. From that height, he must have a magnificent view of the whole town below, and the wide sea beyond, during the day at least. Now he must see mere blackness and white-specked wave crests. And a yellow Golf with its headlights bright at his front gate. You manage to start the car, and reverse hastily—you didn't want him to come down, or cause a fuss. You don't want to meet this man at all.

You manage a three-point turn on the narrow road, and as you steal one last look at the house, the silhouette disappears from the window. You drive as fast as you can down the narrow road and into the nether regions of town.

You turn off the car engine and glide in neutral into the parking space on strewn palm leaves, the lights off. The cottage is in compete darkness. You feel like some voyeuristic intruder, trying to peep in between the boards at the glassless bedroom window, to see if she is still asleep.

The lounge is dead, smelling of wine and candle wax and mosquito repellent. A pool of seawater in the bath shows where her clothes were. The bedroom too is empty. The sheets are folded back and scrunched as if she has been wrestling tigers on the bed. The sheets are full of sand. Your track suit is gone and her satchel—and the journal in it—is nowhere to be found.

6

Panchlora nivea

. . . .

Green banana or Cuban cockroach

> The green banana cockroach, also known as the Cuban cockroach or *Panchlora nivea*, is a tropical species associated with Latin America. Because of its beautiful green colour and its friendly nature, it makes a good pet. Its image has been popularised in the Spanish revolutionary song 'La Cucaracha' about a cockroach that has lost its one hind leg. It lives outdoors, is nocturnal, but may be attracted to light from human dwellings. Cuban cockroaches may also enter your home in summer when windows and doors are left open, so it is advised to erect mesh window screens to help keep them out.

Running is an activity in which you try your hardest to get away from yourself, to put as much distance between the self you have been—the flabby past—and to accelerate to the ideal future, the self you want to become. When you run, you can also sweat out the embarrassment and cringing behaviour and bad faith and insincerity of a self you are but don't want to be. Running is a form of self-flagellation: the endurance of will against your lazy self to reach a higher self.

You run to escape your own dark shadow.

It is a bright golden morning. You run the wide beach from the eSikamanga river, the waves swirling at your ankles, the smell of brine and yellow chemicals (from Richard's Bay) in your nostrils, towards the mirage of the Mswaswe River five kilometres away, deferring the prize of a plunge into the pounding ocean until your body has been punished enough and the sweat and guilt and embarrassment are washed away in the briny surf.

Guided by the glint of sun in the window panes in the foliage, you climb the large dune and watch the view of the restless ocean between two brown breasts. The sea is dark already, with angry white flecks; the river below has silted up, and further to your left the mercurial Manga River is a haze of sand storms. Above you is the cottage with the wide deck and the statue of the sexless and eyeless man standing sentinel.

You think of the other house you stumbled across the previous night—Makaya's house—and try to position it—it must be the other side of town, across the river.

You scout the fence, pass the skull-and-crossbones signs to the cottage, and once you are sure no one is watching you, heave yourself up to the ground level of the cottage and peer over its deck. Wind has swept the sand into snaking patterns, and drifts have piled up against the vacant-eyed sculpture. It is more horrific than before.

'So Mr No-Balls? What have you got say about all this?' The statue stares back at you, a pained expression on its face. Wind scurries over the deck. You creep around the back: the cottage has to have an entrance accessible from the road. Surely the owner does not have to scrabble up a hot dune every time he or she wants to get here? You skirt the cliff around the back, and come against the barbed-wire fence again. But there you spot an entrance, enveloped in jungle creeper, banana trees, spiky palms and dune grass, a green wooden door that looks as if it has not been used for a long time. You tap it lightly with your finger, and then try the brass handle. It is locked. You walk back around to the dune and climb onto the deck.

You peer into the large French window you find on the dune side of the cottage. At first, you see only a dim reflection of your own face, but pressing against it and cupping your hands, you see more. As your eyes adjust, you can inventory the contents of the room. Is this someone's holiday cottage? The room is in dark shadow, but you can pick out if you look to the left or right—not directly at—the contents of the room. A desk, a fridge, some bookshelves. Paintings cover the walls: large rectangular blobs of colour, sweeping landscapes, portraits of black faces. And in the centre of the room, shapes you cannot quite make out. They may be sculptures or statues; more figures like the one slouching outside. On one sun-baked wall inside, the words are painted in red: WHAT IS ART. And in green underneath, in graffiti, you can just make out the rest of the statement: BUT A BURNING VIOLENCE TO FREE US FROM THE FETID GANGRENE OF ARCHEOLOGISTS, ANTIQUARIANS AND ACADEMICS.[1]

And on another wall, in bright blue, you can make out more luminous graffiti: ONLY CHILDREN, MADMEN AND SAVAGES TRULY UNDERSTAND THE NUMINOUS WORLD OF ART.[2]

You survey the paintings again, the sculptures, and feel an icy hand on your heart. Your Adam's apple restricts. This is an artist's cottage, one of those mad artists who locks himself away to paint and sculpt. You can feel his presence here, a powerful, haunted, obsessive Artist, with a capital A. Or her. The room oozes sweat and passion. Every available space is covered with some statue or painting. Everywhere you look, you see pigments squeezed out of tubes onto canvas, oozed clay moulded hot by feverish hands …

'Hello?'

You batter on the door, confident that no one is here. 'Hello?'

But whatever glows from within this cottage, you cannot access it. You turn to face the sea once more, and watch the waves creep slowly into shore, notice how the gleaming pus of the Mswaswe River feeds into the lagoon on your left.

Your first stop on your way to work is the estate agent's office. Mrs Steyn looks up from a computer and smiles over moon-rimmed glasses. 'Dr Turner. What can I do for you? Change your mind? Want to move across to Strandloper?'

---

1   Although it appears that Timothy does not recognise these words, they are taken directly from a manifesto penned by Italian poet Filippo Tommaso Marinetti, the founder of Futurism, who maintained (amongst other things) that academic culture is a disease that needs to be eradicated.

2   This sounds very much like something Pablo Picasso would say, or perhaps it too can be attributed to Marinetti.

You peruse the map on the wall, locating the cottage, the cliff above it, and then a narrow winding road. You place a trembling finger on the red marker. 'Who lives here?'

'Why do you want to know?'

'I … I walk on the beach directly below that house, and I'm curious about it.'

She peers at the red marker, your finger, the blue inked sea marked Indian Ocean. 'That's a private beach, Dr Turner. You are not permitted to go onto that beach.'

'No one told me.'

'It's fenced off. How did you see it?'

'From the beach.'

'Don't go there again, please, Dr Turner.'

'You can't own a beach. How can a beach be private?'

She sighs. 'Actually, Dr Turner, I don't know who lives there. A trust company owns the property right up to the shoreline.'

'So I'm not trespassing if I swim in the sea? They don't own the sea, do they? And what about high tide? If I swim at high tide, am I still trespassing?'

'Dr Turner, it's a private beach. I should have told you when I rented you that cottage that this section of beach is not public property.'

'I just want to know who owns it.'

'A corporation, a … company. I don't know. It's not even our real estate company who deals with them.'

She is lying. She who knows everything that goes on in this little town. 'It's not for rent, is it?' You throw the words after her as she retreats into her cubicle.

It is not just idle curiosity, not just a delicious mystery to be solved. It is the image of the lone artist creating mad works of art that appeals to the *thanatos* in you. It resonates. Connects to a picture you had of yourself many years ago when you were young and wanted to be a writer yourself, before university sowed the seeds of critical self-doubt, before Sizwe Bantu showed you that he had said all you wanted to say already, and better than you could possibly have said it. An echo of something long buried in your soul dislodges: maybe that cottage is yours in a parallel universe, and you are a great artist, not a second-rate literary critic mopping up the words of another.

'And by the way, I do not need a maid, or a gardener.'

She peers out at you from behind her glasses. 'I'm sure you don't.'

'I do not want to have people in my employ as servants.'

She smiles. 'You talk as if you have a choice. This is South Africa, Dr Turner.'

Today is the big day—your inaugural speech, as Zimmerlie calls it, as if you are vying for the Presidency of the United States. Should you remind him that this is an obscure university in an obscure part of an obscure country on an obscure continent, and you have been offered a very tenuous, piddly one-year appointment? But you know what you are really doing here—legitimating their expulsion of Makaya, proving that you are not just some *strandloper* they have pulled off the beach. And you have your own agenda: Sizwe Bantu is unacknowledged here, despised, rejected. But not for long.

Your inadequacies are at a high count. You have tried and failed at this many times before: a non-academic, a pseudo-academic, trying, sneered at by critics, by 'real' academics, a critical failure … one who cannot speak in the discourse of academic theory, in the passive third-person anonymous: *thus it can be assumed that one must distinguish between the vagaries of an undifferentiated discourse and a polyphomous anti-discourse.*

So here you are in the suit of academicians and having to run after the writer, mopping up his words. At least this writer is Bantu, and you are a good mopper in that regard. But perhaps it is not wise to air your obsessions with Bantu here: Zimmerlie dismisses him out of hand; Makaya tears him out of textbooks; if you were more culturally sensitive you would wisely choose a safer topic like the Postcolonial Transgendered Subject or a poststructuralist feminist analysis of a Derridean reading of Kristeva.

Bantu is taboo.

But then Bantu is taboo everywhere. And this is why he is so great a writer: he transgresses boundaries; he smashes comfort zones; he breaks all the rules.

You remember only now the invitation Zimmerlie extended to you to visit him at home to discuss something. Perhaps he could have shed some light on the matter. But it is too late now. He will have to grin and bear it.

Your mind is reeling today with something other than your inaugural speech. The world has tilted. Twice.

You duck into the toilets on the English Department floor and stand by the washbasins, but before you have time to compose yourself, the door creaks open. You scuttle into a cubicle just as someone bangs through the door. Luckily these are not American toilets; each cubicle is solidly bricked in and blocked off from the others in a fastidious British Colonial urge for privacy. You close and lock the door, hold your breath and stare at the back of it, where the usual obscenities have been scratched into the wood.

'That you, Timothy?'

You still yourself, like an animal that realises it is prey, when you recognise the voice—James Ngwenya. And the walls are thinner than you have supposed. 'We're looking forward to seeing you tonight at the party,' the man says from the next cubicle, where he is unashamedly and noisily performing his ablutions.

Now is the time to take the bull by the horns, while you have the screen of a toilet wall between you. 'I don't know …'

'Tonight? There's a big party.' Then as an afterthought, quietly, 'You need an ally.'

'An ally? Why? Have I committed some crime?'

'You're walking right into it, man.' He opens the door and you hear him walking across to the basins where he turns on a cold water tap and splashes his hands.

'What do you mean?'

'Not here. Come tonight, we can talk about it then. You can meet Dr Ma—'

'Listen, Mr Ngwenya.' You try to be dignified, as dignified as you can be while sitting on the toilet and bellowing through a thick, graffitied wall where everywhere you look are the words FUCK, PISS, SHIT, CUNT in a multitude of languages. 'I have a lecture to give this morning. I can't really think at the moment.'

Ngwenya turns off the gushing tap and pulls down the roller towel. 'I know, I'm coming. And so, you'll be pleased to know, is Mxolisi Makaya.'

And then Ngwenya is gone. The door bangs closed and the name echoes through the disinfected room.

*

Bekezulu Hall is a five-minute walk from the English Department, but by the time you arrive, in the heat of a merciless noonday KwaZulu sun, you have lost what little composure you brought with you. And the hall is full. You take your place behind a heavy lectern, where you rapidly drink the glass of water provided, blink green after-images of The Very Honourable Minister plaque, and scour the hall for signs of Makaya. Could he be that frowning man in the front row? That man in casual clothes at the back? The stern-faced man in a suit by the door? No. You would know. Makaya would surely announce his presence. Ngwenya arrives, on his own, and sits at the back, away from the main glob of people.

Zimmerlie and Mpofu take up their place in the front row, next to the Dean and a few grey lecturers. They both look extremely pleased with themselves.

With a nod from Zimmerlie in the front row, you clear your throat and begin. 'Ladies and gentlemen …'

The audience is a Liquorice Allsorts mix of black, white and others. The important men in suits sit in the front three rows, with legs crossed, squashing their private parts and cutting off their circulation. Behind them sit a few scattered administration personnel, other lecturers, and a smattering of students. There are your Honours students, all ten of them, in a solid block of dissent, or encouragement, you don't know which. And sitting prominently in the aisle seat is Tracey, her hair wet, her skin glowing red, and the hint of a frown thrown conspicuously at the speaker on the podium. To make everything worse she is wearing a grey tracksuit, oversized, the sleeves rumpled up, the front displaying in large navy blue letters the University of Melbourne logo.

Clear your throat. Tap the mike. Say 'excuse me'. 'Er' a few times.

'I have elected to speak of the one African Writer who has refused to kowtow to pressures of writing fiction and not history, realism, or journalism. This one man has placed South African literature in the spotlight of the world again, as an authentic, refreshing elixir ...'

You pause for effect.

'Sizwe Bantu has single-handedly taken on the establishment, and has rewritten the rules. ...'

At the mention of Bantu, Zimmerlie looks up. Maybe you should have warned him. Don't worry, you signal to him with a nod, I know what I'm doing here.

But of course you don't. You have no idea what *kuk* you are stepping into.

In hindsight, you should have taken up Zimmerlie's offer to explain why Bantu is a no-no on this campus.

All goes well until the door at the back opens and a man eases into the hall. His hair is white, his head high, and even at this distance, you note the intense focused eyes, reinforced by heavy shaggy brows. He is wearing a traditional shirt, one of those flamboyant articles that Nelson Mandela used to wear as President.

You are expecting him, but even so, he is so incongruent with the picture you have created that you cannot believe this is Makaya. But you know it is him by the reaction of the others. It is as if a little devil, a *tokolosh* they call them here, has run around the hall and pinched people's bottoms. People wriggle in their chairs, crane their necks. Zimmerlie wrinkles his brow, Mpofu sits with a rigid neck, refusing to turn his head.

You doubted his existence. But here he is. In the flesh.

'The cheek!'

'Who the hell does he think he is?'

He is not the bull-headed man you envisioned bellowing down corridors, harassing students, organising rallies. Not the pompous lecturer dictating pious aphorisms for gullible students. Not a man who could be accused of sexual harassment. This man looks feeble, incapacitated, even. Charmingly, gracefully, old.

So the picture shifts again from a lecherous young blood preying on his students. But of course appearances can deceive. And in a way this makes it worse. You are, at twenty-four, unashamedly ageist. The picture of a lecherous old man with a 'girl' your age is even more abhorrent and disgusting.

Makaya turns a stiff neck to his left and right, and he lowers himself into the seat next to Ngwenya. They whisper and nod. Concur.

You bang your notes on the edge of the lectern. But you're okay. More than okay. Isn't this an ideal opportunity to preach to an unbeliever? Isn't this the man who thinks Bantu is shit? The man who obliterated Bantu from the syllabus? Your time has come.

'South African literature has been bullied, poked and prodded and told what it ought to be until it refuses to yield any more fruits. It has dried up. Listen to the rules that have shackled South African writers over the last hundred years ...'

He's listening. He's frowning and tapping his foot on the chair in front of him. You are speaking for his benefit alone. And you have the floor.

'One: because they don't share their total living conditions, whites can't write about blacks. And vice versa. Because they can't possibly get under their skins, writing about, or from the point of view of, race groups other than your own is presumptuous and invalid. But Bantu does it! Two: all South African writing must be political; i.e. it must be about the struggle. If it ignores this task, it becomes irrelevant and dangerously deceptive. But Bantu does it!'

He's shaking his head. He's massaging his neck. He disagrees with everything you are saying. Let him! Your voice booms out through the speakers. For once, you are visible.

'Three: characters must be recognised as types: the sell-out, the returned exile, the white Boer, the committed activist. Both character and plot must be subservient to ideology. Bantu *yakkety yak, blah, blah, blah*.'

Something is wrong. Your words are stones on your tongue. It's his eyes, those wrinkled eyes on you, making you stammer. Ignore him. And of course, Tracey's eyes are on you too, almond-shaped eyes, sparkling with what can only be misplaced admiration.

'Four: South African literature must be accessible to the masses, to an underclass audience, and must eschew intellectual elitism. Five: South African literature must emphasise a documentary realism that depicts the life experience of the oppressed. But Sizwe Bantu! Sizwe Bantu *blah, blah, blah*.'

No one, it seems, is impressed. The speech flows nicely towards its inevitable and obvious conclusion, that Sizwe Bantu is the only African writer worth his salt, heralding the new African Renaissance. It works at conferences all over the world, it works in Australia, but here it feels hollow, cheap, presumptuous. Is it the race thing—a white man presuming to tell Africans what a black writer should write? No, it is the presence of the man at the back who creates that effect—his posture, the turn of his head, the way he crosses his legs, the way he taps his fingers impatiently, all suck your words dry, suck all meaning from them.

'Sizwe Bantu mocks these rules, incorporates them into his writing in a postmodern way, plays with words while Afrika is ablaze ...'

You manage to get through the main argument, but you feel it is all words, just words, glazed over by the audience, and dismembered by the man at the back.

How is he doing it? Like a magician who can render you impotent with a wave of his wand.

Then, there are the sweet plangencies of the ending, the conclusion, and finally: 'Any questions?'

You have been told to leave time for questions, but these two words signal to the audience that they can start yawning and stretching and standing up to leave.

Makaya raises a hand. A murmur arises from the audience. They want their tea and stale biscuits.

You expect sarcasm, not this gentle voice you can hardly hear. You expect an arrogant academic used to having his way. But he speaks as if he is aggrieved, as if your words have hurt him. 'You have just said that Bantu's novels are purely, essentially, quintessentially African. But isn't the novel a bourgeois form, used for capitalist domination of the world?'

'Well, er ...'

'You see, no one reads; no one can afford to read African literature when a book costs more than a month's wages. Why read Sizwe Bantu when there is an AIDS epidemic, poverty, war, injustice? Why would Africa be concerned with a foreign construct like the postmodern novel, and a masturbatory writer like Bantu who does not speak for her?'

It isn't a question at all. It's a pronouncement, a judgement on the inadequacy of your speech. He has swept all your arguments away neatly in one motion. As if you are nothing. As you open your mouth to reply,

Zimmerlie stands, scrapes his chair and knocks over a pile of pamphlets on the chair in front of him.

'Excuse me …'

You think he is going to reply for you. But no. He nods at the Dean in apology, touches Mpofu's hand, and shuffles out of the hall, pressing his fingers to his temples. He doesn't look back. You watch him bang through the doors. You pause and swallow, your Adam's apple tight.

So much for collegial support. You stare at Mpofu who has folded his arms. You are on your own here.

But you do have a reply. How often has this accusation been made? And how often have you been able to defend Bantu against such Philistine sentiments?

'Sizwe Bantu occupies the novel form like a hermit crab inhabits a shell,' you say. 'He borrows not only the form, but the words themselves. In this postmodern world, he samples, intertextualises, palimpsests …'

You can hear the snort. 'You're talking about his plagiarism? You mean derivative?'

'If you, sir, had read your Bantu carefully, you would realise that there is no such thing as an original thought or an original word—they are all second-hand. All that writers can do is juggle them around a bit. Bantu uses plagiarism as a *device*. What Bantu is doing, sir, is merely postmodernising, sampling, to use a musical image, *not* plagiarising, but referring, connecting. Bantu samples, or extrapolates, or textualises, or …'

'Bullshit.'

Whispers ripple across the audience.

Great. This was meant to be the *coup de grâce*, the pyrotechnics display of brilliant intellect to debut the new lecturer, to justify your presence, to legitimate the displacement of the Old with the New. Instead, you're a clown, a stammering foreigner.

And Makaya does not stop. 'Have you run Bantu through our university plagiarism detection software, as we insist our students do to their essays? It comes out all red, all plagiarised. A student gets a big fat "F" for doing that, and Bantu gets awards.'

It is becoming a one-on-one armed combat. Stags lock horns; you have locked words. The lightning crackles from him to you, from you to him. You can taste it, smell it. He obviously wants you obliterated. He wants Bantu obliterated. If this were the Middle Ages, you would be charging at each other with lances trying to poke each other's livers out. But intellectual arguments can be just as psychologically violent.

But for once, you are ready. And it is personal this time. 'If you, sir, had read your Bantu, you would know that your arguments are naïve ...'

'If you, a white man from Australia, had read your cultural innuendoes ...'

'If you, a literary critic, had taken Bantu's repugnance of literary critics into consideration, you would be more humble in your interpretations ...'

'If you, a gullible white man, weren't so blinded by your admiration of the exotic ...'

The words clash, parry, thrust, jab and drive home. Tracey and the Honours class watch with what looks like glee, cheering every statement Makaya makes. Tracey beams at you too, as if you are fighting for her approval.

Finally the Dean stands and waves her hands in the air. 'I think we have gone way past our time, ladies and gentlemen. If there are any other questions, perhaps they could be dealt with during tea?'

The crowd breathes a collective sigh of relief. The doors open and the tea crew begin setting up the tea.

The audience breaks into knots and bubbles. You stand at the lectern, banging your notes together. You are not sure if you have won or lost.

Makaya stands and makes his way against the flow of the crowd towards you. Before you have a chance to get away, he is there. Behind him the Honours students balloon around him. Tracey watches from a cool distance, arms folded, amused smile.

'Sawubona.'

You find yourself shaking hands against your will. He has lined eyes, age spots on his cheeks, and frizzy white hair. But he holds your gaze strongly, and your hand tightly. So this is the man of the people, the face of the resistance who has set himself up in the dark spaces of your mind. The real man is disarmingly gentle. Soft. Kind.

'Dr Makaya.'

He can surely sense your antagonism.

'I did enjoy your talk.'

'Judging by your questions, I find that hard to believe.'

He laughs. 'Even if we disagree about Sizwe Bantu, we have a lot of common ground.' His arm squeezes your shoulder. It is all patronising.

'We do?'

'It's not often I get to engage in an intellectually challenging debate around here.'

'I'll take that as a compliment. But you might have to rethink your animosity toward Sizwe Bantu ...'

'There's a party at my house tonight. We can talk further there. James Ngwenya told me you'd be there. Twenty, Second Avenue. Sevenish. My name's on the gate.'

'I'm really not sure I can be there, but thanks anyway. Very good of you, Dr Makaya.'

'The name's Mxolisi. And may I call you Timothy? Or do you prefer ... Prospero?'

'*Moolisi.*' It is unfair, making a foreigner say a name like Mxolisi, with the Zulu click 'x' the one that scratches your throat and makes you feel a self-conscious fool if you get it wrong, or even if you get it right.

'Come. We have a lot to talk about. I'd like to share some insights I have about Sizwe Bantu that you may not know.'

And with this enticement, he claps you on the shoulder and turns to go. You watch him walk slowly out of the hall.

Your car slices through the night. The Seaview Street tar glitters as the headlights arc across it. And as the VW engine strains up the hill, the black ocean spreads out flat beneath you, while luminous waves roll onto the shore, eating away at the coastline. Lightning flickers in the sky and in that second, the ocean is sheet-metal white. The yellow street signs glisten in the headlights—Christopher van Wyk Avenue, Njabulo Ndebele Road—and the Zulu hills are a dark monolithic sea of shadows on each side of your car.

And why are you doing this, exactly?

Because there is unfinished business here, because of Sizwe Bantu. Because you feel aggrieved, even obliterated, and you have not finished the fight. Because you need to find out more about this man. Because there is something odd about the whole business. Things are not what they seem. You do not even know what they seem, but reality is not lodged as comfortably as it was before.

And because he has quietly and politely bullied you into acquiescing.

Determined to bolster yourself, you pull up your sagging pants, stuff your Hawaiian shirt into your trousers. You wheel into the driveway you scuttled away from over the weekend. The MAKAYA sign gleams gold. This time the gates are open in welcome. You drive up a steep incline to a lawn crammed with vehicles, some dangerously close to the edge of the cliff, cruise past the cars, hear laughter, the clinking of glasses and plates. The smell of burnt *boerewors* chokes the air.

The house has attitude. It dwarfs the other dwellings around it, making them look mean and petty. As far as you can tell, this is the only house that faces the sea, and not just faces but confronts the sea. And it is a round house, a gigantic mud hut with whitewashed uneven walls. You nudge your car up the windy drive through a row of pine trees which lead to the back of the house. You park next to three other beaten up cars on a flat area on top of the cliff which drops steeply away. Through every window people with glasses in silhouette bend to pick up invisible snacks, or lean towards their conversational partners to hear an anecdote or a joke. Sometimes one throws his or her head back in silent laughter.

The house itself, surrounded by collections of whitened, gnarled driftwood, looks organically grown out of the very sands of the eSika-manga beach. The walls are swept unevenly in a curve from ground to roof in the grainy shape and motion of the waves you have swum in that day; ethnic furniture—the kind you see on the side of the highway made for tourists—as well as grass mats, wall hangings, ceremonial fly swatters, and musical instruments propped up on cane furniture are strewn all over a large veranda.

The front door is open, but there is no one in the hallway. On the facing wall stands a huge bookcase. Some people smoke when they are nervous; you browse book collections. And what a collection! African literature, mostly, and the diaspora. Achebe to Zingwane, Ellison, Wright, Martin Luther King, Biko, you name it, it is here. But there is no Bantu.

You slink along the passage through to the lounge where Sony Okusun's music is playing. You are suddenly in the midst of swirling bodies. You squeeze past a dancing couple into the darkness of an inner corridor.

There is no sign of Makaya.

People spill out through the open glass doors onto the patio, and by the pool, the party is also in full swing. The pool itself snakes around the house, and dark bodies bob up and down in the green water, lit from underneath. On the edge of the precipice below, you can see crashing waves, an angry sea bashing at the cliff, and the town's twinkling lights on the other side. You recognise the Honours class: Eric Phala over there, Caesar, Joel and some lecturers you have seen on campus in earnest conversation over at the other end of the bar. Two men chase a woman around the pool. Shrieking they grab her and throw her in, fully clothed.

'Guess who?' Cold slim fish hands cover your eyes. You pull them away.

'Tracey?'

'So glad you came. I liked your talk today. So did the others ... Did you get my email? I assumed it was a university address. Turnert@uem. co.za?'

'I don't have email.'

'Come on in. The water's warm. Warmer than the sea, anyway.'

'Not at the moment, thanks. I've got to do some mingling.' You point towards the yawning entrance to the house.

She slides a wet finger down your face. 'See you later, alligator.'

You watch her slither into the pool, the ripples distorting the shape of her body so she looks rubbery and elongated.

'Timothy!'

You turn.

Makaya is wearing jeans, t-shirt, thongs. He holds a glass of wine in his hand which he passes to you.

'I ...'

'Come and get some food! You must be hungry.'

You are led along the veranda into a cosy corner. Four steaming hot dishes of prawns and rice wait at a small round table. A woman sits next to Ngwenya who nods to her in conversation. Makaya sits you next to her. 'Timothy, my wife, Noliwa. She teaches Sociology at the university.'

'Ah, yes. I've seen you around campus. Brilliant place you have here!'

Conversation thins as everyone sucks and discards mounds of prawns and indigestible cheese and garlic sauce. You sit forward, uncomfortable, stealing glances at the man every now and then. He's not what you thought at all. He seems weak, quavery, insubstantial, a victim rather than an aggressor. But his eyes are fiery, and when his meet yours, you have to look away.

Ngwenya addresses you by poking the air with a fork. 'Their plan backfired, don't you think, Timothy?' He crunches the prawn shells, sucking at their tails, snapping the legs off.

'What plan?'

'Zimmerlie wanted an ally,' says Makaya, in between mouthfuls of yellow rice and rubbery prawns, 'but he didn't realise who he was dealing with.'

You have to be careful what you say. Or don't say. 'How's that?'

Ngwenya cracks a prawn shell and sucks the garlic butter from it, allowing it to drip down onto his chin. Makaya arches white eyebrows.

You have to say it. It's your line in the sand. 'I hope you bear me no grudge for taking your job; it's not personal, I have no … hard feelings. I mean I hope *you* have no hard feelings … ?'

You have rehearsed this line over and over. But now it sounds lame. Hard feelings? *Hard feelings?* You wish you could unsay it now.

Makaya looks at you as if you are aurally impaired. 'Timothy, did those incompetents trick you into believing they could give you my job?'

'I … I … applied for a job, a vacant lecturing position … and they offered it to me. That's what I understood.'

'There is no vacant lecturing position,' says Ngwenya. 'Dr Makaya was unfairly dismissed. The lawyers are demanding he return to his rightful position. And Dr Makaya will sue the pants off them too.'

'Well, they failed to give me those little details.'

They all laugh.

'We're not blaming you, Timothy,' says Ngwenya. 'Not at all. Just letting you know what they should have told you at the outset.'

'Their lawyer says he's holding up for one vital piece of evidence against me, but they're bluffing. What could they possibly have against me except that I taught the students well, and made them think?'

You fill your mouth with prawns and rice so you don't have to speak. But he waits for you.

'Sexual harassment,' Ngwenya says. 'They accused him of sexual harassment, the fools!' Makaya raises a hand for him to stop. But Ngwenya is on a roll. 'The oldest trick in the book,' he continues. 'You want to smear someone, make sure it's with semen.'

Makaya shakes his head. 'The wrath of the ancestors be upon their petty, feeble minds! Trying to get students to testify against me—what stupidity. I want to think of you as an ally. Of mine. If I am reinstated ...'

'When you are reinstated,' corrects Noliwa.

'When I am reinstated, they'll be the first ones to go.'

The food is rich, the wine strong, and your head swims in its undercurrents.

'But let's talk of more interesting things. I didn't invite you here to talk trivialities.' Makaya's eyes never leave you. 'Today you argued well in support of Sizwe Bantu.'

'Thank you.'

'But it is deeply flawed. Deeply flawed.'

'What is?' The attack is so sudden, you feel the annoyance rise in your throat.

'Bantu's writing. What worries me the most is his ... intertextuality—as you call it. Appropriation, I call it, neo-colonialism even. Speaking on behalf of all African writers.'

You sigh. 'It's a well-worn criticism of Bantu. But his vision is all embracing, embraces all African writers ... His vision of the African Renaissance.'

'The African Renaissance?'

Bantu's vision of the African Renaissance glows brightly through all his writing. Like the American Dream, it sustains an attitude of hope about human potential, plastering over the cracks of poverty, illness, squalor, exploitation, violence, corruption, political instability, moulding with an artist's hands a new Africa, using intellectual and aesthetic clay. Bantu talks of the African Renaissance Man: self-confident, self-made, brimming with vitality, able to break from the nightmares of his past and present realities, determine his own destiny, using fortitude, skill, hard work and ingenuity. It is what you believe in, an optimism in Bantu's writing that shows all that is good about Africa. It is why you came here.

Makaya whispers so you have to strain to hear him. He seems to be speaking to himself. 'It's not Bantu's vision. It's my vision. Our vision, not his. He stole it.'

What do you know of the African Renaissance, white boy? says the expression on Ngwenya's face.

'Sizwe Bantu …' You begin. But Noliwa, tactful, intuitive, chooses this moment to unveil a lemon meringue pie which she has been hiding under a dish cover until after dinner, and cuts it into four generous servings.

You slice the pie with your spoon and fill your mouth. 'Very good!'

'And what prevents the African Renaissance?' says Ngwenya. 'Enemies tearing down everything we build up. Zimmerlie and his running dog Mpofu, trying to take us back to the ages of colonialism and oppression.'

You think of the feeble man with a stutter and scars in his head, the headaches, the tired eyes. 'Zimmerlie? He's holding back the African Renaissance? He's just an old man.'

You regret these words immediately. Makaya is an old man too.

Noliwa scoops more pie into your plate. 'It was after the operation,' she says. 'He should have retired after the operation.'

'What operation?'

'Lobotomy,' murmurs Ngwenya, but then presses a napkin to his lips by way of apology to Noliwa, who frowns at him.

'That's why he's clinging to power,' she says. 'He has no one. Nothing. You lose your mind, you lose everything.'

'It was an aneurism,' clarifies Makaya. 'He had an operation, took a year off, and then returned to work. We were hoping he would retire.'

'Apparently this is the second time,' says Ngwenya. 'Six years ago he had one too. Or was it seven?'

'I feel sorry for him too,' says Makaya.

'I don't feel sorry for him,' says Ngwenya. 'He's got to go. He's a— what is the English expression?—a dog in a manger.'

'If he goes, Mpofu takes over. Mpofu has to go too.'

'Zimmerlie never married,' says Noliwa to you as an aside, as if this explains everything.

Makaya explains. 'They're literary critics, Timothy. They have to make war on creative expression. They don't understand what I'm doing because they don't understand genuine creativity. An African university has to discard those old models of literary criticism. An African university nurtures creativity, innovation, embraces more traditional, oral paradigms of learning. Zimmerlie and Mpofu are on the wrong side of history.'

Makaya clasps his wife's hand. 'It'll soon be over. All of it. And then, Timothy, when the dust clears, I hope to claim you as a friend.'

The folding of napkins and dabbing of mouths announces that the meal is finished. Ngwenya stands and wipes his lips with a white napkin. 'It was a lovely meal, thank you.' In imitation, you touch your lips to the napkin too.

They haven't talked about Bantu. You were hoping to ask why he tears African writers out of textbooks, why Zimmerlie looks nervous when you bring up Bantu, why there is such antagonism between them.

'Stay as long as you want, Timothy.' Makaya clasps you hard by the shoulder. "Enjoy yourself. You're among friends here. I mean that. Where are you staying?'

'A cottage nearby.'

'I have a little retreat on the coast here, in the dunes. If you ever need a place to stay short term, you're welcome to stay there. It's empty: I seldom use it now ...'

'Thank you.'

*

For the rest of the evening, you watch the dancing, listen to wild drumming, and drink as much wine as you can hold. A bilious green wave washes through you with excessive violence, threatening to capsize you. You browse the library again, looking desperately for something.

Your sense of betrayal is burning in your throat like a hot curry.

'Hi!' A damp arm drapes itself around you, and you find yourself in Tracey's towelled presence. Her hair is wet, and she presses against you. You smile, but suspect you are a ghastly green colour, and that you reek of alcohol and garlic. You detach yourself from her grip.

'Tracey ...'

'So now you have finally met him, what do you think? I knew you'd hit it off. I saw you having a nice private dinner away from the crowds.'

'Tracey, I need to use the bathroom. I … I'm not feeling that well.'

'Sure, but I'm coming home with you, okay?'

She points down a dark hallway and you push past her through gyrating bodies in flashing strobe lights. But there is a long queue of women, so you struggle further into a quiet corner. You hear clomping feet and high squeals of laughter, so you open a wooden door and step into the back garden.

This is where you throw up. All those beautiful prawns and garlic butter onto the manicured flower bed.

You have to leave. This is no place for you. You wait until Tracey is ensconced in a tête-à-tête with some fervent Indian lecturer by the bar, Ngwenya is dancing in a hot crowd of students, and your exit path is clear. The humid night makes you sweat before you even reach the car. You stumble into the yellow Golf and start it, backing unsteadily into the bushes, barely making it through the wide gates, speeding down dimly-lit black roads, skidding through long elephant grass to your sunken cottage. The more you drive down the snaky road towards the ocean, the worse you feel.

7

Gromphadorhina portentosa
· ·
Madagascar hissing cockroach

The Madagascar hissing cockroach (*Gromphadorhina portentosa*) is one of the largest species of cockroach. Hissing is (in humans) a sign of disapproval (tsk, tsk), and there is no reason to doubt that this is also the case with the hissing cockroach. When disturbed or annoyed, the cockroaches force gas through the breathing pores on their thorax and abdomen. Males use a fighting hiss when challenged by other males. Males also hiss to attract females, and the sound is similar to the human mating calls one hears on street corners and from males at building sites when females walk by (psk, psk).

'Cockroach Liberation' by Sizwe Bantu

(*The Present Tense*, Vol. XXVIIII, Aug. 2003, pp. 345-354)

To stop those ghastly nightmares (in the last one, he had dreamed he actually was one of the cockroaches painted into his painting), the Modern Afrikanist put his artistic endeavours on hold. He became enthralled by world events, and spent his evenings riveted to the television (Azania One). That night, the news again featured the global mass exodus of whites from the United Confederated Tribes and Nations (UCTN) (what was once called the United States of America). The United Confederated Tribes and Nations, the new American government that had miraculously won power last month, had declared in its latest proclamation that all land should go back to its rightful owners, and that all Occupiers, Settlers and Colonists, no matter how many generations back they had lived there, would have to leave within 24 hours, or else apply for residence in the new (or old) country, run by the rightful owners or stewards of the land, who used to be called Native Americans or Indians (to Columbus, all dark-skinned races looked the same). Most whites had elected to leave ("I don't want my country to be become a liquor-saturated gambling casino," said one prominent ex-Congress Member), and the airports were choked with a sea of miserable white faces. Further, the new government had ordered whites to pay compensation for the land they had acquired hundreds of years back, and many preferred to leave, taking their contraband with them.

The Modern Afrikanist watched with great interest one particular clip of Malibu beach in California being forcibly cleared of these "vermin" (to quote the new Minister of Lands and Resettlement) with bulldozers and wrecking balls, "so that they wouldn't even dream of returning to what they had arrogantly called their 'homes'."

Of local interest, of course, was the repatriation of so-called African-Americans, those Afrikans who themselves had been forcibly removed from this continent, and were now being returned to their "rightful homes". This group, it was noted, were treated with more respect by the Tribes, and were being returned to Afrika with pomp and ceremony, welcomed by the Ashanti Empire in the West Afrikan Union of States with all respect. Preparations had been made for their welcome back to the now prosperous and united lands of the African continent (reparations had been made, and wealth returned from Europe in the past ten years).

Following this, the governments of other colonies had fallen. Canada had repatriated its white ex-citizens to France and England respectively; Hawai'i had returned to a monarchy under a descendant of Queen Liliuokalani, and most dramatically, in the country of Koolawala (once the Commonwealth of Australia), the new Committee of Elders had decreed a whites-only emigration policy (to redress the imbalances of the past), and had asked the whites politely to leave their country. They had also been given 24 hours' notice to leave, and the pandemonium had been recorded on television. There had been outrage when an investigative tele-journalist had filmed white children being forcibly removed from their families when they resisted repatriation orders, and sent to detention centres on Nauru and Christmas Island, which housed illegal immigrants.

In Azania, of course, the whites had years ago been driven into the sea (or rather onto ships and planes) and sent back to Holland and England. Azania had of course (or so the television station bragged) set the precedent and been the catalyst for all these events. "We must be careful, though, and learn the lessons from our Azanian compatriates," said the spokeswoman for the Umatilla and Walla Walla Tribes. "We all saw how whites from South Africa spitefully employed a scorched earth policy on their forced removal from that country, sabotaging buildings, filling in open cast mines (notably Kimberley), blowing up bridges and petrol reservoirs. That must not happen here."

The television now showed various demographics in block graphs, pie charts and spidery maps, where pitiful trails of White Anglo-Saxon Protestants led back to their homelands. "It will shrink the world economy," protested one man at the TV camera. "What will come of the global market?"

But some of course had nowhere to go back to, and the station was quick to point out that these new governments were merciful. Under provisions of the new law in the UCTN and Koolawala, whites were allowed to stay if they behaved themselves, though they would be handicapped by restrictive pass laws, group areas acts, and placed in separate areas, or reservations. Many whites of course were already complaining about the lack of adequate facilities in these reserves, and that the land they had been allocated was deplete of resources like water, and they suspected that they were going to be used as labour reserves, which was denied by the Minister of Resettlement. "We don't want these people here at all, frankly, so to suggest we want to use them as labourers is preposterous. We just want them out of sight."

The Modern Afrikanist watched in keen interest. What would follow this, he wondered, a reductio ad absurdum ethnic cleansing, perhaps? Would the Zulus have to leave Xhosa territory, the Ndebele have to leave Mashonaland? The Nguni tribes have to give back Southern Africa to the Hottentots and San? Or would the common sense of the present Pan Afrikanist government prevail, in a united Africa that had seen unprecedented wealth for this continent? And what about those whites returning to England who had French or Roman ancestry? Those Anglo-Saxons who had invaded from the Scandinavian countries? And Latinos in the Americas? Which part of them would have to return to Spain?

But perhaps ultimately, before all this would happen, all humans would have to leave the planet, if we were to be truly non-homocentric in our thinking. No, we would not go and colonise Mars or another planet; we would all become extinct; civilisation itself would wither; human intelligence retreat; evolution suck us backwards until humans once again would become apes, lose our opposable thumbs, stoop over, climb back into the trees, and then back into the seas and become primitive life forms again.

The buildings would crumble, dams crack, and rivers would liberate themselves from their chartered banks. Cities would crumble and greenery snake over all human endeavours. Electricity would fail and the whole virtual edifice of the internet would be gone in an instant.

Yes, in a few thousand years, only the cockroaches would be left.

Even when all the food was gone, cockroaches would pour into libraries, snack on academic journals, make wholesome meals of *Encyclopaedia Brittanicae*, eat whole library shelves, until not a single word would be left, not one recorded thought of human so-called civilisation. So much for humans eating their words—cockroaches would do that for them.

Long live the cockroaches.

Viva Cokcraco!

You do not have a personal email account. You have no internet presence. You do not blog, Tweet, Link in or Facebook (a verb apparently). But at this university the only way information is distributed is via the university email system, so you reluctantly check your university email every day in the library. Normally a string of irrelevant messages skulks in your inbox and all you need to do is erase them. But today, it seems, everyone wants you:

Final dress rehearsal at the student union Prof. Be there or be no-where. We have your Prospero outfit to try on. You're gonna love it!

And from Mxolisi Makaya:

Thanks for the conversation last night. Look forward to doing it again sometime.

From Eric Phala:

You missed the rehearsal at my house. Don't be such a white man!

From Tracey.

Call me on my cell: 043-567-8794

From Zimmerlie:

Timothy, I need to speak to you urgently Come by my office.

And the *coup de grâce* from the university lawyer, Johan Redlinghuis.

CONFIDENTIAL.

You are hereby summoned to give evidence at the closed hearing of Dr. M. Makaya at the University of eSikamanga at 11 am on Wednes-day 4th June in Administration Building 1242. Please don't hesitate if you need to contact me beforehand. The university will be pleased to be of service to you.

Mr J. Redlinghuis, University Attorney

You march straight to Zimmerlie's office. But you find a locked door and a note pinned there: *Prof. Zimmerlie is out sick today.*

'It's his headaches,' says Mpofu, who answers the knock at his door. 'He takes it all so personally.'

'Dr Mpofu. I need a word with you.'

You are ushered into the office. Mpofu closes the door and motions a chair for you to sit in. You wave the email you have printed out. 'Redlinghuis,' you say. Or rather Red Ling House. The way everyone pronounces it here is more like Rud Lung Hiss. 'What is this?'

'Redlinghuis suggested that your testimony would be a powerful indictment. The glued pages, the way Makaya changed the syllabus.'

'You could have asked me first.'

He points to the summons. 'We are asking you.'

'Honestly, I have nothing to say, Dr Mpofu. I don't even know this man ...'

'But you go to his rallies.'

'That was inadvertent.'

'You go to his parties.'

Whoa.

It takes a while before you can think of a reply. 'How does everyone know everyone's business around here?'

Mpofu smiles. 'We know everything.'

It is a game interrogators play to get their victims to confess. Pretend you know and they'll spill the beans.

You scrutinise his face. 'I'm not sure I need to justify everything I do.'

'Redlinghuis thinks that if you testify, you can win them over. After all, the objective testimony of an unbiased stranger counts a lot. Just tell them what that man has been doing. Tell them about the ripped books, their intransigence, the journals.'

'I'm not really one for taking sides in disputes, Dr Mpofu.'

'What? He's won you over? That's hardly in your best interests.'

'No, it's not that. I'm not that interested in fighting your battles.'

'Don't be ridiculous! It's him or us.' Mpofu emphasises his points by poking the desk with his finger. 'Actually it's you or him. Didn't we make that clear? You won't be here if he returns. You'll be out of a job. And beside you don't have a choice. It's like a subpoena. You have to go.'

'What if I don't ... ?'

'For god's sake, the man has sexually harassed his students. It's in your power to stop it. Don't you want to stop this man?'

'I don't think it's any of my business, Dr Mpofu.'

'All you have to do is tell them what you know, what you've seen in class. What he's done ... About the party. I heard how they were all dancing naked.'

'That's ... just outrageous.'

'I have my sources.'

'Then that's disturbing!'

'And I hear you are taking the main part in Makaya's play.'

You stand up. 'Look, I apologise, but I must leave this little interrogation. Gotta go.'

'Timothy, please, your testimony will make or break this case. Your job is at stake, but much more too. The English Department. The university's reputation.'

'Thank you, Dr Mpofu. Have a nice day.'

*

On the way to the car park, you skirt the shaded area where you see them, but it is too late. Lining the green square, banners flutter in the hot stale humidity.

Free Makaya!

We want an Afrikan University!

You recognise the Honours class amongst the two dozen students who barricade the path. Tracey rushes forward. 'You left without telling me,' she says.

'Hello, Tracey.'

But the others have caught up and surround her. They are exuberant, an emotion that you have not seen or experienced for a long time. Even the word feels strange.

'Prospero! Prospero!'

'You weren't at the final dress rehearsal,' says Eric. 'What happened, Prof?'

'I'm sorry. I can't be involved in your play. It's a legal issue.'

They gather around you, and you feel resentment, almost hostility. No, not hostility: disappointment as if your actions represent the entire moral edifice of the universe.

'Redlinghuis,' says Caesar to Eric. 'Or Zimmerlie.'

'Now he's acting like a white man,' says Eric, not so much to you but to the others. 'Before I wasn't sure. I was beginning to have hope.'

'It's got nothing to do with being a white man, guys. It's just not the right thing to do at the moment.'

'Nothing ever has anything to do with being a white man,' says Eric.

'I'm sorry, guys, but you'll understand I'm trying to be professional, and because of certain individuals, it's better I stay out of your very excellent production.'

Joel wags his finger. 'You can't fool us, Prof.'

'He's just kidding,' calls Caesar. 'Didn't you hear Makaya say that Dr Turner was going to support our cause?'

'He's going to support Dr Makaya at the trial,' calls Eric.

'Beware of those lawyers, Prof,' calls Joel. 'Redlinghuis and Idi Amin and Co. They can twist words until a black man turns white and a white man turns black.'

'Thanks, guys, sorry, but I have to go.'

Everywhere you turn, the heat presses down. All you want is to be alone. To be left alone.

At the cottage, you find your clothes in a neat pile, ironed and pressed, and even your underpants squared and folded. The garden shows signs of activity—piles of weeds at regular intervals, overturned soil in flowerbeds. But the fence is secured at the back and the tangle of lines intact. And Thoko is in your kitchen talking loudly, ironing with an antique steam iron she must have procured from under the kitchen sink.

'Thoko!'

'This is Sam, my son.'

A young man grins bashfully from the corner where he is crouching. He stands. 'Pleased to meet you.'

I need to be alone, you want to say. *This is my cottage. Please just leave me alone.*

'Sam has wash all the window and fix the flowerbed,' she says.

You stare dully at the kitchen window, the only one with its glass intact.

'Sam want go to circus this weekend,' she says. 'Circus in Assegai this weekend, but he has no money.'

You stare at the boy. He fidgets, placing his hands behind his back.

'It's just fifty Rand for a ticket for him.'

She points out of the window at the flowerbeds, at the piles of weeds at six-foot intervals on the grass.

'Okay. Okay.'

You pull out your wallet from the suit pocket and find three fifty-Rand notes to thrust into his cupped hands.

'Now I need to be alone, folks. Goodbye everyone.'

Thoko frowns. 'I have not finished the ironing. This iron is so slow. You need new one.'

'Enough! Go! Please.'

The raised voice and finger pointed at the front door is unwarranted, you know. You are playing the master so easily here.

You are shouting at the world, you want to explain, at the heat. At the tangled web of fishing line at the door.

You stamp out of the room and lie down in the bedroom, watching the fan blades turn. You listen to Thoko gather her things with slow dignity.

You wait.

But even when they have gone, you cannot stand being with yourself either. To be alone, you would need to rip off your own irritability and presence in the room. You pull off the suit and lie naked.

Whenever things get too hot, whenever you have to resolve any contradictory selves, you run. You jump in the surf. You let waves cleanse you. You don't deal with the issues. How often has some woman woken in the morning to find your car and your sincere faithful self long gone? How often have you taken both sides in a political argument, only to shrug your shoulders and disown the passionate self who has argued fervently for one cause or another? So here too, you can simply get in your car and drive away, pretend it never happened. In order to survive without being crushed by one side or the other, you have to nimbly step out of these selves altogether. You are the ultimate escape artist.

You have to swim: it is too hot to run. You do not care if you are encircled by sharks or snapped at by crocodiles when you throw yourself in the water. A bank of dark clouds is building up on the horizon, coming closer and piling itself high in the sky. The sea is angry, lapping against the clouds, roaring onto the beach. Thunder rolls across the sky, a distant battle encroaching. You smell rain. Lightning strikes somewhere close, and the heavy clouds skulk across the sea on a purple horizon.

But even the sea will not let you be today. The water is murky brown, restless with relentless waves, and choked with seaweed. Try as you may, you cannot disentangle yourself from its wrapping tentacles of green and yellow rubber barbs. A pungent odour drifts down from Richard's Bay (visible in a yellow smear low in the sky), and hits you low in the stomach.

You kick at the sand, hurl yourself into the waves, chase fiddler crabs into their holes.

You feel better. Much better. You swear at the sky, and no one is anywhere to hear. This is what you need.

Then you run over the quicksand of the marshy wetlands and up the dunes, look up at the cottage.

A curious lightness emanates from this place, as if it is a wormhole through to another universe, or a chink in time where you can go back to your better self, a self you never were, but should have been. In another life, you are this artist in a sanctuary from the world, speaking truth.

You greet the statue, peer into the dusty windows and stand by the door. No one has been here for months, it seems. Sand from the oncoming storm sweeps over the sculptures outside, against the door, and inside looks just as dusty and unchanged. But no, you did see a light here that night you were on the beach with Tracey.

You peer in once again. This time your eyes fall on a painting. In the dusty shafts of intermittent sunlight, you can make out its features: black face, glassy eyes (it is more of a collage than a painting and the artist has fixed glass eyes onto the face), open red mouth showing white teeth and speaking, calling, singing, maybe. The portrait stares back at you, the glass reflecting in the rays of sun that stream into the cottage. The paint has been dabbed in thick globs, in haste it seems, because it has run down over the man's face and over his shoulders, even onto the frame of the canvas.

On the walls next to the painting, you see Leonardo da Vinci-esque drawings.

Everywhere. On the walls, on the desk itself, on sheets of paper pinned to the wall, on the floor, on the chair is the illegible handwriting of the man who lives here. A mad man? A man possessed? A child? A savage?

Underneath the painting is a bookcase, rough wood, uneven texture, which is crammed with books. You strain to make out the titles. Some of them look familiar. You mouth the titles as you read them, your bewilderment turning slowly to acidic astonishment. *African Metaphysics*, you read aloud. *The Great South African Novel. The Five AfriKan Senses.* And not just one copy of each, but several. Here is a string of hard covers, next to paperbacks, second imprints, third editions, and at both ends of the shelf, acting as book ends, two *Bantu's Complete Works*. On the shelf below, journals you recognise as the entire collection of *The Present Tense*.

You turn around, face the storm again and let the wind blow onto your face. Pellets of rain are starting to attack. You take a deep breath and press your face to the pane again. The bottom shelf is almost too dark to see, packed tightly with dissertations, and more journals (*The African Presence; Southern African View*), critical works on Sizwe Bantu, but you can make out a few titles: *Misogyny and the female Other in the works of Sizwe Bantu; Sizwe Bantu and the Politics of Alienation; Sizwe Bantu as African Shaman; The Pre-Oedipal Subconscious in the Politics, Life and Works of Sizwe Bantu*.

And most terrifying of all, a dissertation bound in blue, open on the table, *The African Self in the Novels of Sizwe Bantu*, Timothy Turner, submitted in partial fulfilment of the Ph.D. in English, University of Melbourne.

Wind jostles you against the window frame, and a crack of lightning ends your inventory of the contents of the cottage. You leap off the deck into the blinding torrent of rain. You run along the foot of the dune into the cover of the green mangroves. Red crabs scatter into holes as you squelch into the swamp, past the tea-coloured lagoon, and towards the cleft between the dune and beach, towards the car park. The cold raindrops are like stones. You run for the car which is now sitting in a red pool of mud, pocked with rain. You drive home, peering past the weak wiper blades at the barely visible road. You wipe the inside windscreen with your shirtsleeve because the car is steaming up inside. Thor hammers at the glass dome of the sky. Finally you sail into the driveway, not caring if leaves whack your side mirrors and windshield, and you park in a swamp of cicadas and spattering leaves. A shadow of a small animal scurries off as you step out of the car. You run in the pelting arrows of the enemy to the front door and immediately strangle yourself in fishing line.

It is not a good place to be on your own that night. The rain lashes the house, the wind howls and lightning shatters the sky.

You wedge the yellow surfboard against the back door, check the boarded-up windows, wire up the cottage into a cocoon. Drink a gallon of water.

In KwaZulu, rain is an event, a deluge of emotion. You see why this cottage is not a good place to live. The rain leaks in everywhere. A river snakes in under the front door and floods the bedroom and living room, the ceiling grows heavy and dark and drips ever increasingly large drops onto your desk, your Bantu collection, your books and your bed. The rain slashes through the glass-liberated windows, and the driveway dissolves into a red glacier. You seal off the windows just in time: the lights flicker on and off and then you are plunged into darkness. The fridge putters to a halt. You grope for the candles on the Bantu collection, but the matches are sopping wet and you go through half the box before finding one that works.

You sit huddled over the flame watching the Bantu collection display and your thesis on the bookshelf for a long time. You page through your dissertation, reading it with the eyes of another.

*

Jangling tins and chimes wake you just after midnight. The rain has stopped and screeching insects have replaced the hiss of rain. There are still leaks in the ceiling, and the electricity is still off. But a moon peers through fast clouds in the sky. This time you are ready. Bread knife in your back pocket, you flatten yourself against the door and listen to the heavy breathing, struggling, stamping. This time you have him. You shoulder the door open and grab the shadow looming against the starlight. He falls to the ground as you tackle his torso and pin his arms behind his back. He is not armed. Fishing line cuts into your arm and neck, but he is tangled up in your lines. The tins jangle.

'Now you tell me who you are and why you are spying on me!'

'Timothy? *Yussus.* What the hell?'

'Tracey?'

You let her go, but she is as tangled as you are in the fishing line.

'Ouch, you're hurting me!'

'Tracey, what are you bloody doing here? I thought you were an intruder!'

'Oops.' Tracey pushes you through the front door and wrestles herself free of the fishing line. 'What is it with this goddam fishing wire?'

'Sorry.' You unwrap yourself and her as best as you can. 'Careful … here.'

In the house next door, an oblong of yellow light is turned on in an upstairs window. In that fleeting second you see rain dripping from every leaf, tree, electricity wire and from the metal gutters.

'Looks like we're disturbing the neighbours.'

You place the bread knife down on the counter top, lock the front door, draw the kitchen curtains, and turn to her in the darkness.

'Wasn't that an awesome storm?' she says.

'What are you doing? It's midnight! Are you crazy?'

All you can see is her outline. She steadies herself by leaning on your shoulders as she steps out of yet another tangle of line that has dogged her from the front entrance.

'I came to tell you … we're in danger, Timothy.'

'Danger?'

'They know about us.'

'Us. What us?'

She takes your hand. For a moment, you think it's a play and she is acting.

'There is no us,' you say.

She leans into you. 'They've been spying on us.'

You propel her away from the window and into the living room, bumping into the couch. 'Who's they?'

The wind chimes tinkle and a heavy crash in the bushes outside the front door makes you instinctively duck down, though you are in complete darkness. The neighbour's window is now dark too, and the only light is on the fluffy underbelly of clouds, reflecting the glow from nearby Richard's Bay.

'Stay here, okay? Don't move. I think someone else is out there.'

You fumble for the bread knife again and venture outside. Tracey hugs the door, but does not follow you outside. You check the porch and outside windows. Shadows flee only when you wade through them. Invisible creatures dart through the grass, and crickets screech. You slosh through mud, retrace your steps. The rain begins again.

'Be careful, will you?'

There is nothing to do but tie up the cottage with fishing line again, barricade the door with boxes, check the boarded-up windows to make sure they are secure, and then sit on the sofa with Tracey, staring at the shadowy blob of a rubber cockroach on the table.

'So who's spying on me then? Is it someone I know?'

'They're all spying on Dr Makaya. Mpofu. Zimmerlie.'

'I can't imagine Zimmerlie or Mpofu spying … actual spying on us. Really?'

She clutches your shirt. 'You mind if I stay here tonight? I can't go out again in that rain.'

You both listen to the drumming of the rain on the corrugated iron roof, and watch the splashes as the water drips in regular intervals through the leaking ceiling.

The dream is even more vivid when you recall it the next morning. You have been acting a particularly strenuous part in some Shakespeare play (you have a ready-made past, replete with memories, at the beginning of this dream). The heavy curtains swing closed to thunderous applause. You stand upright after your low bow, and once the stage lights are off, stumble your way backstage. Hands slap your back in praise as you pass fellow actors, stage managers and prompts. In your dressing room (you are a famous actor of considerable repute in this dream reality), you close the door behind you and sit down to peel off the mask you had to wear for the performance. You pull and tug, peering into the mirror to see who you really are underneath this hideous plastic cast. But you pull too much in your intense desperation to get the mask off, and pull off your entire skin. Underneath is ochre clay. But as in many dreams, you show not the least surprise. Next to go are your clothes, and here too, the skin is a white undergarment that slips off too, leaving you naked, the red clay still moist and pliable.

In the mirror, a reflected corner of the room reveals Tracey changing too. She pulls at her clothes, slips off her skin (it is loose and grey) and stands looking at her skinless flesh critically in a full-length mirror.

Instead of being shocked, or embarrassed at seeing her naked, you feel
your own shame. She mustn't see you like this! You hold your hands to
your face, but they too are red mud. She doesn't see you. She is preoc-
cupied with examining herself in the mirror. Under her skin, she is not
all blue veins and red artery wires as you imagined: she is also an ochre
muddy paste, as if she has been plastered by some sculptor and hasn't
quite dried. And this is what she is admiring, examining, considering,
in the mirror: no, rearranging, scooping an excess bulge at the hips,
slapping it on and pasting it onto an arm, taking a lick from an ankle
and smoothing it over her shoulder, touching up her forehead. An alien,
you immediately think. All this time you thought she was human, but
she's alien. And then you look at yourself once more, and despair. The
movement catches her attention; she draws her grey dripping clay hands
to her open cavity of a mouth; and screams. *It's me, Timothy*, you try to
say. *It's only me.* But no words come. In the mirror, you see that you have
no mouth—the entire jaw is missing, and when you try to cover your
private parts in shame, you discover that you are sexless.

The morning sunlight wakes you with jangling bells, an insistent ringing
of your frayed nerves. A dream, it is only a dream! You sit up, gratefully
feel the smoothness of your skin, and peep out of the window. A new
morning sun has melted the night of terror, and the world is freshly
green, with steaming grass, banana leaves nodding as they drip rain
water, the bright blue sky too bright, the car a mess of mud splashed up
to the door handles. You are sleeping on the couch. For a moment you
are bewildered, and then remember the hair-tangled woman sleeping in
your bed.

No, you did not sleep with her. Your armour protects you this once.
You can feel the tug of her tide of emotions, but the tight glass wall
inside you serves you well this time. But it leaves you feeling no better.

The jangling bells continue, and it takes a while to realise that the
chimes are real (they have been ringing in the tail end of your dreams),
and come from the front door. You dress. Through the eyehole of the

kitchen door, you see large breasts, a flowery dress, a hand picking at the fishing line, the nervous and distraught hands of a middle-aged white woman.

You pull three boxes away from the door and open it a fraction. 'Mrs Steyn?'

Mrs Steyn bites her bright pink nails as she stands impatiently on one leg, passing her hand over her severely brushed-back hair. 'Dr Turner. What on earth?'

You open the door and help her with the fishing line, silencing the silver chimes with your fingers. 'Mrs Steyn? This is not the time ...'

She takes this as an invitation, and walks straight through to the lounge. 'I hope you don't mind.' She peers at the boarded-up window frame, and then back at the barricaded door. She hasn't come to check the maintenance of the cottage at eight thirty in the morning, surely? You glare at her for so long without speaking that she grows disconcerted. She walks through to the kitchen. 'Mind if I have a glass of water?'

'No. Go ahead.' While she clinks the fridge open and spies on your dietary dependence on Mrs K, you make sure that the bedroom door is firmly shut.

Mrs Steyn returns to the room with a glass of what cannot be water—more like the stale remnants of your flat Coke from the previous day. She then removes a small glass bottle from her leather bag and pours a generous tot of translucent brown liquid into it, swirls the ingredients together and then swigs the whole concoction down her throat in two noisy gulps.

'I'm afraid it's a little early in the morning for me, Mrs Steyn. Are you trying to still persuade me to move into Strandloper?'

She does not smile. 'Dr Turner, I have a difficult thing I need to clear up. There are some things ... I have heard. Some rumours. I want to know if they are true.'

'Rumours?'

'I must be blunt about this, Dr Turner. We had you all wrong—we thought you were on our side.' As if the drink has given her courage, she lunges past you and before you can stop her, she pushes the bedroom door open and steps inside.

You leap clean over the sofa and stand to fend off the view that will assault her eyes, but too late. You watch in helpless horror as scantily clad Tracey sits up in bed, stretches and yawns. She does not look the least bit surprised. Nor does Mrs Steyn. She shoots a finger at Tracey. 'Get into the car at once. You're going home.'

'I told you I was staying the night out.'

You try to interject, placing your hand between the two women, as if this would stop them. 'Excuse me.' But you no longer exist, it seems. No one hears or sees you.

'You're doing this to spite me,' Mrs Steyn says to Tracey.

You have to assert yourself here. After all this is your cottage. This is none of her business. 'Will you please leave, Mrs Steyn. You are trespassing, I believe?'

'You keep out of this!' Mrs Steyn's pink fingernail waves in your face, then back at Tracey's. 'You're trying to punish me. First that dreadful business with Makaya and now … this! I've been worried sick all night about you. And I told you not to come here again.'

'Mum!' whines Tracey. 'Please. You're *embarrassing* me.'

In a concessional aside to you, she gestures with an upturned wrist. 'My mother.' The last word is thrown at Mrs Steyn with contempt.

Tracey turns on Mrs Steyn. 'Mum, I'm not trying to do this to prove anything or to spite anyone. How many times must I tell you?'

And to you: 'I … I have a confession.'

'That's your mother?'

She flaps her sleeve at the boarded-up window. 'The house that blocks your view?'

'Yes?'

'It's our house. I mean, my mother's house.'

You suddenly see the resemblance between mother and daughter, both grim-lipped, indignant, wild-eyed. Tracey then points down at the wooden floor, the towel on the chair behind you, and the surfboard standing humbly in the corner.

'That's my stuff. I lived here.'

'What?'

'Yes, it's true.'

'But … Khumalo?'

'My father,' she says. 'My absent Zulu father who Mum chased away.'

'Tracey …'

'This is my cottage.'

'This is not your cottage.' Mrs Steyn grabs Tracey's wrist. 'I rented this cottage out. It's no longer your cottage. I forbade you to come here ever again. After that dreadful man …'

'Oh, please don't go on about Makaya again. It's over.'

'Bloody hell,' you say.

'This is my cottage. My surfboard. My things … My mother played a real dirty on me. Renting it out.'

'You leave Dr Turner out of it, Tracey. He doesn't need to know all our business.'

'She changed her name back to Steyn after the divorce. She refused to accept the consequences of her actions. But not me. I am a Khumalo.'

You are in a farce, a badly-written play designed to make fun of the protagonist, put him in a ridiculous situational comedy. That's all you can think: one of those cheap American sitcoms. You take a step back out of their hot circle of words, two, three, notice you are not missed, turn around and march through the door.

'Excuse me …' But no one is listening to you.

You have had the presence of mind to sling the folded suit over your arm, and grab the car keys in your hand as you tiptoe out. Before you are really aware of the decision, you have hopped into the car, started it and driven off through a huge mud puddle which splashes up and over the bonnet onto the windscreen. You turn on wiper blades that spread the red mud over the entire windshield, and drive through more red puddles and craters on the road towards eSikamanga.

8

Saltoblattella montistabularis
South African hopping cockroach

The recently discovered South African hopping cockroach (*Saltoblattella montistabularis*) has evolved so that it no longer has to scuttle around in the dirt, but can leap up to fifty times its body length in one jump. Its hind legs are twice the length of its other legs. It rivals the grasshopper in its ability to escape predators. The 'leap-roach', as it is sometimes called, has made the remarkable 'leap' forward in evolution by discovering that it does not have to grovel in the faeces of other animals, or eat the faeces of other animals, but can live on grass and radically change its natural environment. It leaps when cornered by predators and in its quest for food sources, but also, it seems, expressly for the sake of exploration.

You park in the shimmering car park and dash to the toilets, where you change into your suit. You would have liked to have a shower, or at least a mirror, so you can see whether you look as wrecked as you feel, but you smooth your hair over your head and make do. Then you head for the cafeteria for breakfast. The trial begins in half an hour. The university looks spring-cleaned by the storm, spruced up and ready. There will be no Honours class today, you guess.

A group of students is crowded around a bench. They are struggling with something. One student lunges forward and holds a wriggling black thing, and brings it up to the light. A second student holds a knife, and blood drips down his hand.

Your stomach clenches. You are witnessing some atrocity here. 'Stop!'

You push through the thick crowd and in the centre, the crouched student holds a wriggling furry ball, a kitten with one eye. The other eye is a bloody mess. Another student cups a small bloody object in his hand. The man with the knife stands up.

'Whoa! What are you doing?'

Instead of lunging at you with the knife, as you fully expect, or launching into an explanation, the students drop the cat, and run. The man with the knife slips way, the crowd dissolves, the one holding the small object clenches it in his fist and bolts. Blood drips down his arm.

'What the hell?'

A mewing, eye-less kitten flees into the bushes.

Bystanders are useful to have around. You appeal to them with arms wide-spread. 'What is going on?'

'It's exam time,' says one. 'And those *skabengas* want to be able to see the exam questions.'

'I don't get it.'

'By strong medicine, traditional medicine, by eating the cat's eyes, they can see the questions.'

'And the answers,' adds another.

Another frowns. 'But this time it is to do with Dr Makaya.'

You turn to him. 'What does gouging a kitten's eyes out have to do with him?'

'It is strong medicine, to help him get reinstated.'

'The judges will see the truth.'

'Sorry I asked.'

*

It is one of those moments (and you have had far too many already) when you look up at the sky and ask your non-existent god: 'How did I get myself into this mess?' Here you are on your way to a trial where your employers expect you to testify against someone you hardly know, whose job you are taking, and who has manoeuvred you into a position of white guilt. At the same time, your students and your new-found friends Makaya and Ngwenya expect you to conveniently switch sides and testify for Makaya, and against your own employers.

Fat chance of either.

But maybe it's not up to you. Maybe it's up the gods, or those gods who look favourably on gouging cats' eyes out.

As you approach the Admin block, there is the Crocodile himself bearing down on you. He is wearing a suit and tie, and looks as uncomfortable as you feel in yours. 'Good morning, Mr Ngwenya ...'

The scowl he gives you must mean that he thinks you are about to betray him, betray Makaya and consequently Progress, the university and the whole future of the country, if you can read expressions correctly (which you still can't).

Instead of greeting you, he stares you down and sweeps past you, looking at his watch.

Okay.

You follow him into the Admin building and into the designated room, already semi-circled with distinguished administrators, faculty and students. You are ushered across a very soft carpet to a plush maroon seat in the semi-circle between two men you do not know. A woman sits opposite, in charge of the proceedings, and introduces you to the panel, the defendants and the witnesses. The Dean narrows her eyes in lieu of greeting. Dr Makaya and Mr Ngwenya sit with both arms folded, nodding to the air above you; the Dean jots down a note on her pad, and Mpofu drums his fingers on the table and gives you a wink. Air-conditioners hum and the air is ice cold.

Zimmerlie sits at the back. This is the first time you have seen him since you found out about his brain aneurism. He looks now as if he is about to have another one.

Proceedings begin.

'Dr Turner, you have agreed to help us decide on these charges that have been brought against Dr Mxolisi Makaya. Even though you are a newcomer, we have been told that you have some information which may be important to consider before we come to a decision.'

It is here that Makaya's eyes meet yours. They are steady, burning, powerful eyes. Indeed, Mpofu's nodding head and weak smile confirms all: you are going to betray Makaya.

'This morning's session has been very long, and we hope not to keep the committee here for much longer. Please give a brief account of your dealings with the accused.'

Zimmerlie is staring at you. Makaya is staring at you. Mpofu and Ngwenya are staring at you. Feet tap, fingers fidget, and you take a breath. You have already decided what to say. 'I have had no dealings with Dr Makaya, and therefore am in no position to make any judge-ments on his behaviour in a matter that does not concern me.'

'What?' Mpofu's mouth purses. Makaya's eyes never leave yours. The panel frowns in unison. One consults his notes and speaks, introduces himself as Mr Redlinghuis, a bespectacled balding man with teeth that protrude from both sides of his mouth. He looks nothing like a Red Ling House at all. 'Are you not leaving something out here, Dr Turner? We heard that you have obtained information that incriminates Dr Makaya.'

You speak as if your listeners are hard of hearing. 'As a newcomer, I've had no dealings with Dr Makaya, and so I am in no position to judge his actions.'

Ngwenya nods. 'What he is asking, Timothy, is this: did they co-opt you to extort information from your students?'

Mpofu leans forward and whispers, unbelievably loud. 'Go on, man, don't be intimidated by him. I know he's giving you looks that would kill, but stand up for yourself, man. There's no denying it.'

'What's there to deny?'

'You have evidence. You brought it to us yourself. That's why you are here.' Redlinghuis is not the man you'd imagined: not red, not large as a house, but slight, withdrawn, apologetic. And shiny bald. 'Did you or did you not have conversations with Professor Zimmerlie and Dr Mpofu in which you said you were going to write a statement, where you spoke about Makaya's misdeeds, how he has cut up texts, destroyed university property, disregarded the learning outcomes, and worse, overstepped the boundaries of teacher and student?'

Redlinghuis smiles, showing that he has too many teeth. Some of them still show when he closes his mouth. (The way to tell the difference between an alligator and a crocodile, you think stupidly, is that croco-diles show their teeth when they close their mouths.) 'Do you deny that?'

You push your chair back. 'That's all hearsay; it's not admissible as evidence. Really, guys. Come on.'

Redlinghuis continues to smile (you imagine he cannot stop). 'It is not up to you to decide what is admissible and what is not. Just tell us what you saw in that classroom.'

'What I saw in the classroom was a bright bunch of students pushed and pulled by two sides.'

Ngwenya speaks: 'And you too. You admit that they pressured you to try to incriminate the defendant?'

With a sharp look at Mpofu, who is now staring up at the air-conditioner, you speak. 'They said my job depended on it.'

Ngwenya smiles. 'That if you didn't, you would be out of a job. They blackmailed you in other words?'

'Objection.' Mpofu's fist slams down on the desk.

'This is not a court room, Dr Mpofu. You don't have to object. You may speak.'

'It wasn't coercion. It was common sense. Logical. If Makaya gets his job back, then obviously Dr Turner has to go. I was merely pointing out the obvious.'

You are looking like some kind of dummy here, pushed and pulled, and talked about in the third person.

Ngwenya speaks again. 'But you tried to set up this new lecturer to spy on Dr Makaya?'

'Timothy suggested it. He came specifically to my office to tell me about Dr Makaya's misdeeds. Regularly. He was flabbergasted by the man's antics. True, eh, Timothy?'

You can't help smiling. 'Flabbergasted? Do I look like the kind of person who can be flabbergasted?'

'An interesting word, yes, Dr Turner,' says the moderator. 'But is it true? You were … upset … disturbed by Dr Makaya's unconventional pedagogy? Did you feel he had crossed any … lines?'

You glance at the EXIT sign. It is a short three paces to the door. If you open your mouth now, it will only be to affirm or contradict the reality they are casting. It's like a net, you think, a trap they are guiding you into.

You have a few options. You could stutter and trail off into some affirmation of whatever person they have projected onto you. You could take a stand for one or the other. Or …

The air-conditioner hums. Your fingers press on the mahogany desk. Makaya watches you steadily. Zimmerlie watches you steadily. As if you are the bloody centre of the world, as if it all hinges on you. And maybe it does.

Mpofu speaks. 'Let me just say that Dr Turner is not the accused one here. Dr Turner did the right thing. He found that his students were rebellious, hadn't done the work prescribed on the syllabus, and so—reasonably—asked to see their previous work, which was written in journals. One student indicated that she wanted to confess, apparently, but she was afraid of the man, intimidated by the students who had been sworn to secrecy. Harassed by Dr Makaya into fearful silence. Dr Turner did the only decent thing he could have done. And of course his reticence today to own up to his good deeds may be attributed either to modesty or to the fact that he's being intimidated by Dr Makaya right now in front of our very eyes.' Mpofu indicates Makaya's steady stare. Makaya shakes his head and closes his eyes.

Now it is Ngwenya's turn to defend you. 'This all smacks of your manipulation, Dr Mpofu, of spying, of underhanded dealings. The only evidence here is that you strong-armed Dr Turner into going along with your dirty tricks to undermine your colleague. But once Dr Turner knew that he was being manipulated, he tried to backtrack and stop this process. He soon realised that Dr Makaya is a respectable academic who has the interests of his students and his university at heart, and that these men (here he wags a finger at Mpofu and Redlinghuis) are dirty double-dealing conspirators. It backfired. Timothy soon came to realise that he was backing the wrong horse.'

Mpofu stands. 'I didn't come here to be spoken of in this way.'

The moderator motions for him to sit.

Ngwenya continues: 'This is not evidence of sexual harassment. This is evidence of an awareness of sound teacher-student relations.'

'Can I just say something?' You turn to address the circle. 'As an outsider, my perspective on all this is … Can I speak for myself?'

Redlinghuis smiles. 'Go ahead, Dr Turner.'

'I'm not here to take sides. I'm on both of your sides. None of your sides. If anything, I am on Sizwe Bantu's side and Sizwe Bantu is the only one who has been side-lined here.'

'Who is Sizwe Bantu?' the Dean whispers to her side-kick on the left.

Redlinghuis frowns. 'Is there another witness we have omitted to invite to this hearing?'

Makaya shakes his head in dismissal. Zimmerlie stares at you as if you are completely mad. Which may be true.

But you are not letting either of them get away with it. 'Torn out of textbooks, ignored, misunderstood. Hushed up. Censored. I am not supposed to give a talk on him. Why? What do these two men have against Sizwe Bantu? Sizwe Bantu is the prophet ignored by his own countrymen and women.'

A silence follows. Ngwenya clears his throat. 'What has this to do with the case, Dr Turner?' He turns to the woman presiding over the proceedings. 'This Bantu is a writer.'

'We will be judged by History on our response to Sizwe Bantu,' you say. 'Yet you despise and reject him. Professor Zimmerlie and Dr Mpofu avoid him; Dr Makaya obliterates his voice ...'

Zimmerlie is staring at you as if you are an alien from the deep reaches of space.

Redlinghuis shakes his head. 'I don't quite follow. What has this to do with the case in point?'

'I am against Makaya,' you explain.

Makaya gives you a pained look. Ngwenya stares daggers.

'I am against Zimmerlie.'

Mpofu now frowns at you, opens his mouth, and then shuts it again.

'I am against those who are against Makaya and Zimmerlie.'

Makaya presses his fingers together. Zimmerlie scratches his scarred forehead.

'I am against those against those who are against Zimmerlie and Makaya. Against everything, even being against. I am against being against being against.'

Against becomes a word with no meaning, the more you say it. It is a foreign word—one you have never heard before. Uh-Gay-INXT.

A long silence.

Makaya shakes his head. He must recognise the poem, even if he has cut it out of the textbook. Zimmerlie leans forward as if he is also about to say something. Then he sinks back into his chair and presses his hand to his head, just above the stitches.

You wonder how you are going to get out of this. You have made a stand, but a stand that indicates you are quite unhinged.

Then, as if you have been talking sense, the moderator nods. 'Thank you for your statement. It has been duly recorded. Dr Turner, thank you for your valuable time in helping us clear up a few issues. Any further questions of Dr Turner?'

No.

You stand. Walk out. Makaya, Zimmerlie both watch you go, like birds of prey.

But you have disentangled yourself. Just like that. Simple.

Outside, heavy grey clouds droop over the Admin building. There is no wind, just thick muggy air, and it is hot.

'All for you, Sizwe,' you say aloud. You place a five-Rand coin into a convenient machine sitting in the shade of the air-conditioning unit, and a Coke can scuttles down a chute into a tray by your feet. You drink the fizzy black liquid fast, let it burn all the way down to your stomach. Let the cockroaches come devour me! You crunch the can, like they do in the movies, and then hurl it at the ADMIN sign.

'The Modernist Afrikanist dekonstructs himself' by Sizwe Bantu

(*The Present Tense*, Vol. XXIX, Feb. 2004, pp. 43-54)

The Modernist Afrikanist, in the glow of a fire, and in Cartesian pose, contemplates the possibility that Africa is a construction of the white man. All is whiteness. All he believes was authentic, genuine, original, African, has been borrowed, superimposed, and assimilated.

Africa is easy to dissect. Africa is indeed a construction of the white man. The map navigated by Vasco da Gama was plotted and defined by Europeans. Africa was named by the Greeks *Africa*, or by the Romans *Africae*, not by the Africans. So what was the name given to this continent before it was appropriated? No. No. To call it a continent begs the question: it certainly was not the neat criss-cross of lines and shape determined by the Berlin Conference in 1888. From the Atlas mountains to Adamastor in the Cape, this was European intervention. Did we think of ourselves as a continent, a species *Africansis* before the Europeans called us this? Did we think of ourselves as black before white men came along?

South Africa, a geographic bag rather than identity, all those 19 tribes loosely racially divided. Azania, an ideological construct of one party. So no name, no identity, no country.

Abolish those national boundaries set up by the greedy colonial powers. Begone Portuguese East Africa, and its African pseudonyms Mocambique, Mozambique, Southern Rhodesia, Rhodesia, Zimbabwe-Rhodesia, Zimbabwe. Let the glorious Ashante empire, the Swahili, the Monomatapa, spread across the borders without passports. Let us become our true pre-African selves.

The Modern Afrikanist continues his thought experiment by peeling off layers of what he has always considered to be himself: first to go of course is his skin, the wrinkly elastic epidermis that has caused all the trouble. He hurls this into the fire and it sizzles, writhes, spits in its own fat. Underneath he is pink, fleshy, like all other races.

Next to go is culture and sivilization, that ungainly hotch-potch of decaying tradition, slime and bacteria. It is difficult to wash off: he has to scour at pockets of it, rub himself raw.

Tribe, nationality, identification with herds and flocks go next. I pledge allegiance. *Amandla, awethu*. Primal instincts, biological drives, *vamoose, hamba*. Be gone, Evans Pritchard, Ph.D. Begone!

And then, standing even more naked before the fire, he sloughs gender. Male, female, neuter. Gone. He is not black, not male. Who is he underneath all this macho posturing, this testosterone-driven impulse? If I am not black, white, male, female, who am I? Can I think of myself outside of gender and sex?

I am I, what will be left: a voice, a *res extensa*. Self-consciousness, that ability to define itself as an individual: should that go too? Is that also constructed? Or is the voice in his head, his doubting self, a necessity that must accompany him on his pilgrimage?

No, that must go too: it is a construct, a dualistic Western construct.

And now his genetic make up, physical being, propensity towards habit—it is all gone. So what is left?

A disembodied voice? No, that is Renaissance trickery. Without vocal cords, he is certainly no voice; without a brain, he has no thoughts.

Now that I am unskinned, unmanned, deAfricanised, who am I? What is my real identity?

Invisible. The I of InvIsIble is all. When he looks in the mirror now, he has no reflection, causes no shadow.

Identity is created by putting on layers, not taking them off. But he has to clean the wound before dressing it. Now what does he put on? An African skin, an African identity, a wild golden gleam of a lost sivilization?

Pre-Africa: it all began here. His first ancestor was the mother of all humankind. The African Eve they call her, and can trace her genetic code through the ages. Hail, Pre-African Mother, pure ancestor: you were born here in the centre of this place, wrestled yourself from the animal, plant, mineral world and became human, the first human, here in the core of what is now called Africa …

And then flowing down the Nile, flooding her banks, came the loamy sivilization cradling the human race: Egypt. A black indigenous sivilization: we weren't black then, of course. Others were defined by their lack of our substance. We simply were. Ebony and earth and alabaster pharaohs sat proudly side by side in the now desert of racial divide. We invented mathematics, science, philosophy, religion. We are the centre of the universe in this (so-called) African (so-called) Eden. Not Mesopotamia, that false Eden of a patriarchal white male god who gave rigid commandments, who exterminated whole people with floods and seas and fire, but an African muddy god, an African goddess who gave five organic commandments of the senses: Impulse, InstInct, ImagInatIon, IntuItIon and IndIvIduallty.

You should go home now, but of course there is no home to go to. Your cottage, or what you thought of as your cottage, is Tracey's cottage, Mrs Steyn's cottage.

The trial has left a yellow smear in the air above the campus. You can imagine how it is all going: Makaya, Ngwenya on one side with their lawyer; Zimmerlie, Mpofu and Redlinghuis on the other; the presider sifting through the evidence: guilty, guilty, guilty of all charges brought against him. Ngwenya defending him: 'He was nobly trying to institute an African university, and the crime before us, ladies and gentlemen, is the reactionary obstruction of progress perpetuated by this turncoat Timothy Turner.' The evidence is self-evident, and no amount of scurrying and covering with intellectual dust will disguise it. The fact is, you don't care anymore, one way or the other. Only that you are seen not to fall into one camp or the other. Not to favour one petty academic over the other. They tried to trap you, and you have escaped.

*

Dear M,

I think I have found myself. Is that what you wanted? You said I didn't appreciate you, couldn't see who you were, but how could I? I couldn't see myself. You weren't sure who I was. Nor was I. Now I am. I took a stand for myself. I took off my mask of self in public and stood naked before them. But they still cannot see me. You still cannot see me, not my true self, the self behind all these masks.

But it feels good to be myself. For the first time.

Sincerely
T

*

You do not have to wait long for the verdict. After a solitary lunch in the cafeteria, you hear the singing.

You expect the worst. The gavel poised over Makaya's hanging head. Guilty. Guilty. Guilty. You dutifully cross the shade of the Humanities Building and watch your students clump and dance ready for their protest march. You expect tear gas and dogs and outrage. But a jubilation (another emotion you are not that familiar with) greets you.

VIVA MAKAYA! A LUTA FINIS! MAKAYA VICTORY!

Students *toyi-toyi* in large clumps, pounding the red earth, linking arms and snaking their way across the car park to Admin, which is cordoned off by the familiar red and white plastic barriers. But the revellers are not in a hostile mood. They have won; theirs is an Afrikan university. You hurry alongside the building in the shade, but they have seen you. 'Dr Turner, Dr Turner! We won! We won!'

Eric holds out his hand. 'We won! The New Struggle is won!'

'Dr Makaya won the case?'

'An overwhelming victory!'

'But how?'

'The evidence they submitted against him was obtained illegally,' says Joel. 'The judge invalidated it.'

'And we heard, Dr Turner, that you refused to co-operate with them. That you stood strong for Dr Makaya!'

'*Viva* Dr Turner!'

You tear away from the mob, looking anxiously for signs of Ngwenya or Makaya. But they are nowhere. Admin is stone cold, buzzing loud with a masking air-conditioning unit, locked up.

The demonstration has grown into a party, and there are rumours that Dr Makaya himself will address the crowd in Freedom Square.

'We knew all along he would prevail!' calls one student.

'No more Hamlet!' calls another.

'Join us! Join us!' Caesar raises a stick on which is impaled a very burnt, smoking piece of *boerewors*. You shake your head.

You scour the mob for signs of blonde dreadlocks and bells and beads, but cannot find any.

*

'Timothy, Timothy, Timothy.' Mpofu calls you in to Zimmerlie's office.

You stare at the boxes half full of books and ask the stupid question. 'What are you doing?'

'You haven't heard? We have to pay recompense. Each of us.'

'Me?'

He stares at you. 'No, no. You … not you.'

'Dr Mpofu.'

'He's coming back. He wants his office back, and I am not going to stand here and watch everything we stood for crumble. I don't want to see his gloating face.'

'What happened?'

'You were there. You made sure the evidence was discredited!' He thumps a pile of singed books into the box. '*Umendo awuthunyelwa gundane.*'[1]

'I don't quite understand.'

'Nor do I, Dr Turner. Why would you cut the branch you're sitting on? And Professor Zimmerlie? He's taking it very badly. He had high hopes for you. We had high hopes for you. Pass me those books over there, will you? The Shakespeare tomes ... No one at this university will be needing them anymore.'

You drive home. The sun is much too hot. Even the sea writhes in discomfort, and the land in the far distance shimmers, revealing its illusory nature. Your blood pulses in your veins, and sweat glistens over your skin. And the heat of the car makes it worse. The plastic seats exude fumes; the road ahead is a shimmering, black, gooey mess.

The cottage is deserted. All foreign bodies have been expelled. Tracey has skedaddled with her mother. The only sign of life is a brown shiny cockroach sitting on the crust of a pizza on the kitchen table, which looks as if someone has polished its hard back (the cockroach, not the table or the pizza crust). Tracey has left no sign of her visitation, except a faint body odour which hides in the crevices of your sheets. Her ghostly body shape, albeit deflated, is also left behind on the unmade bed. A glass that has recently contained brandy and Coke stands primly on the dresser where Mrs Steyn abandoned it. You look in vain for the inevitable PLEASE VACATE THESE PREMISES note.

---

1   Literally: 'You can't send a mouse to spy out your intended marriage'. Mpofu is saying that you can never know what's going to happen in the future.

You change out of your suit, shower and drive your car as fast as you can down through the reserve to the sea.

The storm from the previous night has done a good job of rearranging the beach. The Mswaswe River now cuts high banks to the sea, an urgent brown deluge. Tree branches, logs and other debris cover the sand.

You climb the dunes, which have shifted and rearranged themselves into a foreign terrain.

The cottage is piled with wet sand against its front door and windows.

You wait for a heavy five minutes at least, thinking, wavering.

You grip the rusted s-shape door handle and turn it. The door, surprisingly, opens. You push it slowly inward and it sticks halfway. Sand has piled up against the door inside, and the floor is damp. You listen to the hot breeze. A musty darkness awaits you inside. You hear your heart beating. The dunes shimmer in time with your heartbeat.

You smell candle wax. Staring back at you from the opposite wall are the protruding glass eyes of a melting man. You steady yourself by holding onto a rough bookcase to your left. You stare out of the corner of your eyes until you adjust to the darkness of the room. It takes a while: you are blind, and boxes of green light on your retina project themselves onto the darkness. Your feet refuse to move, as if you are standing on a glass plate on Sydney Tower. You wait, calm your breathing. You detect other smells: paint, paraffin, glue. The open door creaks. You walk slowly past statues, paintings, bookshelves, and finally stand before the first painting that you saw from the outside. Myopically—it is dark in this corner—you have to peer close up. It is not a painting. It is a collage, a landscape of the sea and Mswaswe river—banks of sand on the left, and towering dunes on the right. But it is not the subject matter of the collage that jolts you, it is the texture. You run your fingers over the bumpy, oval shapes to make sure.

You stare at the hump backs, the heads, the proboscis of each creature, the black eyes, even—my god—the feelers intact. A thousand sleeping cockroaches, varnished, painted red or green or amber, neatly undulated in forms and patterns that are unrecognisable close up but from a few feet away are the eSikamanga sugarcane fields, the blue sea, the dunes and the river.

A warm wind blows through you, though you are shivering. You have often wondered what a cockroach painting looks like, even wanted to snatch up a scampering cockroach, paint it blue or green and stick it on a canvas to see the effect. And haven't Bantu followers all stuck rubber-varnished cockroaches on their mantelpieces in honour of the great writer? But no one, you are sure, has ever gone this far.

The inside of the cottage is a different place to the grimy vision from outside. The chair is covered with the same grainy cockroach design. You turn to the small mat on the floor, the chest of drawers, the lampshade, the bookcase, the sofa—all are cockroach-covered. You scrutinise each item in turn. Each cockroach has been hand-picked for size, painted with blue, green, brown, pink, and then varnished and glued neatly into place. The chair is covered in baby cockroaches; the bookcase large, coarse ones; and the mat, hardy monsters.

You have always thought, and you have even written in your thesis, that it was all conjecture, that the *Cokcraco* story was a work of the first African sense of Imagination. Certainly no one would be so outrageous as to actually make cockroach furniture.

Unless ... unless ...

You stop at the desk in the centre of the room. On the top is an open book—a journal. A computer screen and keyboard have been pushed to the back, and on the side you see an old Olivetti typewriter, a sheet of paper in its jaw.

```
The sea is a poem.
```

The next line is crossed out heavily in upper case Xs and another line has been banged out:

```
I ache for the sea, yet I fear it
   does not recognise me.
```

At first confusion clouds your brain. Then the sky cracks and the thunder voice of god booms down.

Bantu's writings speak of a golden brown sand and a crashing thunderous blue sea.

You can hear the eSikamanga waves pounding on brown sands, the beating of your heart, and the voice of Bantu speaking loudly in your ears. You feel the desk, also cockroach-covered. Each covering, whether sofa or chest or bookcase, is a magnificent piece of work in itself, but its significance outshines its intrinsic worth. You brush your hands over the paintings, the walls, the furniture, then finally gaze at the Bantu portrait itself. And finally understand. The melted man stares back at you with his convex insect eyes seeing everything, his Joker's smile filling the painting, and his glossy ochre skin glinting with some lacquered substance that looks still wet.

'Sizwe Bantu!' you say to the echoing walls. 'Sizwe Bantu.'

Your heart is pounding. You can hardly stand, you are so dizzy.

This is Bantu's cottage. This is where he lives and works.

And on another sheet of paper on the desk, here is a story that has not been published yet, half typed: 'The Illusion of African Literature.'

```
"There should be silence," it begins. "All the words are
trees that have to be sacrificed, cut down. Every
wriggling word takes up space, pollutes the air,
chokes the world with excess material. We cut down
whole forests to write silly words. Trees are better
than books."
    "But books," I said, "can raise consciousness,
awareness, enlightenment."
    "At the expense of the environment?" she said.
"Most books are pulp, and writing is vanity."
    "But words can make you aware of the environment,
can open our eyes to the trees. You can only write
about not writing because you have written."
    "I will be silent hereafter. As you say, the next
step, the wise step after all this babble of academia
is silence — to listen and not talk. I've learned to
talk and now I've come to listen."
```

The dialogue stops abruptly here and the next few lines are scribbled out. You can make them out under his heavy ink: "Words are trees? Silence growing, nourishing, greening the world. All these words ... " Thereafter blank paper, yearning to be filled with his words.

A creak on the floorboards behind you tells you that you are not alone, that you have been discovered.

A man, in silhouette, stands in the doorway. He shakes his head as if he has a stiff neck. In his hand he holds a weapon, a 9 mm pistol.

You turn to face him, raise your hands in surrender, but also in bewilderment. He is tall, a large man, and in silhouette he looks familiar, makes a gesture—a familiar gesture—as if he is going to fire a shot. 'Don't shoot! Please. I'm ... a fan. I should never have ...'

9

Periplaneta albus
·············
White cockroach

What observers believe to be albino cockroaches are actually newly moulted cockroach nymphs or nymphets. Like lizards and snakes, cockroaches shed their skins, or cuticles, and the new skin underneath is initially white and soft, before it blackens and hardens. This metamorphosis, from black to white to black, has led to the myth of the 'albino cockroach', which in some cultures is revered as a sign of blessing or an omen of good luck. Frantz Fanon, the Algerian, is no doubt influenced by this shape-shifting phenomenon, and alludes to it in his seminal work *Black Skin, White Masks* (1952).

The shadow of the tall black man melts and moulds into a white-haired professor with an Afrikaans-English accent.

'Zimmerlie?' You listen to the waves bash the shore in a relentless rhythm. You watch the man's lips tremble in some tight emotion. He is pale, deathly pale, his lips a sharp jagged line. He aims the pistol at you as if it is a torch. You hold onto the cockroach bookcase, breaking off one or two baby cockroaches in your attempt to stop the world from spinning. He is framed by the archway of traversing cockroaches. The gun is still pointed at you. He is wearing, uncharacteristically, an African shirt, chevrons around the neck, San figures dancing up and down his chest and arms.

'What are you doing here?' You spread your arms to encompass the statues, the paintings, the writings, the bookshelves, all Bantu, all of his universe.

When Zimmerlie speaks, you can hardly hear him. 'What am I doing here? You're the intruder. What are you doing here?'

'I thought. I thought ...'

You stare at the gleaming gun barrel still pointing at you. Zimmerlie's eyes dance. He is mad, you suddenly realise. He's mad and he has a gun. If you are quick, you could lunge at him and disarm him. Sweat runs down your brow.

In your subconscious, the pieces of an intricate puzzle have already slid into place. But your mind persists doggedly, stubbornly, with the painfully slow process of unravelling the knots.

Sweat runs down your brow. It is true then. You have found the home of the writer you have been following all of your adult life. He lives here. Here are the cockroaches. Here are the books. He lives here in the very town you live in. But you feel no exultant joy at the discovery. You are instead focusing on the dark barrel of a gun, aimed at you by a mad man. Still listening to your thumping heart, which now bangs loudly in your ears so that you can hardly hear your own voice. 'Where is he?'

Zimmerlie laughs, a hollow echo in the dark room. 'Who?'

'Bantu. He ... lives here, doesn't he? This is his house.'

'Yes. He's not who you think he is.'

Zimmerlie sits at the desk and plays with the weapon, looks down the barrel, then holds it at arm's length pointing at the window and squints through the sights. His lips are pursed, his eyes full of fire. *Humour him*, the voice inside your head whispers. Try to hold your voice steady. You think: does this man have blood on his hands? 'What do ... do you mean?'

Zimmerlie measures the heavy weight of the pistol in one hand, and then places it down on the desk. He stares at you with glazed eyes.

'What are you doing in his cottage? Why are you ... ?' You stare at the gun, then feel behind you for the wall. You have the mad idea of creeping along to the door without him seeing, but he is scrutinising every twitch and movement. Has he murdered him?

'He speaks to me, I am his scribe ...'

'What do you mean?'

'I write for him.'

'You ... ? Is he disabled in some way?'

'You could say so.' Zimmerlie's laugh is hollow, full of pain and bitterness.

The truth hammers at your glass wall, but your obstinate imagination pushes it aside as if your life depends upon it. A desperate scenario unfolds in your desperate mind. Bantu is a cripple; Bantu depends on this insane man to write his books; Bantu is at the mercy of a mad man who suffers brain aneurisms. You think of Stephen Hawking and other writers who need physical help in order to write. Of a Stephen King novel where the writer is trapped by a mad fan and forced to write what she wants. 'How ... exactly?'

Zimmerlie finds this cruelty amusing. 'He is unable to use normal vocal cords, or physical hands. Yes, you are helping me to understand Bantu. He is disabled, of course! And *my* disability enables him to exist!'

You stare at the madman. A hundred cicadas screech in your head.

'But I can't go on. He's killing me.'

You stare at the gun on the desk as Zimmerlie paces the room. Should you make a lunge for it?

'I wish you would have come earlier. I wanted to talk to you about art. Art and madness. To see if you could make the connection. You know Bantu so well. I may have found a way to make things easier ... an understanding ... you had the capacity to see beyond, to understand pure voice. To help me. But you didn't come. My burden is mine alone.'

He picks up a manuscript off the shelf and presents it to you. You try not to let your hands shake too much as you take it from him. It is written in Royal Blue Washable ink in an A5 CNA black book. You creak open the first page and hold it towards the yellow light. It is a mess of blotchy crossings out, and a steady flow of ink all throughout the book. You read the opening words. 'Creativity is the greatest weapon against tyranny.'

'Bantu,' you say.

It is *The Great South African Novel*, in its first draft. You recognise the opening sentence, written in Bantu's own hand. You know Bantu's handwriting. You have studied it in the University of Melbourne library in microfilm, in published excerpts from manuscripts.

Zimmerlie gesticulates around him at the papers flapping in the breeze, like wounded birds. 'Such a literalist! No one sees the invisible, the ghostly world. I try to make it flesh and blood, my flesh and blood. ...

I sacrifice myself for him ...' His tangled wild wisps of hair sweating over his brow are like the tangled white thoughts in his mind. 'He's a spiritual voice. He's a ghost.'

Zimmerlie is either inarticulate, or mad, or you are obdurately stupid. His words are like stones. They have no meaning.

'I need you to understand,' says Zimmerlie. 'It's not something I wanted to do. Bantu torments me. I can't stop. But I have to stop; I can't go on with my life as it is. You must understand me.'

You snatch the open copy of the unpublished manuscript and fan it open in a rainbow arc. Zimmerlie folds his arms. 'Bantu wrote it. Through me. I am not invested in it at all, you must believe me. Bantu is the voice of all African writers I admired. I found myself writing one day words that I knew were not mine, but were borrowed, sampled, from other African writers. I had no choice but to follow the voice in me, to write ... to listen, rather, to the voice within me.'

You watch his lips move. You watch Zimmerlie's eyes glance at the weapon within his reach. But he makes no move for it. Instead, he waves his hands in the air, as if trying to erase your words. 'Listen, Timothy, you must understand. Bantu is ...'

You strike the table with the bound manuscript and it spills out over the floor, a sea of white. Haven't you modelled yourself on the real Sizwe Bantu all these years? Haven't you listened to Bantu's voice in your ear, in your beating heart, in your soul?

Zimmerlie picks another book from the bookcase and places it on the windowsill. You turn stiffly. Manganye. *Being-Black-in-the-World*. He flicks through to a passage that you know well. 'To create is to create dangerously[1] ...' he reads.

'You took it from ... this writer?'

'No,' says Zimmerlie. 'Manganye took it from Camus. I took it from him. The idea lives, it transmigrates ... Is it a crime to ... ?'

'Plagiarise? That's how you did it. Makaya was right after all!' You bang your fist on the bookcase, and cockroach shards splinter up at you.

---

1 Manganye, N (1973) *Being-Black-in-the-World* (Ravan Press, Johannesburg). Manganye maintains that creativity is a dangerous activity, especially in the contexts of oppressive societies (he was writing at the time of Apartheid). Manganye is quoting Albert Camus who expresses a similar sentiment.

He clutches his chest again and scrambles for what you think is the pistol. You leap over to the table and sweep it off the counter onto the floor. You kick it away from him in a move you learned from Hollywood westerns.

He stares at you and motions desperately for a glass of water.

'Jesus!' You keep between him and the gun as you reach for the glass.

He pours two pills into his hand from a vial on the desk, and swallows them. He winces. 'I don't have much time, Timothy. But you must understand. You must listen to me. Bantu is real, as real as your voice, as my voice. The phoney is the man who thinks he has an original thought, who thinks he is the author of the novel or poem.' His voice is rasping, and he is wincing from pain. 'The real writer acknowledges the spirits, the ancestors, the words that come from another.'

'For Christ's sake! What are you saying? At least he—Manganye—acknowledged it was Camus! People think Bantu said this. But Bantu is a ripoff of Manganye?'

'And Achebe and Marechera and Armah and … He lives through all of them.' Zimmerlie fingers the spines of the books neatly packed in the bookcase. 'Out of print. Who reads *Black Sunlight*? Who reads *Why are we so Blest*? Who reads *The Man Died*?[2] Who can understand? All unread—the great voices of African literature need a medium, a resurrection, a true … renaissance.' He sighs. 'People all over the world are reading Bantu—he presents African writers again. It's a way for them to be heard, yes, through an imperfect channel, but I had no choice—I heard Bantu speak to me, and I had to obey …'

Zimmerlie scratches his scar. 'I never wanted to be Bantu, don't you understand? I'm John Zimmerlie. I don't want to be Bantu. It's not a choice. I try to think of it as a gift. I try to be grateful for it, for him. But he's killing me. I need air!'

He pushes through the open door onto the deck and leans against the railing. The muggy, humid air won't do anyone any good, you think, but you follow him out and stare at the wild Indian Ocean.

He speaks to the air. 'I was a modest academic with my English Literature Ph.D., my dabblings in African Literature. But then I started

2   Zimmerlie is alluding to great African literary classics that are out of print and therefore inaccessible to the general public: Dambudzo Marechera's *Black Sunlight*, Ayi Kwi Armah's *Why are we so Blest?*, and Wole Soyinka's *The Man Died*.

getting headaches, and suddenly one day, I found myself in unbearable pain, and I ended up in hospital with a double aneurism. I feared the worst. The doctors said I would not live long, that it would happen again. So I took a sabbatical, a year off; I rented a flat in Durban to recover. I didn't want to walk around like Frankenstein's monster, with a stapled head. Mpofu took over as acting chair of the department. Makaya was away in Ohio …

'And then it happened. A volcano in my brain exploded in bubbles and bubbles of ideas and images. I started painting the images in my brain. I couldn't stop. Then sculpture, then the cockroaches: they kept coming—not real ones, but the Dali ant-like ones in my brain. They were more than real. Then the writing—I couldn't stop. Ideas poured out of me, words, long sentences, inspired thoughts, all day, all night. And the voice was not mine. It was another person, a spirit, a ghost. Sizwe Bantu, he called himself.'

He looks you in the eyes. His white hair flies in the wind around his face. 'Haven't you ever been inspired? Heard voices, been compelled to write down a thought in the middle of the night, been burned by an idea, forced to come out with it?'

Yes, you want to say, but there were never any words to write down.

'I published using Bantu's name. It was his writing; I had no right to call it mine. And it took off like wildfire. I didn't know what to do, except submit to being a scribe. The money came. I moved out of my old house, formed a company, bought this property on the beach, moved the cockroach collection here. Tried to keep it separate from my life. Whenever Bantu attacked me with more words, I would come here, write, purge myself and then hope that he would leave me alone. I took my job back again, hoping to return to normal. But he didn't leave me alone. It got worse. I found myself writing at work, at night …'

Zimmerlie is talking into the air, to the sky, to the wind, not to you. 'They warned me, but I kept going, going, the headaches, the gap between thinking and writing: my critical faculties seemed to recede, the more I wrote. The right brain taking over, or rather Bantu taking over my brain, an avalanche of cockroaches, more and more Bantu … too much. My god, you think I had a choice?'

You do not know what to say. He's gesticulating wildly at invisible tormenters in the air.

'It was no coincidence that brought you here, Timothy. It was synchronicity—you were the one sent to deliver me, to free me from this burden.'

'You've got to be kidding!'

'I thought you … a Bantu man … would be able to understand … that I could at last tell someone who would understand.'

'Enough!'

He is mad then: your first observation at that very first meeting was correct. Here is a man possessed, not by the spirit of Sizwe Bantu but by his own insanity, a grand illusion that he has foisted on everyone else, including yourself. You want to scream, to hit out, to smash things.

Zimmerlie lapses into a deep silence, a silence that sucks the very light out of the cottage and leaves you in a dark space without words or weapons. You stare at purple waves crashing onto the beach. Suddenly the rage in you propels you to the door, to get away.

'Wait, Timothy, I know you are upset. But the knowledge you have is dangerous, you can't just walk away from it.' He lunges after you, claws your shoulder, but you wrench free and leap down off the deck into the sand. You are afraid he will bolt back into the cottage for the gun and shoot you in the back. You zig-zag in the dark, guided by the moonlight on the waves. The sea is loud, but you can still hear his wavering voice. 'Come back, Timothy, you can't leave me here like this.' You look back to see his skeletal frame against the sky, but he does not follow. 'Timothy!'

The pounding waves thunder, but you do not plunge into them, as much as your body aches to. 'Cokcraco! Cokcraco!' the cicadas screech. You run along the edge of the sea and pound your feet into the sand. You find your car, fumble for the keys for long seconds. Can't get the right one in the ignition. Then the solenoid clicks and the engine roars. You slam the gears into reverse and drive hard up the road.

He has your soul; you cannot escape; he is inside you. All of Bantu's words are his words, and they are inside you. Like a lover you embrace into your heart who then betrays you, you do yourself damage. You are nothing; you have no refuge; nowhere to go.

You drive harder, screeching up to a hundred kilometres an hour up the road to eSikamanga. The engine whines in high gear up the dune roads. Only in Seaview Street do you feel safe, under the shady umbrella trees where your cottage hides. But the thought of walking into a cottage that contains a puny shrine to a false god, a shrine to Zimmerlie, is almost unbearable.

Midnight. The stars twinkle as if nothing has happened; the hot wind blows hard through your window; you sweat and tremble. A strong sense of déjà vu knifes itself into your being, something to do with M, with Tracey, with being trapped in a self not of your making. Some small frightened animal (a wild pig?) cries somewhere outside. Nature is malevolent, indifferent, deceptive, treacherous. The universe has played tricks on you, because you have been dull-witted enough to believe in synchronicity. You stare at the ceiling of your cottage in the half moonlight. You try to make sense of the spasm of words that knots in your head and thumps and thuds in your blood. Sleep has fled, as if you have forgotten how to sleep at all. Part of the reason is fear: he will come after you; you must be vigilant. Now you know his secret, you are not safe. But this you dismiss as irrational. No, the enemy is inside you. The enemy is your fuzzy self.

Language has betrayed you. You have been incoherent all along, unable to express yourself in words. Aphasia is rotting your inner being, rusting your vitality. Your words are stammering repeats; you used Bantu as a way out of the misty imprecision of your world, yet now you are imprisoned deeper in it.

Self? The plastic self? The divided self? The pliable self? The trouble is, you have worn too many masks, too many selves, and the real self has disappeared, has become the vanishing self. Without words, you are truly lost. Now that he, Sizwe Bantu, is dead, where are you?

When you use the word 'self' you know that it is an illusion. The self is In-Actual-Fact a construction, a confusion rather of a number of systems of thought, a discontinuous electrical message network of various desires, ideological beliefs and responses, language, forms and hormones. You have no choice who you are. You have no say in where you are born, your gender, race, or social position. You are judged by these things and defined by them.

You stagger to the kitchen for a drink of flat Coke and return to the lounge where you sit on the sofa and sip it like champagne, staring at the glinting Bantu collection. You pick up *The Great South African Novel*. Weigh it in your hands and then slam it onto the floor. Kick at it. Then aim a blow at the table itself. The leg cracks and the table overbalances and falls, tumbling all the heavy objects to the floor. Bantu's poem 'Against' flutters and knifes into your shin. You snatch at it and tear it into tiny pieces. *The Five AfriKan Senses?* You throw the book across the room.

You picture the compost heap at the bottom of the garden. It has lived only in the blurred periphery of your daily life as has the garden itself. You stalk out of the house, feeling the night air cling to your skin like plastic. Trip wires ensnare you, and bells ring in warning, but you rip through them. Guided by the milky light of the stars—the moon is hiding—you cut your way through the long grass and grey dusty creepers to the fence at the back of the house. Here is the festering stench of rotting vegetation and manure, and the waste of Western civilisation (Mrs K's pizza boxes, rusty Coke cans, an old worn car tyre). Eager for action to cure the malaise of a sleepless night, you scurry back to the kerosene lamp in the kitchen and pour the vile liquid into a glass that still contains a trace of Coke and brandy and a white mould that has begun a mini civilisation on top of it. You hunt for the matches, and find the bashful box behind the gas stove.

Next you gather as many Bantu books as you can carry in one swoop and totter outside to the heap of gleaming flies and fumes. Dump them. The *doof* sound and the resultant explosion of dust and angry flies is as satisfying as if you have already performed the deed, yet you hurry back with malicious intent and gather more. You pick every scrap relating to Bantu from the floor. The poster, the card stands, the rubber cockroach, the mounted frames, and yes, even your thesis. Wistfully weigh it for a moment, then think of the man who has written all these words, and the man he has written them about, and are propelled by an invisible force towards the heap of memorabilia.

You light a match. The wind snuffs it out. You cup your hands and light another, and another. Throw them down in disgust and instead pour the kerosene over the books and rotting vegetation. Then light a match and throw it quickly onto the gleaming liquid. It catches immediately and you can hardly jump back in time. The flame, a curious green thing, dances and runs along the lines you have designated, then catches onto the flimsy paper shreds of 'Against'. It holds onto it with teeth and then bites into an article, flicks through and samples a heavy *Collected Works*, then abandons it and finds more interesting matter—a pizza cardboard box. It flicks across it, tasting the remnants of your sad liaison with Tracey, then returns to the business at hand. You run for more kerosene, your heart racing, your head pounding, but your spirits lifting. 'More kerosene!' you call, and sprinkle it on like a Catholic priest with a chalice of incense. 'There is no such person as Sizwe Bantu!' You dance nimbly around the fire, more to avoid the singeing heat and crackling attacks of the flames which surge towards you in their reckless hunger, than to celebrate. A can explodes and the firework crackles into the night sky, blipping out the stars and swathing you in a black warm blanket. A terrible smell like the burning of human flesh fans towards you and warns you to keep your distance. The putrid flesh of Bantu, you say, who doesn't have flesh or blood. The rubber tyre is now burning solidly and slowly and creating a black cloud over the smug town of eSikamanga. You run, spluttering, into the house. Black insect-like scraps of ash float by and cling to the walls of the cottage, or drift higher and higher into the sky.

After a shower you feel no better. The bitter taste in your throat is still strong, mostly from the stench of the rubber tyre, but also from the remaining Bantu in you. Burning his books means nothing. The weight of his world that you have just tried to cast off still lives in you. He is a poison you have to slowly expel. But it is a beginning.

Bantu is no longer watching from the sky. But the habit of being under your god's omnipresent gaze is difficult to break. Or is there another watcher behind Bantu you can sense? Another one behind him, watching you, on the beach, on the outside of this universe, watching you? How can you ever be free? But you have removed one layer at least. You feel airier, butterfly light, unshackled by Fanon's curse.

You wrap the cottage with fishing line, barbs, trinkets and wind chimes, ram the surfboard against the door and pile boxes against the window. You sleep after this, but not in your bed, which is inhabited by a restless phantom and now a layer of homing black butterflies which have found their way through your window. You have to curl onto the sofa with your blanket and pillow, and shut the bedroom door before you can drift off into a dead sleep.

'Death of a Cockroach' by Sizwe Bantu

(*The Present Tense*, Vol. XXX, Aug. 2004, pp. 4-12)

One day, as the Modern Afrikanist was taking a break from his work, contemplating whether to replace the blue cockroach that had crawled off and smudged his cockroach painting, or to leave its absence as an effective statement, he found a dead cockroach in the bottom of the Coke can, and spat out feelers, legs and body juices. He had been drinking dead cockroach; no wonder it had tasted bitter.

He was no great discerner of colas. He drank Coke and Pepsi with equal lack of discrimination. He was oblivious to the subtleties of the images associated with each, produced by the multinational corporations in attempts to get people to think they were buying good times, the real thing, popularity, the Modern African way, when all they were doing was buying carbonated water with caffeine, inverted corn syrup (sugar in KwaZulu Natal because of its plentiful supply), phosphorus, and bad teeth. When he could, he tried to get Royal Crown Cola, the remembered favourite from his childhood bottle store in Ulundi. He had even tried Dr Pepper, but found it too artificial, too plasticky, too American.

No, he didn't begin to liquidise cockroach and sell it as a new brand of soft drink. But from here on, he liked to think of Coke/Pepsi as liquidised cockroach. It was black and fizzy, just as he imagined a crushed cockroach would taste. It also had the acidic burning in his stomach that concentrated cockroach would produce. He would drink Coke or Pepsi when he was painting, sculpting, drawing, and use it for inspiration, its destructive, invasive foreignness militating against his stomach juices. And this is how he celebrated the process of art.

But just when he was getting into the swing of things, the Modern Afrikanist's flat was again invaded. The cockroaches had been absent for so long, that his nightly excursions had become routine. At first he delighted to see his prodigal creatures return and celebrated by watching them scuttle over his food, out of his taps. But as they grew more and more voluminous, he decided to dust them down with white powder.

It did not work. There were too many of them, or maybe they had grown immune, adapting to their hostile environment, and they looked a new breed, a more determined wave of invaders who had strategised and schemed, and planned their campaign of defiance. Even though he carted out hundreds of dead cockroaches every day, even more live ones returned with a vengeance. They poured into the flat from all those crevices, from all those secret places up in the rafters, behind the walls, in the dark cistern cupboard, through tunnels that led from the streets below, up the air-conditioning vents, along water pipes, through garbage chutes. He had plenty of material for his art now, and what's more, a crisis, a disruption to his art, which would itself make great art, but he needed time, reflection and distance in order to produce it. And of this he had none.

Cockroaches carry diseases, he reminded himself. They cause food poisoning (both Salmonella and Escherichia), leprosy, bubonic plague, typhoid, parasitic worms (Helminths). It is for good reason that they are loathed. What had he been thinking all this time?

When he woke one day with cockroach feelers on his face, his flirtation with experimental cockroach art was over. He returned that evening with three cans of Roachkill III. Cockroaches were all over the kitchen: on the bread, in the packets of sandwiches, in the pots; indignantly upset when he stamped his feet at them, they only retreated a short distance then returned, impudently—with impunity, these impunitious creatures.

He sprayed clumps of cockroaches, descending on them in surprise, covering them with glistening insecticide, and then watched grimly as they slowly writhed, kicked and stammered their farewell to this world in their raspy cockroach voices.

Where had his compassion gone? He was in defence mode: they were attacking, and his response was reflexive. *Them or me.* But once he had emptied all three containers onto large clumps, into illegal gatherings of cockroaches, they still came. They still were fearless. They knew they could outlive him. Even when he hurled the empty cans at them, they didn't even scatter, a few of them impertinently clambering onto the bright yellow design of dead cockroaches on the cans themselves.

The Modern Afrikanist hadn't gotten rid of them but he had certainly taught them a lesson. They would flee when they heard his footsteps. He would spy them quivering in cracks. All those cracks! There must be millions of cockroaches living behind these walls. What a fool he was to think this was a place of sanctuary, when under his floorboards he could hear them scrabbling and writhing and clawing at each other in the dark. There were just too many holes. Just when he thought he had a cockroach cornered, it would mysteriously vanish into a crack in the skirting board. Then it would appear somewhere else. Had this block of flats been built on a dark crypt of loathsome prehistoric creatures, sealed for centuries and now open to the modern world?

That day he bought more Roachkill and a bag of Polyfilla, determined to seal them out of his living space. But still they came. He pasted white filler all along the skirting board over every crack, up on the ceilings, along crevices, but still they came. He would wake up at night to hear them having a party in his kitchen. He sealed the breeze-blocks in the walls; he sealed windows tightly at night; he wedged paper under the door, and still somehow they got in.

He would get up at night to surprise them in the kitchen, mad, spray blindly all over as he switched on the light. They learned that at no time they were safe, unless they heard the front door bang as he left the flat. Sometimes he would surprise them by leaving, but then return a few minutes later to find them already at his food. He swept piles of the daredevils into corners as a lesson to the others. He had lost the ability to see them as creatures of wonder. He had ceased to paint.

As the days went on, he saw that he was winning the battle. His throat was getting dry, but he had to keep up the spraying—the cockroaches were relentless and to slow down now would be to show weakness. His eyes were brimming red, smarting, and he had developed a wheeze and a hollow cough. And he slept very lightly, afraid that a cockroach might crawl over him. And when he did sleep deeply, he dreamed that they were all over his body, their jagged feet tickling him, burrowing into his crotch, snuggling under his arms to nestle.

Then he fell sick: he had obviously picked up a bug of sorts from these vile creatures who had been crawling all over his food. Even his breadbin was not safe. He sprayed it inside and out. Cockroach symptoms spread throughout his body: fever, sore throat, squelching stomach, which not even the Coke could soothe. Every time he ate something, he had to rush to the toilet, spray the cockroaches aside, and squeeze out cockroach-coloured stools of digested cockroach. He would stare in disgust at the liquidised cockroach his body had produced in the bowl, and flush it, scrub it, spray it. Had they been crawling in his mouth while he slept? That would explain the twitchy feeling in his stomach, as if dozens of jagged feet were scrambling through his tubes of digesting food. The essence of cockroach was inside him. Worse than dreaming of being a cockroach, they had inhabited him, spitting on their food to digest it (or was that flies?) then he ate it, this yellow cockroach diarrhoea on everything he touched—in his bath, on the toilet seat, on his plates, in his glasses, in the very air he breathed.

For days he languished in bed in a fever, tossing, throwing up, voiding his bowels … feeling imaginary legs running over him. He would burn with rage to hear them scuttling in the kitchen, taking advantage of his weak condition. He would crawl, can in hand, into the kitchen or bathroom or wherever, spray them then fall into a hot sleep, only to dream of them coming pouring out of holes in the wall, shitting on his food, salivating on his food, sawing their feelers together in glee.

But he had a new plan: starve the buggers out. If he had no food in the house, if he fasted for 48 hours, he would cure himself of diarrhoea and they'd have to go somewhere else. He cleared the kitchen of all foodstuff, sprayed empty bins and cupboards, and kept only bottles of Coke in the fridge, which he sipped weakly every now and then, homoeopathically, this effervescent spirit of cockroach. He drank and drank, hoping to purge himself of this evil. Bubbles prickled down his throat, gas bloated his stomach, he belched foul-smelling cockroach breath, and farted loud cockroach smells.

The next day he was weaker. He decided to stay in bed, nurture his delusions, and the hunger artist he was, to create works of art from the visions that came from his condition. But all he could do was watch limply as one cockroach after another crept out into his room, emboldened by his condition. They hadn't found any food, the bastards, yet they came sniffing, feeling their way, whatever it was they did. Another poked its way out of a crevice he thought he'd filled up. And another.

Yet another. He watched, paralysed with hate, but with underlying triumph—he had the can of spray in his hand. Gathered his strength. As he reached for the can, a few cockroaches hesitated then continued their business tormenting him ... He sat up slowly, found the nozzle, and unable to keep from smiling, aimed, pressed. Nothing happened. Spray seeped onto his hand, then air. He shook the can, tried again. The spray of air died away like a last breath. The cockroach scuttled at his first act but didn't hide. It sensed his powerlessness. He flung the useless can against the wall. A cockroach nearby inspected it. He could count five, six, seven, now eight large cockroaches—big black shiny ones—ten, twelve, long as a finger, fat as a sparrow.

Leave me alone, he shouted, you've punished me enough. Go away.

Cockroaches hear, as we know, only through vibrations felt through their legs. They didn't respond. Then he felt a quiver on the sheets, and there was a cockroach by his feet. He kicked out and the cockroach was hurled into the air, and writhed on the floor on its back.

But then it flapped a pair of horrible insect wings and flew. It flew! He never knew cockroaches could fly. It vibrated science fiction story wings, flew past him and landed on the wall behind his bed. He banged clumsily on the wall behind to unsettle it, tried to flick the cockroach away with his comb. But it spread its paper-thin wings again and flew into the living room.

There was one last bottle in the kitchen. He dragged himself to the counter, banged away the roaches clustering on the counter, and pulled it weakly down. He was not going to waste it squirting onto individual cockroaches, or into the air. He had to protect himself. Cockroaches were now flying around the room, given free rein. He sprayed the repellent all over him: legs, arms, face, chest. That would keep them away. He sprayed clean and hard so the spray was greenish liquid drenching his skin. It was good. It would cleanse him. He began with his feet, up his legs, groin—it stung horribly here, but it had to be done—stomach, back, arms, neck, and face. He screwed up his eyes but a lot still got into his nose and ears. His eyes burned anyway. He sprayed his lips heavily: if any cockroaches dared to get near here ... His throat burned like fire, his stomach turned in revolt—all those nasty creatures inside after his food. His skin cried out, but now he was safe. His tongue had the bitter taste of diethyltoluamide. His nose ran, his eyes watered and smarted, but in glee he watched triumphantly as the cockroaches drew closer to the bed. They were in for a surprise. Sudden death would overtake them. Then he lay still waiting for sleep, breathing very uneasily. He imagined being found dead the next morning by the caretaker of the flat, who wanted his three months' unpaid rent: cause of death—cockroach poisoning, but he preferred the thought that the cockroaches would carry him away and devour him bit by bit until they too choked and died, all of them, all the millions behind the walls, all with human diarrhoea.[3]

<hr />

3   Although this is a much better story and more erudite, it appears that the source Bantu used for this concept is an obscure short story, 'The Flat', about a man who poisons himself by trying to eradicate cockroaches in his apartment written by Paul Williams and published in the South African journal *Contrast* in 1988. Interpretations of this story (both Williams and Bantu versions) range from a simple realist description of cockroach pests to allegorical readings about the nature of colonial power and its paranoic self-destructive tendencies.

10

Periplaneta australasiae
. . . .
Australian cockroach

The Australian cockroach (*Periplaneta australasiae*) is a large, uncultured, boorish, shallow species of cockroach, winged, and brown in colour (probably because of the abundant sunshine in the region), though it began as a white, or albino, nymph (see Chapter 9). It can be easily mistaken for the American cockroach, although it is smaller and has distinguishing yellow streaks along its sides near the wings. Similar to the German and American and Asian cockroach, it is an introduced species. Because of commercial shipping routes, it has spread throughout the world, and can be found as far away as Canada and Great Britain. The Australian cockroach is a scavenger, and is very agile, able to hide in small cracks and holes, and once entrenched, often very difficult to dislodge.

The voices batter you all night, crashing heavy onto the shore of your consciousness. By morning, the fire is out—you are somehow expecting it to still smoulder—but ashes still float and dance in the air. The car, wet with dew, is pasted with the fragments of Bantu's *Seven Invisible Selves*.

You dress tightly in your suit, inhabiting it as much as possible, knotting the tie against your Adam's apple, liking for once the harsh abrasive material, the cut around the shoulders, the firmness with which it props you up. It makes you walk in a certain way; it makes you behave in a certain way; it holds up your sagging self nicely around the waist.

You drive slowly, almost reluctant to disturb the misty town. You have the roads to yourself. The road to the university is whitened by the ghostly mist and so is the Thomas Mofolo Forest on either side.

Whiteness hides behind trees, wraps itself around road signs, and hovers ahead of you, and behind, but dares not come close. It dissipates at your presence. Or perhaps your Golf GTI has the power to dispel fog. You rev the car up to 120 kph to catch up with the lingering KwaZulu breath, but sleepy and slow as it looks, it always disappears a few metres ahead and then closes in behind.

How would a real Timothy Turner act, without having to hide behind a mask, or a stuttering voice? A real Timothy Turner would banish the fake Bantu. And it wouldn't end there. A real Timothy Turner would expose him in the literary world. He would write article after article on the fallen Bantu, maybe even make his name in academia by exposing this counterfeit writer. You can see the book now: *The Fake Black Self: The Novels of Sizwe Bantu.*

In the fog you see Zimmerlie's pallid face, his smile, his crinkled eyes wincing in what must have been pain. You blink to rid yourself of the vision of this man. You can still feel his cold hand clutching your shoulder. You stretch your neck, massage the tight muscle spasm, but the sensation persists. And you can hear the man's voice as clearly as if he is sitting in the back seat:

> sIzwe Is not my name, because no shell can be ME
> the nameless wordless "I"[1]

You shake off the hand, the voice. You are used to ghosts of your own imagination playing tricks. You are also used to listening to a ghostly Bantu in the sky, after all those years of creating a phantom mentor out of his words.

*

The library is open, thank goodness, but contains no students, only a scattered herd of staff. You find an empty booth and sit at the already humming computer screen. The search engine defaults at Google, so you type in 'brain aneurisms' and watch what comes up.

Is it true? Can a brain aneurism make you into an accidental artist? Apparently so. It is called temporal lobe epilepsy, or TLE. *Brain*

---

1   From *Seven Invisible Selves* (2008).

haemorrhages, you read, *alterations in the temporal lobe (sometimes sponta-neous) could result in heightened perception.*

> "I see things slightly different than before," says Bryan Ferendinos. "I have visions and images that normal people don't have. Some of my seizures are like entering another dimension, the closest to religious or spiritual feelings I've ever had. This disease has given me a rare vision and insight into myself, beyond myself. Without TLE, I would not have begun to sculpt, to write, to paint, to create. With this gift, I have extraordinary experiences of transcendent wonder, luminous insight."[2]

You type in 'writing + aneurism'.

Sometimes, you read, people with brain aneurisms suffer from a condition called hypergraphia. The temporal lobe, that part of the brain responsible for the creation of meaning and language, can cause idea creation, graphomania, increased creative output, and the illusion that a voice is dictating, that this creative output is not from you.

All those cockroaches, those words in that voice inside your head for seven years—was it all simply the waste product of malfunctioning brain cells? Is Art merely—should you say 'merely'?—an aberration, a malfunction of the brain?

You type in 'art as aberration'.

It seems so. Van Gogh's great works were caused by temporal lobe epilepsy ... Van Gogh suffered brain trauma. There is still some controversy over whether mind-altering substances could possibly have contributed, but whatever the cause, his art was a result of brain malfunction. And the list goes on ... Dostoevsky, Flaubert, Tennyson all suffered from TLE (as it was flippantly acronymed in the articles you read). Whether or not they knew the physiological cause of their seizures, they all incorporated their symptoms into poems, stories and myths. They fell into trances, heard voices, saw visions, and created incessantly. They suffered from migraine headaches, epilepsy, and some were also famous for their rages.

> "I think of this as a gift," says George DeLand. "It's not a disability. It's

2   Oliver Sacks in *Musicophilia* (2008) describes the case of the Accidental Artist, a pianist who, after being struck by lightning, suddenly developed an obsession with composing music. He wrote the Lightning symphony which was performed in New York. There is also the case of the man in England who, after a brain aneurism, began to plaster his walls with paintings. He couldn't, it seemed, turn off his creative talent.

not a malfunction of the brain, but an opening up of the brain, a return to what should have always been. The doors of perception have been cleansed. We should all be creative like this: the taps gushing, our hands sculpting, writing, painting, playing music, not all sealed off in dead words, criticism, linear thinking. We are a right brain species."

*

It is a scene you regret witnessing, and it only lasts ten seconds or less, but the images are seared into your heart. As you walk out of the library, you see blonde dreadlocked hair swishing. On impulse, you call out: 'Tracey!'

She turns. She is hugging a book close to her chest. She looks at you as if she is tasting stale cockroach. She opens her mouth as if she is about to say something. You too widen your eyes, and are about to say something. But there are no words to say. In this moment, anything could happen. You could rush into each other's arms, her green eyes could well up with tears, and you could stroke her hair. She could spit into your face. She could smile, shrug her shoulders at the capricious world.

Then the moment passes, she closes her mouth and tosses her hair back over her shoulders. She turns and walks away, slowly, self-consciously.

*

You sit in an empty cafeteria and order coffee. You drink it scalding, enjoying the pain, seeking courage from its dark bitterness. When you have suitably composed yourself, you stride briskly into the English Department corridor, directly to Zimmerlie's office and rap on the door.

'Yes?' The room is bare, save for the empty shelves and Ngwenya sitting impatiently on the edge of the desk.

'I was looking for …'

'Zimmerlie? Bad news. He's just resigned. And so has Mpofu.'

'Makaya, actually, I was looking for Makaya.'

'The good news, of course, is that Makaya has been reinstated. He agreed to an out-of-court settlement of 250,000 Rand. And I've been asked by the Dean to head the department in the transition.' He gestures for you to sit.

Ngwenya's body posture already tells you what you need to know. 'Admin … Admin has some more bad news for you, I'm afraid. They can't approve of your lecturing position.' He opens his generous arms in an expansive arc. 'It's been a terrible shock.'

He doesn't look as if it's been a terrible shock. He glows with well-being and self-righteousness. You hold his gaze and say nothing, so he continues. 'We argued your case for you, but the University President vetoed our recommendation.' He shrugs his shoulders to show his fatalistic, helpless relation to the malevolent, capricious universe. 'The Dean knows more about it than we do. If you want to have a word with her, she's also in this morning.' You continue to sit. 'You'd better ... see the Dean.'

You wait a measured thirty seconds—a long time when you are trying to stare someone down. But Ngwenya is not willing to play. He marches to the door, holds it open, and points down the corridor. You stand, wipe your feet on the mat (why, you don't know). Your (former) colleague holds his breath to let you pass.

A cool secretary waves you through an open door. As if you are going to the dentist, you clench your jaw tightly. The Dean, the same woman you have seen at the lecture, and in the trial, is frank. 'You've heard the bad news?'

Now that you have had the practice, you find it easy to stare down this woman. But the Dean skilfully avoids you by peering at her computer screen and clicking her mouse. 'Dr Turner, the President has recommended that your appointment be terminated with effect from Monday. We'll pro-rata your pay, but I'm afraid ... Professor Zimmerlie had no business hiring you in the first place.'

She turns the screen so you can read.

(1) Dr Turner's conduct. ... Evidence of Dr Turner's sexual harassment of students, particularly one Tracey Khumalo, see attached signed statement by a Mrs Steyn (mother); and attached photo.

(2) Conspiring with Professor Zimmerlie and Dr Mpofu, who are both under investigation for conspiracy ...

But you can read no further. 'Sexual harassment? You are accusing *me* of ...'

The Dean speaks to the screen. 'Your behaviour and your public humiliation of our respected colleagues here have done you a lot of damage.'

'My behaviour? Damage? Excuse me? Who the hell made this accusation?'

'Fortunately for us, you were not officially hired, so we have no need to even justify your dismissal, but we wanted to make it clear why you were to be given notice to leave. The fine print'—she smiles and taps the bottom of the screen with a red fingernail—'suggests that the charge will be dropped if you leave …'

'I never sexually harassed anyone …'

She folds her arms and looks directly at you. 'What do you mean, Dr Turner? Your behaviour with that student was very inappropriate. We have photographic evidence, we have a witness who verifies that she visited you at your house, and stayed the night.'

'Bloody hell. Mrs Steyn … ?'

' … is a very influential woman in town and a good friend of a number of university staff.'

You stare. This time it is she who stares you down.

'Admin will give you a cheque if you go see them now. You are relieved of your duties.' She lunges at you and shakes your hand hard as if you have just completed a dangerous mission.

You find your way to the Admin block, you are given a cheque, and you are ushered out of the building after surrendering your ID card. You walk passively, your legs automatically striding ahead as if you were a normal, confident human being. You walk calmly to your car without saying goodbye to anyone, and drive off onto the main road and back to your little cottage in eSikamanga. You feel nothing. Perhaps once or twice you laugh out loud, at yourself, drily, ironically, but otherwise you silently watch the scene as if you were a movie maker creating a long shot of a man driving home in silence along a beautiful forest by the roaring, crashing, blue Indian Ocean.

It is still early when you arrive at the cottage, and the sun pours golden slanted rays through dusty gaps between trees. A fire burns to the west, and smoke signals billow into the sky.

The future yawns open. You haven't paid any deposit for this cottage, thank god. Your job was surety. You tumble all your possessions into the trunk of the car. You don't have much, now that you have demolished and incinerated the Bantu collection. Speaking of which … you brush through the glistening dewy grass to the compost heap, which is now a black heap of wet soggy indistinguishable matter. You pick out a few items that are still recognisable: the gold lettering of your thesis, CONSTRUCTING THE AFRICAN SELF IN THE NOVELS OF, as plain as the pungent smell of rubber, glints in the light. Half of the dissertation has not burnt at all, and the pages furl out in a display to the world. You can still read some of the words: *And thus, Bantu's … Moreover, it is nevertheless inflammatory of Grey to insinuate tha.* … And the 'Aphasia' short story which you read the other night is intact, crouching behind a blackened Coke can. You reach for it, then change your mind and instead pull up a handful of dead leaves from an untouched part of the heap and scatter it on top. Your hands are blackened and red from the clay soil and rotting compost, but the fragrance of dead vegetation and insects smells good. A nest of frantic white ants crawls onto your suit sleeve, and you brush them off with a muddy hand. Your tie leans forward and dips itself into the ash, and you wipe a sooty hand on a white shirt by accident. You plunge the half-thesis back into its burial ground and smother its cover with ash so the gold lettering cannot be read. Then you walk away, your shoes now squelching, the socks muddy and the trouser legs splashed with soil.

Inside the cottage, you take off the suit, wondering why you had not taken it off before playing with the compost heap. It will need major dry cleaning before you can wear it again. *Wear it again? Why would you want to do that?* You change into shorts and t-shirt, and crumple up the suit on the sofa. It will only dirty the car. It will be a nuisance. Leave it where it lies! You empty out the fridge of any valuable edible items, throwing the rest onto the rubbish heap. When you are ready to drive off, you simply close the front door and walk away.

*

The beach looks as if a hurricane has rearranged it. Debris is strewn all over. You find logs from Richard's Bay paper mill, and the rivers have twisted new estuaries away from the main beach. You stand by the only dependable reference point: the sign.

IT IS DANGEROUS

TO SWIM IN THE LAGOON

BECAUSE OF

SHARKS AND CROCODILES

'And prytty ladyes,' you shout to the dunes. You look up for any watching figures. But you are alone. For once there is no voice inside you. Bantu has been extinguished. You can listen to your own voice without the mediation of another telling you what to think. In the waves, you no longer hear the echo of Bantu's poetry beating its wings.

You run and dance and swim and yell and swear and sweat out the suit, sweat out the whiteness, the poison, the words, the seven fake selves. You are an onion, hoping that there is a self intact under all this. You hurl your body into the waves, and they delight in hurling you back onto the sand, shooting fizzing briny water into your nose and eyes and ears. You scream at the universe. You swim across the strong current, pushing yourself as hard as you can, then, exhausted, let the sea roll you onto the beach and the sun dry you. The waves dance and froth.

*

Dear M,

I return to you voiceless, self-less. I was hoping to go on a hero's journey, a quest, and return with something substantial – myself perhaps, or a golden fleece, or a magic potion that would make you see me, acknowledge me, love me, even, but no: I return with nothing, with less than nothing, with crashed illusions.

For a brief moment, I imagined that Art would rescue me, or at least transform experience and pain into truth and beauty. But art, I discover, is a dysfunction of the brain. The sane person has no need for art. Love too, is a dysfunction of the heart and soul: a whole person has no need for the other, does not crave or obsess, or write letters which he never sends.

I am empty, M. I have poured myself out, and there is nothing left to say.

Your truly,

T

*

On your way out of town, you drive slowly, out of respect for the dead self that you have left here. You wind all four windows down to let the salty breeze whip your face and dry your shorts and t-shirt. You steer with one finger, accelerate with one big toe on the accelerator, and tap the roof with your hand. The car furrows through the hills, and though you have decided not to, you cannot resist looking in the mirror back at eSikamanga. The roads are shimmering already from the heat, and the mists you have earlier driven through are gone, replaced by other phantoms, mirages on the tar, watery patches where the whole countryside looks flooded. The town presses itself flat into the haze in the valley, and a smoke column rises golden brown into the sky.

YOU ARE NOW LEAVING ESIKAMANGA

You push the accelerator to the floor and lean back, ready for the two-hour journey to Durban. Bantu's words are now ashes on your lips, smouldering white, black, red, grey and dead: you can see through the mystery of them now, and they take on a mundane meaning: a white writer trying to be African, desperately coming short, because a white man can't be African ... tumbling through you now, newly interpreted, words now embodied with Zimmerlie's stuttering voice: *Am I white? Am I black? I wear my face backwards. No one judges me by my skin colour; Sizwe is not my name, because no shell can be me ...*

The absurdity grows even more absurd as his words repeat on you: here is a white man masquerading as a Black Consciousness Pan-Africanist—AfriKanist, you should say—writer. Picasso stole Cubism from African culture; Elvis stole rock 'n' roll from the African; Paul Simon stole South African black music; Richard Attenborough stole the struggle and celluloided it for mass consumption; even Andre Brink took *A Dry White Season* from a poem by Serote. Every so-called white attempt at rendering visible the black man was merely a white man's exploitation of the black man. Brink's book became more famous than Serote ever did; Simon's *Graceland* is hummed in every country, while Stimela still have to pay their own fares on the train. Donald Woods is the hero of Biko's struggle, rock 'n' roll is as American as apple pie,

Cubism is a European invention. Instead of Bessie Head, people read Alexander McCall Smith.[3]

But then a sudden swell of condescending pity for this man arises in you. You shouldn't feel so smug: you have betrayed a frail, brain-damaged, old man who offered you his soul. Your stomach cramps and a spasm of words bursts into your brain. The words attack like stinging insects against the windshield of your soul.

You have to dismiss Bantu as the ravings of a madman, the outpourings of a man with a brain aneurism. It was only Zimmerlie, you say. He merely stole ideas, as Makaya says, from 'real' African writers. But the 'only' sticks in your craw. The 'merely' feels reductive; the 'real' shallow and simplistic. You cannot shake off the words that easily. You can burn them, tear them out of textbooks, but they are still hovering above you. You cannot stop them.

As you near the turnoff to the freeway, a siren latches onto the morning air. An ambulance with red flashing lights swings off the freeway onto the eSikamanga road towards you. A fire engine follows, announcing its important mission with a loud farting bullhorn.

You pull the steering wheel to the left and skid onto the gravel to let them pass. An ESIKAMANGA PATROL police car charges past too. You crane your neck back to see where they are headed. A curious gnawing at your brain unsettles you for a moment, but you shake your head and pull back into the road. *Just go, just leave.*

The sirens grow louder rather than softer as they plunge into the valley of the town, calling you back. Come to think of it, that fire you saw earlier was too near town to be a sugar cane burn. A dread grows in your stomach,

3   Paul Simon's musical album *Graceland*, a curious hybrid of American lyrics about Simon's divorce and African rhythms, was written by the New York pop icon in collaboration with many South African musicians and was criticised for breaking the ban and appropriating South African black music for his own ends; Richard Attenborough's movie *Cry Freedom* is ostensibly about Steve Biko, the anti-apartheid activist murdered by the South African regime, but focuses more on the white journalist Donald Woods' experiences, and uses American actors instead of local African actors to play the major roles; Andre Brink's *A Dry White Season* similarly focuses on the crisis of conscience of a white man and his plight, and becomes a world best-seller, whereas African writers describing similar events, such as the poet Serote, cannot make a living with their writing; similarly, Bessie Head, a Botswana writer who wrote of village life in Botswana, is largely unknown and died under stressful circumstances, whereas white writer Alexander McCall Smith has won literary and popular acclaim for his series *The No. 1 Ladies Detective Agency*, and perpetuated stereotypical and caricatured perceptions of Botswana in Western popular consciousness.

and the knot tightens, the louder the sirens become. In the mirror, you see emergency vehicles creeping (at this distance their speed is sluggish) up a hill, along First Avenue, Second, and then up a rough dirt road, and on top of this hill sits a mushroom of smoke. In the smoke you see a face, a wincing face with a scar on its head, which a ghostly hand comes up to scratch. It has no mouth: the cloud has moved away in the wind and left a smudge where a mouth should be, but nevertheless this apparition speaks in the crackling, insistent voice of Professor Zimmerlie:

> I am I. I am not my body or my roots, I am not my skin.
> I am a soul, a spirit, an ageless, sexless, raceless being.

You watch the cloud dissipate into a cirrus shape; the words crackle into sounds of the siren, the wind, and the cicadas in the mopane trees at the edge of the road. You have to decide now, because once you are on the freeway, there is no exit for the next twenty kilometres. You swing the steering wheel to the right and drive back into the misty town you have just abandoned.

WELCOME TO ESIKAMANGA - PLACE OF MYSTERY.

You follow the trail of the sirens, guessing where they are going, or rather following an intuition that you know where they are going. You pass Second Avenue, on a narrow winding road that dead-ends at a red track. From here on you follow the dust, drive the winding red snake through thick creepers and the ever widening view of the magnificent blueness around you.

The sirens lead you to the back of a familiar building, a cottage perched on the edge of the world, and here the emergency vehicles have parked in a half laager formation, as if to trap the enraged fire. You see the ambulance with its rotating red light on the roof, its back doors wide open to reveal a hastily abandoned mini hospital inside; the police car, the words ESIKAMANGA PATROL emblazoned on the side, and with an equally hastily flung open driver's door. You do not see much of a fire, but blue smoke pours out of the windows and from under the door. Firemen unravel hoses and douse the cottage in an excess of water, and the smoke hisses and increases in volume before finally petering out. The cottage is still standing (you have somehow imagined it to be a blackened shell), but you can see by the scorched windows that the inside must be in ruins. A thin spiral of smoke still seeps through the top of the roof. An excessively loud police radio crackles with static, and some nasal voice repeats '43 Jack Romeo Alpha over. Come in. Do you read?' over and over, like a kid playing at cops and robbers. Then the answer comes, in crackly static over the radio in a voice only you can hear:

> The difference between pretending to be what people
> want you to be and humouring them by acting in a
> certain way is quite indistinguishable.

You watch as the firefighters now rush to the door and push it open, peer inside and point their hoses into the darkness like weapons, and then beckon their comrades. Two medics step out of the ambulance and follow. Then a police officer. Another firefighter rolls up the hose. The fire is out. You park the car and climb out. They have all disappeared into the house, and you follow.

The cottage is charcoal. The furniture is smouldering, the bookcase and desk eaten away, the manuscripts turned into grey ash fluttering out of the windows. The statues are charred, and all their accoutrements are burned off.

The firefighters ignore you—you expect them to shoulder you off the property, but this is South Africa, not Australia. You step through the open door and see the police officer and ambulance medics crouching over something on the floor.

It is a body overcome by the smoke. The clothes are singed slightly, but not burned. You see white hair, an African shirt, and the scar on his head. You step forward but stop when you see that the movements of the body are those of a puppet whose strings have been cut, moving only at the behest of the medics. They turn his head around, check his pulse, his eyes, his reflexes, and then let his head and arms flop down on the hard floor. One policeman waves away the black flakes that follow him. Another shakes his head, taking note of you for the first time.

'He's dead.'

The police officer sidles up to you, offering to shake your hand, perhaps mistaking you for some authority figure with a legitimate reason to be here. 'Suicide,' he says. 'I hear the poor bastard was fired from his job. Looks like he tried to burn the place down too.'

The medic shakes his head. 'Looks to me more like he had a stroke. This must have been an accident.' He indicates the ashes. You follow the sweep of the man's hand. Every piece of Bantu is torched. The cockroach furniture is burned to shapeless hulks, the books are black corpses, the papers escape out of the window and door towards the beach in their first taste of freedom. The words crackle in your ears:

> Words are excrement. What's in this black shit anyway?
> To think some people spend their lives sifting through
> other people's shit!

The other medic points to Zimmerlie's chest, and then at a melted pool of wax, and then to the phone on a nearby desk. 'It looks as if he had a seizure, and he must have knocked over the candle, see? When he had the stroke, tried to reach the phone.'

'Good job there was a fire. Otherwise we wouldn't have found him at all.' The medic taps his foot on the skirting board. 'Who are you, anyway? Friend of his?'

Your throat constricts. The words you utter surprise you. 'Yes, of course, a colleague from the university …'

'I'm sorry.'

'Spooky place, innit?' says the policeman.

You pace up and down, examining the lost artworks. A painting: a blackened mess, cockroach corpses burned into the canvas, colour turned grey. You step out the door to see if the sculpture outside has been damaged. No; it sits as stonily as ever, staring out at the sea.

The two men hoist the dead man onto a stretcher, and you follow and watch the wispy, white-headed man nod as they heave him into the ambulance. His arm flops off the stretcher in macabre farewell.

> I cannot be freed unless you listen, read, open the door
> and let me out. I will not exist unless you imagine me,
> create me.

You drive slowly behind the three vehicles, at the back of a makeshift funeral procession. But at the highway, the three vehicles in front turn right towards Assegai, and you turn left towards Durban. You chew your lip all the way back to the city and turn the radio up loud to fill the silence.

Review: *The Time-Pest*: New Strugglers
University of eSikamanga Student Times

Following its success in local performances to packed audiences in Assegai and eSikamanga, and at the University, the New Strugglers have embarked on an ambitious and successful runaway national tour of South Africa with their riveting play based on Shakespeare's *The Tempest*.

This is a splendid production. The touch of genius is where Prospero, like Godot, never arrives. The white coloniser thus becomes a most effective, sinister, invisible presence in the play, and haunts it by his absence.

Director of the play, Professor Mxolisi Makaya (Head, English Department, University of eSikamanga): 'Well, we figured that Prospero is not one man anyway, but represents that amorphous collective of all white colonialist oppressors.'

Sterling performances by Kaliban (Caesar Langa) and Eric Phala, as well as John Matinde, whose classic lines ('Don't be such a white man!') made the audience howl with laughter.

The crowning performance though has to go to Tracey Khumalo (Miranda) who, with her sharp words, banishes the double-dealing Prospero and thwarts his schemes, to triumph as the heroine of the play at the end.

Energised with the success of *The Time-Pest*, the New Strugglers hope to follow their success with a classic Athol Fugard play adapted for contemporary South Africa, entitled 'Sizwe Bantu is Dead.'

Nomsa Thando – student writer for the *Times*

There is an epilogue:

Australia is a foreign place. You have altered since you have been back. You feel alien here, as if your organs of perception have been forever changed. Africa has become a place in your heart, a territory beyond geography.

You're walking in the dead rain, on a low grey pier, a long slab of concrete into the wintry ocean, when a voice calls out in the wind.

Yo!

You look around—you see no one on the beach but a family with dogs in the hazy distance. The Melbourne concrete skyline rises ahead of you. Its city noises are ghosts in the distance.

Hey white man!

You stare into the misty air. 'What?'

Nothing more.

As you climb back up the dune to your car, you feel short of breath, as if your chest is being squeezed by some invisible angel.

Recite.

'What? Who?'

On your way home, you feel a heady compulsion to write something down. Words pour into your head. But the traffic is horrendous. When you get home, you have to scrabble for a notebook and pen, and begin to write.

The words attack thick and fast. They pour onto the paper, slippery and bubbling hot. You don't know what you are writing at all, and you watch in amazement as the words flow, one after the other, in perfect grammatical order and sense. Yes, they are your words, but you have no idea where they come from; you don't recognise them at all. You watch them in fascination as they pour out of you, miracles, flowers growing out of concrete, butterflies flitting and alighting on your page. Your words, your thoughts, you think, as your hand writes and you watch, trying to read them as they come out. When the notebook is full, you have to write on the inside back cover, then on the back, then on the margins of pages you have already filled with your spidery handwriting. Perhaps this is the resolution, the healing you have been waiting for— writing something of your own at last, not something second-hand. But when the spasm has passed and you lie exhausted on the couch, holding the notebook up to the window square of golden light, you do not think so. You recognise them. They are not your words at all.

> The sea is a poem—
> crushing, scraping battering on my wasteland shore.
> The sea is inside me:
> It claws onto the beach of my restraint;
> It sucks and surges;
> It writhes in restless energy;
> It pulls and pushes within me;
> And I dance to the tide of the moon.
>
> I ache for the sea
> to wash away my city clichés,
> Purge me of all niceties.
> Say the words and I shall be healed.

References

Bantu, S, 2002,'Cokcraco' in *The Present Tense*, Vol. XXV, Feb., pp. 36-40.

Bantu, S, 2002, 'The Cockroach Artist' in *The Present Tense*, Vol. XXVI, Aug., pp. 43-50.

Bantu, S, 2003, 'Afrikan Metamorphosis' in *The Present Tense*, Vol. XXVII, Feb., pp. 66-77.

Bantu, S, 2003, 'Cockroach Liberation' in *The Present Tense*, Vol. XXVIIII, Aug., pp. 345-354.

Bantu, S, 2004, 'The Modernist Afrikanist Dekonstructs Himself' in *The Present Tense*, Vol. XXIX, Feb., pp. 43-54.

Bantu, S, 2004, 'Death of a Cockroach' in *The Present Tense*, Vol. XXX, Aug., pp. 4-12.

Bantu, S, 2005, 'Sivilization' in *The African Presence*, Vol. 2, Mar./Apr., pp. 31-34.

Bantu, S, 2006, *The Great South African Novel* (PowerHouse Press, Johannesburg).

Bantu, S, 2007, 'The Bloody Horse' in *Modern South African Stories* (AD Jonstra Press, Cape Town).

Bantu, S, 2007, 'The Tale of the African Lizard' in *Ubuntu!* Vol. IX, pp. 23-24.

Bantu, S, 2008, *African Metaphysics* (PowerHouse Press, Johannesburg).

Bantu, S, 2008, *Seven Invisible Selves* (PowerHouse Press, Johannesburg).

Bantu, S, 2008, 'Technology as Colonising Discourse' in *The African Presence*, Vol. 4, pp. 35-45.

Bantu, S, 2009, *The Five AfriKan Senses* (PowerHouse Press, Johannesburg).

Bantu, S, 2010. *The Cockroach Whisperer* (PowerHouse Press, Johannesburg).

Bantu, S, 2011. *Cokcraco and Other Stories* (PowerHouse Press, Johannesburg).

Bantu, S, 2012, *The Complete Works* (PowerHouse Press, Johannesburg).

Chesterton, LK, 2010, 'Women Speak in the Silence of the Text' in *The African Presence*, Vol. 3 Sept./Oct., pp. 1-19.

Fanon, F, 1952, *Black Skin, White Masks* (Grove Press, New York).

Houghton, C, 2009, 'Bantu's Misogyny: Maids, Wives, Temptresses, Whores, Goddesses, Madonnas' in *The Present Tense*, Vol. XXX, Aug., pp. 13-46.

Jones, JM, 2008, 'Anagrammic Dyslexia in Sizwe Bantu' in *Ubuntu!* Vol. X, Summer, pp. 34-43.

Jonson, J, 2013, 'The Post-Apocalyptic Guide to Parochial South African Towns Buried in the Past' in *Crowded-Planet*, pp. 122-123.

Kafka, J, 1915 [1972], *The Metamorphosis* (Bantam, New York).

Kundera, M, 1978 [1980], *The Book of Laughter and Forgetting* (Knopf, London).

Manganye, N, 1973, *Being-Black-in-the-World* (Ravan Press, Johannesburg).

Marechera, D, 1992, 'The Bar-Stool Edible Worm,' in *Cemetery of Mind*, ed. Flora Veit-Wild (Baobab Books, Harare) and *Scrapiron Blues*, ed. Flora Veit-Wild (Baobab Books, Harare), 1994.

Ndebele, N, 1983, *Fools and Other Stories* (Ravan Press, Johannesburg).

Pantheon, J, 2013, 'Bantu, a Disembodied No Man' in *New York Times Review*: Dec. 4.

Sacks, O, 2007, *Musicophilia: Tales of Music and the Brain* (Vintage, London).

Serote, M, 1972, 'What's in this Black Shit' in *Yakhal'inkomo* (AD Donker, Johannesburg).

Turner, T, 2009, 'Bantu's Practice-led Research' in *The African Presence*, Vol. 4, Jan./Feb., pp. 41-49.

Turner, T, 2009, 'Bantu Waives Britannia's Rules' in *The African Presence*, Vol. 9, pp. 12-17.

Turner, T, 2011, *The African Self in the Novels of Sizwe Bantu*. Unpublished Ph.D. thesis, University of Melbourne.

Turner, T, 2013, 'Seapoem' in *The African Presence* Vol. 10, pp. 77-82.

Watt, T, 2008, 'Bantu Unveils the Masks of our So-called Civilisation' in *The Present Tense*, Vol. XXI, Sept., pp. 3-45.

Wesson, M, 2010, 'The Original and the Edited Bantu' in *Bantophilia* Vol. 1, issue i, pp. 55-65.

William, C, 1934 [1980], 'This is to Say' in *Collected Poems* (Faber & Faber, London).

Williams, P, 1988, 'The Flat' in *Contrast*, Vol. 67, Winter, pp. 58-64.

Acknowledgements

My gratitude to Kate Elkington for her close reading of the first draft, to Linda Nix at Lacuna Publishing for her sharp editorial eye, to Shelley Davidow who believed in my cockroaches, and to Timothy Williams, the cockroach-rescuer.

Paul Williams
July 2013

About the Author

Paul Williams' memoir *Soldier Blue* won Book of the Year in South Africa, 2008 and his novel *The Secret of Old Mukiwa* won the Zimbabwe International Book Fair award for Young Adults in 2001. His educational readers have been set in schools across Africa and his stories and critical articles have been published in *Meanjin*, *Text*, *Social Alternatives* (Australia), *Chicago Quarterly Review* (USA), *New Writing* (UK) and *New Contrast* (South Africa). He has a PhD in Creative Writing from the University of Wisconsin, USA, and lectures in Creative Writing at the University of the Sunshine Coast, Australia.

More information about Paul and his books is on his personal website: http://www.paul-a-williams.com

www.ingramcontent.com/pod-product-compliance
Lightning Source LLC
Chambersburg PA
CBHW020610030726
47497CB00007B/2176